EISHA'S SEARCH

Eisha's Search is a magical, mystical myth. It is magical, because if comes purely from the world of imagination. It is mystical, because it comes from personal experience of the divine truths the story tells. It is a myth because it is about the life of the soul yours, mine, and everyone's.

Therefore, it is not confined to our everyday experience of time and space. It happens in the marvelous anywhere, anytime. Nor is it a story only for children, or only for adults. It is for the young at heart of all ages who love the adventurous and truth-full realms of inspired Imagination.

Karla Van Huysen

Karla currently lives in Telluride, Colorado with the love of her life, Shemryn, and her cat Hemmingway. She is also an Art Therapist for children. She attended Naropa University in Boulder, Colorado. She does not have formal training in Art, and did not begin making art until she was twenty-one years old, and living in Aberdeen, Scotland. One morning she visited a castle so magnificent, that it demanded she drop whatever she was doing, and simply sit down and sketch it. She has been drawing and painting ever since.

Marchiene Vroon Rienstra

I love journeys! I was born during my parents' journey from America to India. Ever since, I have journeyed to far away places. These marvelous journeys have shaped my life as I have searched for Wisdom, Beauty, and Who I really am. I have discovered that the journey and the search are life itself, and that every destination leads to another.

EISHA'S SEARCH

Written by Marchiene Vroon Rienstra
and
Illustrated by Karla Van Huysen

Bookman
Publishing & Marketing
Providing Quality, Professional Author Services
www.bookmanmarketing.com

This book is a work of fiction. Any resemblances to any persons, living or dead, is completely coincidental.

© Copyright 2005, Marchiene Vroon Rienstra

All Rights Reserved.

No part of this book may be reproduced, stored in a retrieval system, or transmitted by any means, electronic, mechanical, photocopying, recording, or otherwise, without written permission from the author.

ISBN: 1-59453-536-1

This is a bed-time, dream-time story for children and the women and men who love them, and care enough to listen.

It takes place in the Islands of the Inland Sea—a magical, mysterious place that is deep inside this world, and beyond it.

Eisha, the heroine, is every-girl and every-woman. Her search is an important one for us all.

Will you join her?

DEDICATION AND GRATITUDES

This book is dedicated to my nieces and nephews, especially to Daron, Theresa, Anton, and Lenore, whose open hearted and excited listening, and ongoing encouragement to "Write more, Aunt Marty," cracked open the shell of this mystical, magical story.

In addition, I wish to express my gratitude to Karla, my soul-sister and artist extraordinaire, whose enthusiastic response to the story, and skillful illustration of it, have made this book an adventure in the making, and a feast for the eyes of the soul.

I am also deeply grateful to those authors whose stories have inspired me to write in this genre: C.S. Lewis, George McDonald, Madeleine L'Engle, Frank Baum, Lewis Carroll and others. Joseph Campbell's profound understandings of the importance of myth in our lives, and Carl Jung's active imagination process have provided a foundation from which to write this sort of story with confidence.

Finally, I am grateful to my friends who put in hours of loving labor to read the rough drafts and offer their suggestions: Sharon, Lillian, Donna, and Colette.

Always, I am grateful to my dear husband John, whose loving support makes it possible for me to write stories like this, just for the pure joy of it.

TABLE OF CONTENTS

Introduction		1
Chapter One:	The Cave	3
Chapter Two:	The Serpent	15
Chapter Three:	The Star	22
Chapter Four:	The Stone	29
Chapter Five:	The Castle	35
Chapter Six:	The Ship	47
Chapter Seven:	The Island Of The Horses	58
Chapter Eight:	The Trial	66
Chapter Nine:	The Sacred Horse-Herd	73
Chapter Ten:	The Willow Grove	80
Chapter Eleven:	The Sacred Tree	85
Chapter Twelve:	The Storm	94
Chapter Thirteen:	The Secret Entrance	100
Chapter Fourteen:	The Golden Grove	109
Chapter Fifteen:	The Stone Circle	115
Chapter Sixteen:	The Women's Story	121
Chapter Seventeen:	The Preparation	130
Chapter Eighteen:	The Ship Of The Desert	138
Chapter Nineteen:	The Oasis	145
Chapter Twenty:	Desert Danger	152
Chapter Twenty-One:	The Beggar	159
Chapter Twenty-Two:	The Challenge	166
Chapter Twenty-Three:	The Dungeon	175
Chapter Twenty-Four:	The Hidden Passage	183
Chapter Twenty-Five:	The Plot	191
Chapter Twenty-Six:	The Escape	199

Chapter Twenty-Seven:	The Race	209
Chapter Twenty-Eight:	The Hunt	215
Chapter Twenty-Nine:	The Misty Isles	221
Chapter Thirty:	The Meeting	227
Chapter Thirty-One:	The House Of Joy	234
Chapter Thirty-Two:	The House Of Sorrow	243
Chapter Thirty-Three:	The Playful Place	250
Chapter Thirty-Four:	The Last Voyage	258
Chapter Thirty-Five:	The Swampeys	265
Chapter Thirty-Six:	The Forest Folk	273
Chapter Thirty-Seven:	Safe Passage	282
Chapter Thirty-Eight:	The Queen Mother	289
Chapter Thirty-Nine:	At Last	299
Chapter Forty:	Your Ideas, Questions, Drawings Etc.	308

INTRODUCTION

    This is a magical, mystical myth. It was inspired by C.S. Lewis's children's books, *The Chronicles of Narnia,* and by George McDonald's children's books, including *At the Back of the North Wind, The Princess and Curdie,* and *The Golden Key.*

    Like their stories, this story is magical, because it comes purely from the world of imagination. It is mystical, because it comes from personal experience of the divine truths the story tells. It is a myth because it is about the life of the soul—yours, mine, and everyone's. Therefore, it is not confined to our everyday experience of time and space. It happens in the marvelous anywhere, anytime. Nor is it a story only for children, or only for adults. It is for the young at heart of all ages who love the adventurous and truth-full realms of Imagination.

    It is my favorite place to be, and I am delighted that I found an artist to illustrate this story who dwells in and draws from these realms. Here are Karla's own words about her art.

"I have longed to make pictures for books since I was five years old, the night my parents read me "The Velveteen Rabbit" on our cozy old couch in Grand Rapids, Michigan. A few months ago, Marty handed me her manuscript of "Eisha's Search" with a twinkle in her eye and a smile tugging at the corners of her mouth. As I curled up with my tea and dove in, I knew by the third chapter that I had finally found the challenge, the inspiration, and especially the Home inside this book that I have been seeking for a very long time.

Each illustration is intended as a gift to you, the reader, to interpret, color, frown or smile upon however you wish. It has been thrilling to navigate through Eisha's world, carrying only a Sharpie pen and a full heart. It is even more thrilling now to share her journey through the insightful eyes of you, the reader. I hope you will enjoy the drawings as much as I have enjoyed making them for you.

If there are any of your own drawings that you would like to share with me, you can find me at <u>www.karlavanhuysen.com</u>"

You will notice a couple of unique features about this book that will help you make it your own in a special way.

First, at the end of each chapter is one of Karla's wonderful drawings. You can color it if you like. On the other side, the page is blank so you can draw your own picture to illustrate the preceding chapter, or write your own responses.

Second, the fortieth chapter is for your questions, your insights, and your ideas about what happens next. Who knows, it may inspire you to write a book of your very own! The pages are blank, so you can fill them in as you please. If there is anything you would like to share with me, feel free to email me at: Marchiene@earthlink.net.

CHAPTER ONE:

THE CAVE

It was the middle of the night. The bed was shaking. Eisha sat up, her heart pounding. She heard the loud sounds of things crashing to the floor. When she looked out of the window by her bed, the stars were swaying. Suddenly there was an urgent whisper in the dark.

"Run, Eisha, run! You must escape this earthquake. Go into the desert. You know the way. There, you will find whatever help you need. Take this with you."

Eisha saw the dark figure of her grandmother at her bedside, and felt a bundle being pushed into her arms. She was too frightened to think or protest. Stumbling out of bed, she took the bundle, ran out of her bedroom, through the corridors of the castle, and out into the night air. The ground was still shaking beneath her feet as she ran, and behind her she heard screams as the walls of her castle-home tottered and fell.

A few moments later, the earth stopped it's heaving, and Eisha found herself beyond the castle grounds at the edge of the desert. Behind her lay a pile of ruins that buried all she knew and loved—even her grandmother, who she loved more than anyone in the entire world. Ahead of her lay an unknown desert. A full moon shone in the sky, flooding the desert with light, and the stars gleamed like the light of distant fires. But Eisha found no comfort in their light.

"Why did grandmother tell me to go into the desert?" she sobbed as she stumbled forward among the sand and rocks, with tears streaming down her face. "How will I survive? What help can I possibly find here? And what will I do, all by myself, with no home, no family, no friends, and nothing but this bundle she gave me?"

Because Eisha had learned to trust her grandmother, she trudged on into the desert in spite of her questions, pushing the strands of her long brown hair back from her forehead, and wiping the tears from her cheeks. Her bright blue nightgown, which she had been wearing when the earthquake hit, clung to her sturdy legs and ankles. Her shoulders drooped with sadness, and her arms ached with the weight of the bundle she was carrying. Her sandals kept slipping off her feet, until finally, in exasperation, she took them off and walked barefoot in the cool desert sand until she was too tired to walk anymore. Then she laid herself down on the ground, pillowed her head on her bundle, and fell asleep.

When Eisha awoke, the sun was high in the sky. Her green eyes filled with dismay as she saw nothing but sand, rocks, and scrub for miles in every direction. The sand met the sky at the horizon, except in the west, where a range of mountains thrust dark, jagged peaks into the sky. "Where am I?" she wondered anxiously. "And which direction should I go?"

A growl from her stomach reminded her that she needed something to eat and drink. "I hope there's something in this bundle, or I won't last long," she thought as her fingers eagerly tugged at the knots that secured the cloth around its contents. Finally, they came loose, and Eisha saw several packets of dried fruits and nuts, some round, flat bread, and a large flask of water. Gratefully, she ate and drank as much as she dared, not knowing how far she had to go. As she ate, she remembered that her grandmother had once talked about the mountains that lay west of the desert, and of someone she knew who lived there. "Maybe that is where she would want me to go!" thought Eisha. She got up, wrapped up her bundle, put on her sandals, and began walking westward towards the mountains.

All day she walked under the blazing sun. The only shade she could find was shed by clumps of scrubby bushes, and that is where she stopped to rest and eat and drink. By evening, the mountains seemed only a little nearer, and as the sun sank, her heart sank with it. How would she ever reach them at this rate? Her food and water would run out soon.

Then Eisha remembered her grandmother's promise that she would find the help she needed in the desert. It was all she had to keep her from giving up. "I wonder if she knew the earthquake was coming?" thought Eisha as she sat down on the desert floor to rest. "She often seemed to have a sense of things that were going to happen. I remember how she walked with me at the edge of the desert, beyond the walls of the castle grounds, the night before father died. She said then that I might feel as if my world had come crashing down around me! And I did. But even that was not like this!" And the immensity of Eisha's loss swept over her in a great wave of grief. She collapsed onto the desert floor, weeping, and cried herself to sleep.

Once, during the night, she awoke, and looked up to see two stars right above her that somehow reminded her of her grandmother's eyes, and she fell asleep again feeling comforted. She awoke in the morning with a lighter heart, and ate the last of her food. Saving a little water for later in the day, she began walking again.

Shortly after mid-day, Eisha chanced to glance behind her, and could hardly believe her eyes. A huge Lion was running toward her! Springing to her feet in alarm, she ran from it as fast as she could, her long brown hair flying behind her. For a while, she was able to stay quite far ahead of the Lion. But then she became too tired to run any further. A huge rock loomed off to her right, and she dashed behind it. "Perhaps I will escape the

Lion's notice here," she thought, and she huddled in the shadow of the rock, hoping against hope that the Lion would somehow pass her by. She did not dare peer around the rock to see where it was. She simply sat as still as she could, leaning against the rock, with sweat trickling down her face. Gradually, she stopped panting, and began to relax a little. There was no sound in the vast stillness of the desert. She shut her eyes against the glare of the sun...

When Eisha next opened them, she saw, to her horror, that the head of the Lion was bent over her face and throat, its breath hot in her face! In desperation, she hurled herself out from under the Lion, and began to run again. To her amazement, she found herself running as never before, as swiftly as if she were flying, as lightly as if she were a bird! The mountains to the west, which had looked so distant, began to loom large on the horizon. She glanced over her shoulder and saw that the Lion, who was running after her again, was dwindling away into a tiny, distant speck. In spite of her relief at this sight, she kept running on fear-winged feet until she saw that she had completely lost sight of the pursuing beast.

Then, with a deep breath, she slowed down and looked about her. She was at the far western edge of the desert. The ground was no longer flat, and between the rocks there rose a steep, winding path that led upward through fragrant shrubs into a forest of pines. Eisha decided to follow the path upward. Soon the rocky ground was covered with ferns and flowers, mosses of all kinds, and piles of pine needles. She began to walk still more slowly, letting in deep breaths of the mountain air. On Eisha went, higher and higher, until, at a turn in the path, she came to a gap in the pine trees. A great row of shining snow-white mountain peaks towered beyond the trees against a deep blue sky. The sight brought her to a standstill as she gazed in awe at the splendor of the mountains, and the depths of the vast ravines that plunged down from the side of the path on which she stood.

Eisha did not move for a long time. It felt good to be still after running for so long. She sniffed the pine-scented air and savored the quiet that surrounded her. Gradually, the shadows of the trees began to lengthen. The sun's evening slant lit the mountain ranges with gold, and sent shafts of amber light into the depths of the forest on her left. One of those shafts happened to fall on a small hut, which stood against the base of a gigantic rock. A light like that of the setting sun glowed softly through the arch of the hut's doorway. It seemed to bid her come and take shelter against the approaching night and whatever beasts wandered the darkening forest. Eisha eagerly followed the beckoning ray of light through the forest shadows as they swallowed up the lingering rays of the setting sun. As night took over the forest, she reached the doorway, and with great relief stepped into the hut.

Its back wall was the huge mountain-rock against which it was built. A little stream of water trickled down its stony face into a small, scooped-out hollow in a rocky ledge that ran the length of the wall at about the height of her waist. The floor was covered with a thick layer of moss. There was nothing else in the hut.

Eisha was very hungry by now, and even more thirsty. She saw nothing to satisfy her hunger, but at least there was the water. Plunging her face into the clear liquid in the rocky hollow, she scooped handfuls of it into her mouth and over her face. Somehow, the water assuaged both her hunger and thirst. Still, it did not prevent a huge wave of weariness from suddenly washing over her. She threw herself down on the moss-covered floor. It cushioned her aching body as comfortably as a bed, and before long, she closed her eyes and knew no more...

When Eisha awoke, it was dark outside. Whether it was the same night or the next, she could not tell, for she had no way of knowing how long she had slept. In the hut, however, the same soft glow of light that had shone through the forest, beckoning her to come in, now gleamed all about her. It was as if many candles lit the room, though not a candle was to be seen. The mysterious light danced with the shadows on the ceiling and in the corners of the hut. Eisha sat for a time in the silent play of soft light and shadow, wondering.

Presently, she thought she heard, ever so faintly, the sound of a strange voice singing. It seemed to come from far below her, for when she got down and put her ear to the moss, it was slightly stronger. She lay and listened. Then tears of longing and memory, joy and sorrow, began to roll down her cheeks, for the song unsealed them so they could flow from the depths of her heart, which had for a long time been as dry as the desert she had crossed. Memories of being cradled and rocked, of lullabies and loving arms, awakened and mingled with her flowing tears. She saw her grandmother's face bent over her, glowing with love. Her mother's face had disappeared when she was a little child, and her father's face seldom appeared in her memories. It was her grandmother's face and form that filled them, and oh! How she longed to see that face and form again, now, in this strange place!

Finally, she lifted her head and saw, dimly, through tear-filled eyes, that the mysterious candle-like light that filled the hut seemed a little brighter near the door. Quietly, she crept on hands and knees, until she came close to the threshold over which she had stepped—how long ago, she did not know. There, the light glowed through an opening in the floor. She peered into it, and saw that a ladder, seemingly woven of rope in all the colors of the rainbow, hung suspended from the floor of the hut. She could not see the bottom of the ladder, for it was very long, and the light was brighter the further down she looked.

A longing to go down the ladder seized Eisha, for she felt that somehow she would find the singing at the heart of the light below. She squeezed feet-first through the narrow opening and found herself stepping from one rope rung to another as her hands clung to the sides of the ladder. The rope gave a bit with every step. Under her weight and downward motion, it began to sway. She grasped the rope more tightly, noticing that as the light grew brighter around her, the shadows beyond the light deepened, for the ladder hung suspended in a cave whose sides disappeared into those shadows in all directions. When she looked straight down, she saw a light like the heart of a candle's flame. From that light came the sound of the singing that had loosened her tears.

With renewed determination, Eisha descended. The rope was silky to her touch, and its rainbow colors, skillfully woven together, seemed to contain a promise that her descent was not in vain. The light glowed ever clearer and brighter. The shadows danced farther and farther away. The soft singing grew stronger. All at once, her foot, reaching for yet another rung of rope, touched solid rock. It was hard and cold on her bare feet. Carefully releasing the rope ladder, she turned around.

The sides of the cave stretched and curved themselves into a single spacious room. At its center sat a Lady with the long white hair of the very old. She wore a simple gown of blue the color of an autumn sky. Her loose hair veiled her face, for she was bending low over a hollow in the rocky floor at her feet.

Eisha softly took a step closer. The source of the light seemed to be in the hollow, and it lit the Lady's face as she lifted her head. To Eisha's surprise, her face was smooth and young. Dark eyes shone there, and as she looked into them, Eisha felt she gazed into depths beyond all telling. Something about the face was familiar, but Eisha could not tell why. The Lady gazed at her in silence, and Eisha realized that the singing had stopped.

"Oh, please," she blurted out. "Don't stop singing. I came all the way down here for the song and the light."

The Lady made no reply, but returned her attention to the hollow at her feet. Eisha followed her gaze, stepping nearer so that she could see into the hollow. There lay an infant Child, cradled in the light whose glow filled the cave and the hut far above. The glow of the light seemed almost solid, as if one could touch it, and gathered in folds below and around the Child, who lay sleeping with a look of complete peace on its face. Eisha gazed at the Child lying in the light, and a great ache filled her heart. She longed to hold it and care for it. Instinctively, she felt that this Child held in its being the secrets of her heart.

All at once, Eisha became aware again of the singing that had drawn her into the depths of the cave. She looked up at the face of the Lady, who was still gazing at the Child. But no sound came from her lips. Rather, the singing seemed to come from the shadows behind her. Eisha turned and gazed intently into the shadows. The light flared up for an instant, like a flame springing from a glowing ember. In its glow she saw, emerging from the shadows, the great shape of the Lion from whom she had fled in the desert! She screamed and began to tremble all over as she sank to the ground next to the Child and the Lady, hiding her face in her hands as if to keep from seeing what she saw.

"Don't be afraid," said the Lady from somewhere above her. "Listen, my daughter! It is the Lion you fear so much who is singing the song that moves you so deeply."

"But," gasped Eisha, her face still covered with her hands, "the Lion has been chasing me and almost devoured me out there in the desert!"

"You were running away; that is why it seemed to be chasing you," replied the Lady gently. "But the Lion meant for you to come here all the time. It let you go and gave wings to your feet so you could fly to the mountains. It has been here waiting for you, singing for you, luring you to the light and the Child and me."

Eisha sat straight up and uncovered her face. The Lady and the Lion were gazing at her, and there was love in the Lady's eyes, and sorrowful joy in the Lion's.

"The Lion will not pursue you," continued the Lady, "unless you leave the Child and the Light. For it is your destiny to tend this Child. I cannot stay any longer, for I have waited a very long time for you to take my place."

Eisha stopped trembling and looked long and hard at the Lady. "You look like someone I know," she said with some hesitation, "but I can't figure out why. And you look very young and very old all at once. How can that be?"

"To tend the Child of the light is to grow younger while growing older," said the Lady. She smiled and continued. "You can only live this truth—it cannot fit your mind. And when you are ready, you will know who I am, and why I seem familiar to you."

Eisha was quiet for a long time, glancing now at the Lady, now at the Lion, now at the Child sleeping in the cradle-clothes of light. All was silent. Finally she spoke.

"Where will you go, Lady-Mother?"

"There are other children of light with no one to tend them, lying deep in other caverns. Now that you have come into your own cave, only you can care for this Child. Will you do it?"

"Will I be down here all alone?"

"No. Beside the Child, the Lion will watch over you and sing the songs that free tears and let joy and sorrow flow. Be still, sit in the song, care for the Child, live in the light, and all will be well."

Eisha looked at the Lion, its fur gleaming dull gold in the light, its eyes shining, its song, like a cat's purr, vibrating in its body and throat. She took a deep breath, then walked over and embraced the Lion, laying her cheek against its throat, and feeling the song deep within. It vibrated through the Lion's body into her own, and such joy welled up within her that she felt she could not bear it for more than a moment. She stepped back from the Lion, and held out her hands to the Lady. A radiant smile broke over the Lady's face like dawn over the sea.

"I am the one your grandmother hoped you would find here in the mountains," she said softly. "The Lion was the help she promised you, though I know you didn't see it that way!" They laughed together, and the Lady took Eisha's hands into her own.

Eisha said, "I am willing to care for this Child. I know that something very important depends on it."

The Lady looked into Eisha's eyes, and kissed her lightly on the forehead. Eisha felt as if a star were imbedded there forever. Then the Lady arose, turned, and walked slowly away from Eisha and the Child. Step by step she ascended up the rainbow-hued ladder, and as she lifted each foot, the rung on which it had stood disappeared, until finally the Lady and the ladder vanished into the shadows far above.

"There truly is no going back," said Eisha as she sat down and bent over the sleeping Child.

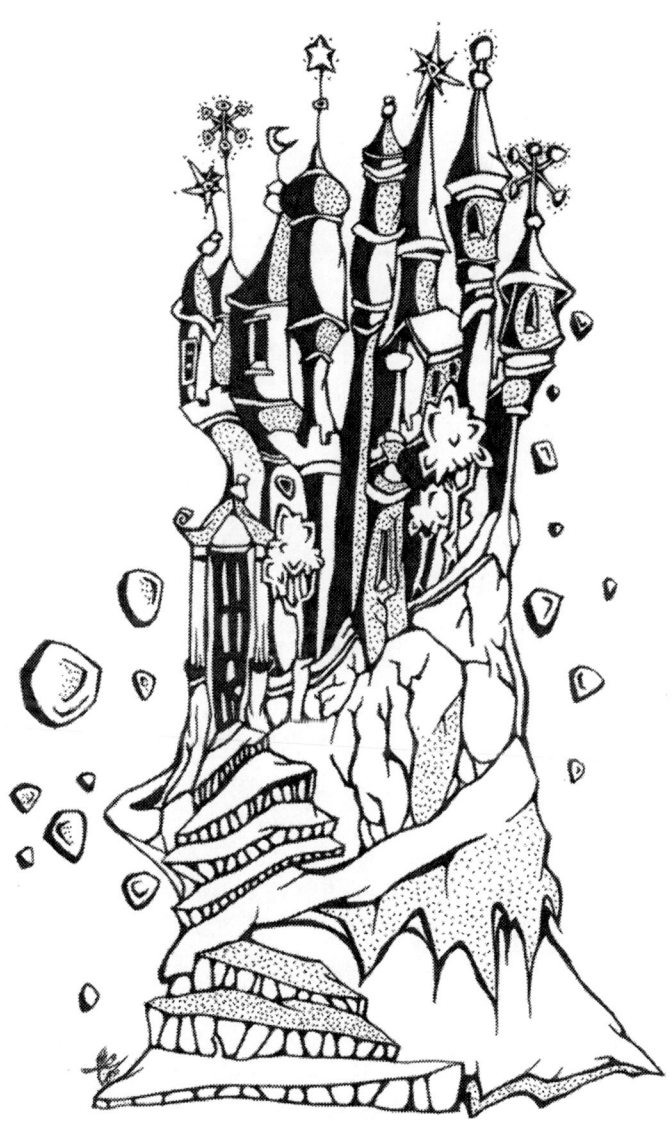

"The ground was still shaking beneath her feet as she ran, and behind her she heard screams as the walls of her castle-home tottered and fell."

CHAPTER TWO:

THE SERPENT

Out of the shadows behind the Lion, the form of a Serpent uncoiled itself, and slithered slowly towards Eisha as she sat holding the tiny Child who was the love of her life. Its long, undulating body was covered, not with the usual scales, but with feathers like that of a peacock's tail. The Lion grew silent. There was no song as the Serpent spoke.

"My lady, listen to me."

Eisha looked up, startled.

"What is it you want?" she asked. "And who are you? Where did you come from?"

"From the darkness behind the Lion, in the far recesses of the cave," replied the Serpent. "I come to call you to the forest above, which you left so long ago."

"I cannot go," replied Eisha. "My place is here, with the Child."

"For how long?" asked the Serpent.

"I don't know," she replied, and a slight frown creased her brow.

She had no idea how long she had been in the cave watching the Child.

The Serpent persisted. "Perhaps I am the sign that the time has come to leave."

"But—why should I?" asked Eisha.

"There are many reasons. There is great need for you in the world above. You alone can fill those needs. You have only to see, and you will believe me. Come, come away."

There was a long silence. Eisha gazed at the Child who lay in her arms. How could she leave it alone? How could she cease to care for this little one to whom she had given her heart?

"The Child will be safe; see how peacefully it sleeps," murmured the Serpent, as if reading her thoughts. "What can harm it, hidden away here far below the forest, lying in its cradle of light?"

Eisha looked about her, searching for another reason to stay.

"But there is no way out," she said. "The rainbow ladder by which I came down is gone."

"Ah, but I can be your ladder," replied the Serpent. "See how large my coils are. The roots of the feathers that cover my scales will give you footholds, and your hands can grasp my feathers. It will not be difficult. You will see."

Eisha considered. It had been a long time since the Lady left her to care for the Child. She was hungry for human contact. The Serpent's words about need in the world above tugged at her heart. A vague restlessness stirred within her. For a long moment, she looked into the face of the Child. Then she rose to her feet, placed the Child gently and a little reluctantly in its cradle of light, and faced the Serpent.

"Very well," Eisha said. "If I am needed now in the world above, I will go."

The Serpent uncoiled itself and rose up on its tail, till its head towered high above into the thickening shadows of the cave.

"Come," came its voice from on high. "Come out and see."

Eisha stepped onto its tail, and slowly, steadily climbed up its feathered body towards the opening above. The feathers glowed with the colors of sapphires, emeralds, and amethysts in the flame-like light. The roots of the fibrous feathers bit into her bare feet. As she climbed upward, the shadows around her deepened. Once, when she stopped for a moment to catch her breath and ease her aching feet, her glance fell downward toward the Child that she had left. Suddenly she became aware of the silence. The song that had surrounded her for so long had stopped. With deep misgiving, she gazed into the shadows at the edges of the light and saw to her dismay that the Lion had disappeared. Her heart filled with questions.

In that moment of her hesitation, the Serpent moved swiftly, drawing its length upward. Eisha was carried rapidly towards the roof of the cave, forcing her to cling tightly to the feathered coil beneath her. She became dizzy from the upward speed and swaying movement of the Serpent. Closing her eyes, she fell on her stomach in the Serpent's feathers and hung on with all her might.

All at once, the movement stopped. Eisha felt herself fall onto hard ground. She opened her eyes and saw that she was lying at the door of the hut she had entered so long ago. It was winter, and the trees of the forest that surrounded it were bare and brown. A faint dusting of snow lay on the ground; and in it she saw the track of the Serpent, who had swiftly slithered away, leaving nothing behind but a peacock-like feather in her hand.

Eisha shivered. She looked down at the threshold of the hut. The opening through which she had gone down and come up was closed! Not knowing what else to do, she re-entered the hut. It was cold and bare. The moss on which she had slept was brown and stiff. The water, which ran down the back wall, was now frozen into icicles. Remembering how well the water had nourished her, she broke off a piece of the ice to ward off hunger and thirst. Then she looked about her, wondering what to do next.

Near the door, she saw a pair of boots, and a thick, long brown cloak hanging on a peg. Eisha put on the boots and wrapped the cloak around herself. Delicious warmth enveloped her. "This will protect me against the cold in the world outside," she thought to herself. "And since that is where the need is, that is where I will go." With a sigh, she stepped out of the open door and began walking into the forest, looking for the need the Serpent had spoken of. It was all she could do now, for there was no going back. In her heart was a strange emptiness, and her arms began to ache to hold the Child. Filled with doubt about what she had done, she sank onto the snow, leaned against the trunk of a huge oak tree, covered her face with her hands, and began to weep.

After she had cried for a good while, Eisha became aware that the sound of other weeping was coming from beyond her. She opened her eyes, uncovered her face, and saw a band of ragged children walking nearby. All of them were crying, shivering, and looking utterly miserable. Eisha got up and approached them. "What is the matter?" she asked. "Why are you wandering through these woods in the dead of winter without anyone to take care of you?"

The children stopped crying and stood staring at her. One of them spoke. "We're lost and cold and hungry, and we don't know where to go."

At this, several of the smaller children began to wail loudly. Eisha's heart went out to them and she said, "I'm lost too. But maybe I can help you. There's a little hut nearby. Come there with me. We can huddle together and tell each other stories!"

The children nodded numbly, and followed her as she led them through the forest and into the hut. They all sat down on the floor together. The moss offered a dry, if prickly, cushion. Eisha took off her cloak and invited the children to share it. As each one took a corner, it grew and grew so that its warm brown folds enveloped them all in a delicious blanket of warmth. The children became still, comforted by the warmth of the cloak, the closeness of each other's bodies, and Eisha's caring.

In the silence, the growl of empty stomachs reminded her of their hunger. Rising from the ground, she picked a frozen icicle from the back of the cave. "Here," she said, "pass this icicle around and lick it, each of you. It might help your hunger and thirst." The children did as she asked. A look of delight lit up their faces as they passed it to one another. "It tastes like strawberry!" exclaimed one who loved strawberry better than anything in the world. "It tastes like chocolate!" exclaimed another, who, of course, loved chocolate better than anything else. Each one tasted what he or she loved most, and the little icy lick each had was enough to ease their hunger and thirst.

Then, worn out by their weary wandering, the children fell asleep, one by one, like a pack of puppies curled against each other. The cloak lay gently over them all. Soon Eisha too fell asleep, and dreamed of a wonderful song, and a Lion chasing her through the forest.

"It's long, undulating body was covered, not with the usual scales, but with feathers like that of a peacock's tail."

CHAPTER THREE:

THE STAR

Eisha's eyes flew open. A silver shaft of starlight rested on her forehead and eyelids. It came through the open doorway of the hut from a single brilliant Star that gleamed in the darkness. She sat up, and the children huddled next to her stirred in their sleep.

A longing to get up and follow the Star into the woods seized her. But how could she leave the children? Eisha looked down at their sleeping forms, and tenderly arranged the folds of the brown cloak around them. Then she looked up at the Star again. Its light seemed to her to be resting on her forehead, and suddenly the memory of the Lady's farewell kiss welled up within her. If only she could see her loving face again!

Eisha rose from the floor, and walked out the door, leaving her cloak behind as a covering for the children. The night was still and cold, and the Star a swirl of silver light, luring her into the forest. She found herself stepping across the clearing that separated the hut from the forest. At its edge, she stopped and looked back at the hut where the sleeping children lay.

Suddenly a huge, dark shadow fell across the space that lay between Eisha and the hut. Her heart raced in fear. But she held her ground, resisting the impulse to run into the forest as fast as she could. There were the children to think of. She forced herself to stand still and look hard at the shadow. It was the

Lion! Its eyes gleamed in the dark, and it seemed to be looking straight at her.

"Where are you going?" The words were growled, rather than spoken, but Eisha understood them.

"I-I don't know," she stammered. "I just came out here to look at the Star."

"And why did you just turn from following it into the forest?"

"I was worried about the children. I didn't know if I should leave them alone in the hut, after they put such trust in me."

The Lion stepped closer, and its tail switched a warning back and forth. "Are they your children?"

"No," replied Eisha slowly. "I came upon them in the forest. They were lost and hungry and crying."

"Yes. And you sheltered and fed and comforted them. That was all right. But I want you to realize that I know and love them more than you do. You have done your part. They are to be left in my care and keeping."

"You mean—I'm supposed to leave them there in the hut?" asked Eisha.

"You must," replied the Lion. "There is no going back. Your way lies inward into the forest."

Eisha felt a flood of loss, then a burst of relief, and a glimmer of joy. They mingled and flowed in tears down her face as she stood before the Lion. "Will you lead me back to the Lady and the Child?" she asked. "Or will I never see them again?"

"The Star and I will lead you," said the Lion gently. "If you follow, and do not turn back again, you will find the Lady and the Child. But it will be a long and different way this time. You can never go the same way twice."

"But- what will happen to the children?" asked Eisha, gazing at the hut.

"That is their story, not yours," answered the Lion sternly.

Eisha stood for a long while, staring at the hut where the children lay sleeping. Finally, she took a deep breath, faced the forest, and said, "I am ready."

At these words, the Lion drew alongside her, and she could feel its fur next to her skin. It radiated protecting warmth in the cold night air. As they walked together into the dark shadows of the forest, the Star blazed anew above the treetops, and from deep within the Lion's body came the sweet sound of the song that had drawn her deep into the cave to the Child and the Lady.

"Put your arm around my neck and I will keep you from falling," said the Lion as they walked further into the forest. "And when you get tired, just stop and kneel on the ground, and I will carry you."

Eisha nodded and they walked along in silence. After awhile, the Lion's purring song began again. The Star shone brilliantly above them. Surrounded by the song and the starlight, with the warm furry feel of the Lion's body next to hers, she walked peacefully into the night and the forest.

Her peace was shattered all at once by the sound of crying. Her heart could feel that it was the children, awakening to find her gone, and wailing in fear and confusion. A deep sadness welled up within her. Her body felt heavy, aching, and weary. She sat down on the ground, and covered her face with her hands.

Beside her, the Lion stopped, and waited.

"How can I go on?" she cried. "I don't know what to do. I don't know where I'm going. I'm not even sure anymore who I am. Oh, what will become of me?" And she began sobbing as if she would never stop. The Lion stood silently beside her. After awhile, it sank to the ground. Feeling its warm breath on her face, Eisha removed her hands and looked at the Lion with stinging, tear-blurred eyes. The Lion gently licked the tears from her face. The tender gesture opened the spring of tears in her again, and throwing her arms around the Lion's mane, Eisha buried her face in it, and cried uncontrollably, her shoulders shaking, her body tensing and releasing with sobs.

Finally, she stopped and sat very still, her cheek against the Lion's mane, her arms wrapped tightly around its neck. The cries of the children had almost faded away, though now and then her heart ached in response to a muffled cry that still penetrated the distance and stillness.

"Come," said the Lion gently. "I will carry you for awhile."

Eisha climbed laboriously onto its back, her whole body stiff and sore with sorrow, weariness, and loss. Then the Lion walked slowly on into the forest. The shadows of the trees swallowed them in darkness. Now and then, when she looked up, she caught a glimpse of the Star that had kissed her forehead and lured her away from the safety of the hut and the care of the children into the unknown depths of the forest. Still the Lion walked on, carrying Eisha deeper and deeper into the shadows.

After what seemed like an eternity, when she felt she could not stay awake and upright a moment longer, the Lion came to a halt and lay down. "Time to stop for awhile," it said. "You have journeyed far and are worn out with grief and guilt. You need rest." With that, it gently rolled her off its back and began gathering pieces of wood in its mouth and piling them in the center of the small clearing in which they had stopped. Directly overhead, the Star shone down, its beams seeming to reach out toward the earth below. Brighter and brighter they grew, until, as Eisha watched in wonder, they touched the pile of wood the Lion had made, and it burst into flame. And oh! What flames they were! Orange and blue, yellow and green, red and purple, they flared up, flickering and leaping toward the Star. It was as if they had been sparked by the distant, blazing star-sun into a fiery dance of blazing joy upon the earth.

Eisha crept closer to the Fire and sat down. She gazed into its flames, and their fierce, fiery beauty warmed her body and penetrated into her whole being. She felt the sore grief and sad weariness seeping out of her whole body until she melted like warm butter into a puddle of sleep.

Once, in the middle of the night, Eisha awoke, and saw, on the other side of the Fire, the dark shape of the Lion, a great sitting shadow with eyes that gleamed as bright as the flames, gazing steadily at her. For a moment, she felt a stab of fear. Who was this Lion, after all, and where was it leading her? And for what purpose? But the memory of its tongue gently licking tears from her face blunted the fear. The sound of the Lion's purring song mingled with the sizzling, searing sighs of the Star-Fire's glowing embers, and Eisha let go of her doubts and fears. Her eyes grew heavy once more. She put her head down and in her last waking moment imagined she glimpsed, in the heart of the flame, the Child, and the Lady bent over it, watching and waiting.

"As they walked together into the dark shadows of the forest, the Star blazed anew above the tree-tops."

CHAPTER FOUR:

THE STONE

Eisha awoke in the darkness with a start. The fire was a pile of cold, gray ashes. The Lion was no longer there. She shivered, and felt the cold dampness of pre-dawn dew seeping through her clothing into her skin. She was no longer tired or sleepy, but she was afraid. All about her stretched an unknown forest, dark and foreboding. She sat alone in a small, empty clearing. The only sound was her own breathing.

"What now?" Eisha wondered. "Shall I wait to see if the Lion returns? Shall I go on? But—where shall I go? And how shall I get to wherever it is I am supposed to go?" No answers came. Nor did the Lion.

Finally, after sitting with these questions for a good while, Eisha heard the chirp of the first waking bird breaking the silence as if to say, "It's time to get up!"

She rose slowly to her feet, and took a few stiff steps towards the woods, away from the ashes of the Fire that had burned at the center of the clearing. "I'll walk around the clearing first, before I go into the woods," thought Eisha. "Maybe I'll find some sign of the Lion or some clue about which way to go." She walked slowly, looking carefully at the ground, and peering frequently into the woods. But she did not find what she was looking for. She walked a second time around the clearing, and a third. She had almost completed the fourth round when she spied a vivid green patch of moss that was made up of hundreds of tiny, brilliant green star-shapes. In the midst of the moss, a few little white flowers glowed in the growing light of early morning. She was drawn to their fragile beauty, and got down on her hands and knees to examine them more closely.

Suddenly, the moss under her hands gave way. Her arms, head, and shoulders plunged deep into a dark emptiness. Eisha fell headlong into the black hole that had been so cleverly concealed by the moss-patch. Down, down, down she went, falling, falling, falling into the darkness, her arms in front of her, her legs and feet flailing out behind her. It seemed she would never stop, and Eisha was sure this was the end of her.

After awhile, she had the strange sensation that time had slowed way down, and with it, the speed of her fall. She began to notice things around her—the sound of trickling water, jewel-like gleams of light in shades of green, purple, and blue glimmering in the rock that surrounded her, and, ever so faintly, the smell and sound of ocean waves far below.

Then there was a shift, and it seemed to Eisha that time and the pace of her falling fast-forwarded to a speed that made everything a whirling blur and took her breath away. She tried to scream, but could not. The sound rose up from her throat, and was pushed back into it. She was falling so fast she felt as if her stomach would drop out of her open mouth at any moment. Just when she thought she could not bear it for one more instant, Eisha felt a mass of hair and fur in her face, and her body thudded against the warm flesh of an animal. For a moment, she lay there, too frightened to move, trying not to breathe. In that long, silent moment, she heard a familiar purring song.

Eisha lifted up her head, and found she was lying on her stomach on the back of the Lion! She sat up, straddling it with her legs. Ahead of her was a large opening through which she could faintly see waves of water whishing up on a beach. She and the Lion were in a cave. Its floor was covered with the same moss that she had stopped to examine in the woods far above.

"I must have fallen right through the heart of a mountain!" she exclaimed.

"Indeed, you did," said the Lion calmly. "And a long fall it was. I have been waiting here for a good while for you."

"Oh!" answered Eisha. "Well, I'm glad I landed on you. But why did you leave me by the campfire alone? How did you expect me to find you?" Her voice was filled with relief and indignation all at once.

The Lion looked over its shoulder into her eyes. "I am not gone from you, even when you can't see me. But sometimes, you need to search to find me. Still, do you think, after all this time, that I would let you get really, truly lost?"

Eisha gazed into the Lion's eyes, and after awhile said simply, "No. You wouldn't. I'm sorry I didn't trust you."

For reply the Lion began its purring song, and its vibrations moved into Eisha's body. She clasped her arms confidently about the Lion's neck, laid her face in its mane, and said, "Please take me where I need to go next."

The Lion bent its great head, and crouching close to the mossy floor, moved toward the opening of the cave. It stopped just at the threshold.

"Look down at the ground just behind you," said the Lion.

Eisha looked, and saw, lying in the starry green moss, a beautiful purple-green-and-blue Stone. It shone like a precious jewel, and at its center she could see a tiny white flower-like crystal, a stone version of the little white flowers that blossomed in the moss-patch through which she had fallen.

"Pick up the Stone," said the Lion. "It is the heart of the heart of the mountain. It has lain here for many ages, waiting for the right person to find it and pick it up and treasure it."

Eisha leaned over and took the Stone from its mossy bed. She looked in awe at its jeweled beauty as it lay, heavy, cupped in the palm of her hand.

"Your Heart-Stone will often be useful to you," said the Lion. "It will guide you along your way. When you are in the right way, it will glow brilliantly, as it does now, and lie heavy in your hand. Should you go astray, it will grow dull and lose its weight. Always keep it with you. It is the gift of the mountain's silence and steadfastness. With it, you will be able to find your way to the journey's end."

Eisha nodded, and with her Heart-Stone clutched in one hand, and the Lion's mane in the other, rode the Lion out of the mountain cave onto the shores of the sea.

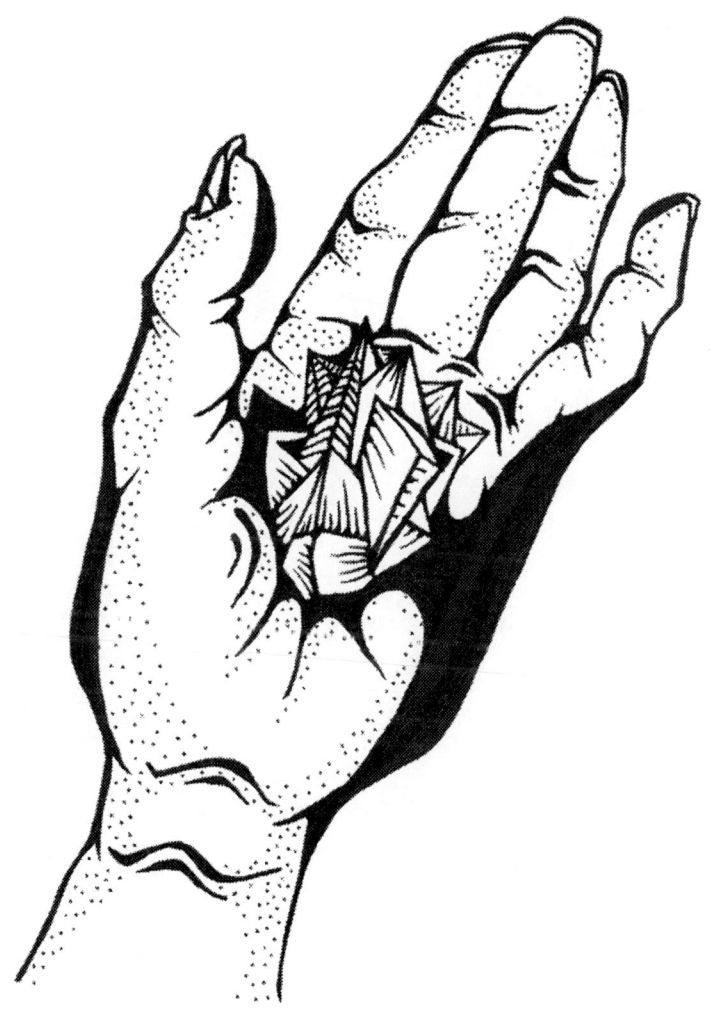

"She looked in awe at its jeweled beauty as it lay, heavy, cupped in her hand."

CHAPTER FIVE:

THE CASTLE

It was night as Eisha and the Lion emerged onto the beach. A few stars shone dimly through a mist that mingled water and sky. Behind them, a great, forested range of mountains loomed black against the night. The beach was deserted, except for a large sand castle that towered as high as Eisha stood when she was on tiptoe.

"Oh!" breathed Eisha. "What a beautiful, big sand castle! I wonder who built it?" She slid quickly off the Lion's back and walked toward it. The Lion watched her go with sadness in its eyes, then turned and walked into the shadows at the edge of the beach.

Eisha scarcely noticed, so entranced was she by the sand castle. The nearer she got to it, the more attractive it became to her. With its turrets and towers, battlements and ramparts, it looked something like the castle in which she had grown up, only much smaller, of course. A great, arched wooden door stood open, as if in welcome. She knelt down so she could see into the castle through the open door.

"If only I could shrink a little so I could go inside and look around," Eisha thought. She sat down on the sand, peering through her knees into the doorway. But she could see nothing to satisfy her curiosity. She walked around the sand castle several times, looking for another way in. Finding nothing, and not

35

knowing what to do next, she sat down on the sand to rest awhile. She had been awake since way before dawn, and the fright of her long and unexpected fall had worn her out. She sighed, yawned, stretched out on the beach, squirmed about to make herself comfortable, and closed her eyes.

For a time, memories of Eisha's childhood swirled in her mind. She relived the times she spent in her grandmother's room at the top of the tallest tower, listening to the wonderful stories her grandmother wove right along with the jewel-colored tapestries that slowly emerged from her loom. She saw herself playing for hours alone in her own bedroom in a round turret looking east towards the sea. She smiled as she remembered how she would dress up in old clothes from a big barrel in her room and re-enact the stories she had heard, with herself as the heroine. She frowned as she remembered the times her father would catch her in the middle of her play, and scold her for wasting so much time using her imagination instead of her mind. "You should concentrate on your lessons," he would say gruffly. "They will do you a lot more good when you are grown-up." But Eisha had never believed this was so because her grandmother always encouraged her to use her imagination, and even create her own stories.

"How I wish she were here now," thought Eisha, and her eyes filled with tears. "I've lost her, and my home, and everyone I ever knew. And now I've lost the Lady and the Child too." Then she buried her face in her arms as she laid on the sand, and cried herself to sleep.

Hours later, when Eisha awoke, the first thing she saw was the Morning Star, hanging low in the sky over the water. Its bright shining sent a path of silver that rippled across the sea straight to the sandcastle. Eisha stared at the Star, and it seemed to her that it was the same one that had kissed her on the forehead as she lay sleeping in the hut with the lost children. As she gazed at the sky and sea, she noticed, ever so faintly in the distance, the shadow of what might have been a sail, crossing the silver star-path that shone on the dark water. Then it was gone, lost in the night's darkness.

Eisha shook her head, rubbed her eyes, and looked about her. The Star had reminded her of the Lion. She got up and walked about the beach, searching the shadows. But the Lion was nowhere to be seen. Now what was she to do? At that moment, her eye fell on the sandcastle that had attracted her so much. Its dark walls glimmered in the faint light of the stars. A light shone in the doorway. Eisha noticed, with surprise, that now the door seemed to be just her height. Or, she was its height! In any case, the castle was definitely bigger now, or she was smaller—she wasn't sure which. Its towers and battlements rose high against the starry sky. Quickly, she walked up to the castle, and pushed the door all the way open.

She found herself in an empty room that obviously served as an entry into the rest of the castle. For a long moment, Eisha hesitated, wondering if she should go further. Without remembering to check her Stone, which she had slipped into a handy pocket, she decided to go on, and chose a door that stood slightly ajar on her right.

The room in which Eisha found herself was filled with heavy, dark, ornately carved furniture. The chairs were upholstered in patterns of all kinds. The floor was covered with oriental carpets of intricate design, and thick, maroon velvet drapes covered the windows. There were shelves and shelves of books in matched sets with gold lettering. A fire burned low in the grate of an ornately tiled fireplace. The air was hot and stuffy, and the whole room overwhelmed her with a cluttered, busy, closed-in feeling. She turned to leave, when a voice spoke behind her.

"Wait!"

Eisha turned back, and saw a thin, gaunt-looking man with fierce eyes and a dark, pointed beard staring at her with a stern look.

"Who gave you permission to enter here?" he demanded.

"No one," she replied.

"Did you not see the sign on the door?"

"No."

"It says 'Men Only.'"

"Why?"

"Because it's a scholar's study."

"So?"

"These books were written by men for men. This room was created by men who write and study important things for other men who write and study important things."

His words brought back memories of the times she had wanted to stay in her father's study and read some of the books. But he always made her leave, saying it was no place for a girl. Back then, she had been disappointed at his words. But now she felt differently as she looked around the room and sniffed the air. She wrinkled her nose in distaste. "I don't even want to stay in this stiff, stuffy room!" she said to the tall man who stood glaring at her.

A look of surprise and a hint of disappointment came over the man's face. "Well, I'm glad you know your place," he huffed.

"I don't," answered Eisha. "I am a stranger here. But I do know that this room is not my place." So saying, she walked back out of the door into the entry. Across from where she stood, she could see a stairway through an open door. "I wonder where that leads?" she thought to herself, and decided to go up the stairs. They wound round and round, the steps getting steeper as she climbed upward. At last, the stairway ended in a long hall. As far as she could see, the walls were hung with great, gold-framed portraits of solemn looking men in dark clothing. A number of doors opened off the hallway. She chose the third one on the left and opened it.

She stood at the threshold of a large, rectangular room. In it were many massive tables. Men who looked a great deal like those in the portraits sat at the tables talking earnestly. Every now and then, one would pound a gavel on the table, and a number of voices would boom out, "aye." Plates of food and goblets of wine stood on the tables, but only occasionally would anyone take a bite or sip. At the far end of the room, opposite the door where she stood, there was a stage. A few women were standing there, apparently making speeches to the assembled men, but few looked at them or listened for more than a moment or two, for they seemed to be pre-occupied with themselves and their business.

At that moment, one of the men caught a glimpse of her and called out, "Hey! Girl! We need some more water here," and he held up an empty glass as evidence. Eisha was startled.

"Where do I get water?" she heard herself saying, somewhat to her own surprise.

"In the kitchen, of course! Surely you know where that is!" said the man, and there was an edge of scorn in his voice.

Eisha blushed, and turned to find her way to the kitchen. "It's probably down on the main floor," she thought to herself, and took the first downward stairs she could find. It took her a while, but eventually she found the kitchen, and the water, and pitchers in which to pour it to serve to the men upstairs. When she came into their room, and poured the water for them, they paid little attention, simply taking what she was doing for granted, as if it were her job.

At first, Eisha didn't mind pouring water for them, and then, following their orders, bringing them various foods from the kitchen. It gave her something to do in the castle, and it wasn't all that hard. But after awhile, a part of her began to be resentful about what she was doing. "Why can't they serve themselves?" she asked herself. "What's so important about all their meetings?"

But something very powerful inside her compelled her to keep serving the men, day in and day out. She found a little room near the kitchen with a cot where she could sleep at night. She helped herself in the kitchen to whatever food she needed. And the days and nights went by until she lost track of the time she had been in the castle.

It was a strange sort of life, for she had little contact with any place or any one in the castle except the room in which she served her days, and the men who worked there. Once or twice, she tried to ask them questions while she was serving them, but they let her know in no uncertain terms that her questions were not allowed. Her place was to serve. Period.

Now and then, Eisha would run into a woman or two in the kitchen, but they would not speak to her when she tried to start a conversation, and acted afraid of her questions. They seemed terribly busy, but Eisha did not see them in the room with the men whom she fed and watered each day. "Maybe they are serving men in other rooms," she said to herself, and realized there was a taste of bitterness in her words.

Then, one evening at suppertime, as she was climbing the stairs from the kitchen with a heavy tray of water-pitchers, she suddenly remembered her Heart-Stone! How could she have forgotten it all this time? Eisha eagerly reached for her pocket, and the tray went crashing to the floor, spilling all the water onto the steps and onto her clothing. But she did not care. She was staring at the Stone as it lay in her hand. It was light in weight, and dull gray in color. "I'm in the wrong place!" she cried out, remembering the words of the Lion. "I've got to get out of here, before it's too late! How could I have gotten hooked into being a serving maid to the men upstairs!" And she began to scold herself as she walked, empty-handed, up the stairs and then down the hall to the all-too-familiar room. All the resentment she had stifled in herself surged through her as Eisha angrily flung open the door.

"Where's the water?" asked one of the men, looking up in a startled way from his papers as she burst into the room.

"I'm not bringing you any more ever again!" said Eisha loudly, and was surprised at her own boldness. "I'm not one of your maid-servants!" And with these words she turned her back and left the room, slamming the door behind her. Another wave of anger swept over her, and she was surprised at its force. "Who do they think they are—ignoring the women on the stage and ordering me about as if it was my job to wait on them!" she muttered to herself. "I'm getting out of here!" And she raced down the long hall, a little afraid she would hear the heavy footsteps of an offended man behind her.

When she reached the stairs leading down toward the kitchen, she took them running, two steps at a time. But it was dark; she missed her footing, and fell. She felt her body hitting the sharp edges of the stairs as she tumbled downward. Then everything went black.

When Eisha came to, she was lying in a crumpled heap at the bottom of the stairs. Pain washed in waves over her, and she groaned as she tried to stand up. Her legs buckled, and she collapsed back into a heap on the floor. It seemed she had no choice but to lie there in the dark, and wait until she was able to get up and grope her way forward, or until someone found her.

"I wonder if I've broken anything," Eisha thought. "I know I'm badly bruised!" She closed her eyes, and tried to get in a comfortable position on the floor. Suddenly, a long-buried memory flooded into her mind. She was a little girl, standing behind the door of her grandmother's room, overhearing a conversation. Her mother was saying to her grandmother in a choking voice, "I can't stay here, Mother! I am losing my self! I have no room of my own, no space for my soul, no voice to say what I see or sing what I feel. This castle is no home for me—it is a prison, and my husband and his cohorts are the jailers! They don't see me as a person—only as someone who is here to serve their purposes. They won't even let me use the name you gave me, but say I must use my husband's. I cannot bear it."

"Then you must flee, my daughter," Eisha heard her grandmother say. "I will care for Eisha in your place, for I have the power and freedom to do so. You will be of little use to her if you lose your soul."

"But I can't bear leaving her!" Eisha heard her mother cry. "I love her so much, I would rather die than never see her again."

"You will die inside if you stay," replied her grandmother. "You will live if you leave, and you will live to see Eisha again." Then there was the sound of sobbing.

The memory faded, and Eisha lay in the dark, shaking. "I thought my mother had died! That's what my father told me!" she thought. "Maybe she's still alive! But where would she be?" A swarm of questions buzzed in her mind, but waves of intense pain overwhelmed them, and Eisha blacked out again.

When Eisha finally came to, the pain had subsided. Carefully she pulled herself up onto her feet. She was stiff and sore, but at least she could stand. "I must get out of this castle," she said to herself. "But which way do I go, and how do I find my way in the dark?"

Then Eisha remembered the Stone again. Quickly, she reached into her pocket and took it out, but could not see its color at all in the darkness. However, she could feel that it was still very lightweight. "Maybe if I walk about, it will get heavier when I move in the right direction," she thought.

And that is just what happened. The Stone lay light in her hand when she turned north, south, and east. But when she turned west, it grew heavy. With a sigh of relief, she walked westward, step by slow step in the darkness, until she bumped into a door with a knob right in the center of it. When she reached out and turned the knob, the door opened, letting her into a small, dimly lit chapel filled with carved wooden pews that faced east towards a glowing round stained-glass window. At its center was a pure white lily, surrounded by a circle of thorns. Six sections, each in the form of a petal, radiated out from the center in alternating hues of deep red and blue. Eisha guessed that the light coming in through the window must be from the moon shining in from the east. The soft light, filtered through the stained glass, revealed a small group of people seated in the pews. Some sat with bowed heads. A few gazed at the window. Still others wept, their muffled sobs mingling with the soft organ music as it rose and fell in mournful melody. Now and then, someone would rise and leave the chapel, stopping first to stand for a moment before a table beneath the window. Eisha noticed that the table held a large empty crystal bowl, a loaf of stale, moldy bread, a burned out candle, and a closed black book. "How curious," she thought.

"Long ago," whispered a voice beside her, "there was a bowl of fresh water, but it evaporated. There was fresh bread, but it grew stale and hard. A candle burned beneath the window, but no one tended it, and the wax drowned the wick. The book was open, and many read its words. But after awhile, no one kept those words in their hearts, and now it is a closed book."

Eisha turned and saw beside her the tear-stained face of a frail old woman. Her sad words, mixed with the mournful, empty feeling of the chapel, brought stinging tears to Eisha's eyes. "Why has all this happened?" she wondered.

She must have spoken her question aloud, for the old woman said, "Because of the castle, and the kind of rooms in it, and what the people do in them. In the beginning, the chapel stood by itself on the shore. It was filled with people who came seeking. But over the years, the children of the seekers stopped searching and created this castle to protect the chapel. The castle grew more important to them than the chapel."

She sighed and gazed around her. The moonlight glowed more brightly through the window, as if a cloud had passed from before its face. The circle of stained glass glowed like a jewel in the dark eastern wall of the chapel. The old woman stretched out her hand toward the window, and her voice grew strong, ringing in the dimness with a prophetic note. "The day will come when great waves will tear down the walls of the castle. Only the chapel will still stand. Then seekers will once again come, and find a lively and rich peace that passes understanding." With these words, the old woman slipped into the shadows and was gone.

For a long moment, Eisha stood very still, letting the old woman's mysterious words sink in. She knew she understood only a little of what they meant, but she wanted to remember them. Then, clutching her precious Stone in her hand, she turned from the window and table, and walked towards a door in the west wall of the chapel. She pushed it, and the door opened easily, letting her out into the moonlight that shone on the beach.

"Why can't they serve themselves?" she asked herself.
"What's so important about all their meetings?"

CHAPTER SIX:

THE SHIP

Eisha took a deep breath of the cool night air, and then another, and another—as if to draw the very light of the moon and stars into her lungs. She walked away from the castle, and as she did, it got smaller, or she got bigger, until it looked no more than the size of a sand castle built by a child on a lazy summer afternoon.

With a sigh of relief, Eisha felt the stone grow heavier in her hand as she walked, and when she sat down in the sand at last, and opened her hand, the stone glowed and flashed blue and purple in the moonlight, and the star-flower crystal at its center beamed bright as the Morning Star that shone on the horizon over the sea. The moon was shining just above the mountain peaks, and its light cast their dark shadows almost to the water's edge.

Weary, sore, and shaken by her castle experience, Eisha stretched out in the shadows on the sand, lying flat on her back, so she could look up at the star-filled sky. The cool sand shifted under her weight into the shape of her body, and somehow she felt as if the sand were absorbing the pain from her body. Then she slipped into a deep and healing sleep as the waves whispered watery secrets to the pebbles that lined the beach.

When Eisha awoke, the moon was setting, sending a stream of gold gleaming across the water. As she watched in delight, a black triangle moved across the golden stream, silhouetted against the setting moon. It was the sail she had seen hours earlier in the misty starlight, but now it was much clearer and larger. Back and forth it tacked, crisscrossing the golden moon-path, growing bigger and bigger as it came towards her. Meanwhile, the moon was melting like liquid gold into the water, and the sky was growing pale with the coming of dawn. Behind her, in the woods, birds started to sing their greeting to the new day.

Now, the ship's sail hung slack in the early dawn calm as the incoming tide slowly and gently carried it towards shore. A long line of pelicans soared low over the water beyond the ship, their bodies and wings a mottled brown against the pale coral of the sunrise sky. The sea mirrored back the coral in shimmering, dancing reflections. All at once, the fiery disc of the sun burst from behind the horizon and caught the ship in orange rays of light as, with one last heave of the waves, it came to rest on a sandbar a few yards from the beach where she sat.

With an exclamation of surprise and delight, Eisha looked closely at the ship. It was made of wood, beautifully polished and molded. The sail was a silken blue, the color of a clear summer sky at noon. A rope ladder hung from the ship's edge, its bottom rung just touching the sand and water near her. She started toward the ladder when she remembered her Heart-Stone. In her opened hand, it flashed a brilliant blue. As she mounted the ladder, it became perceptibly heavier. She was on the right way!

Putting the Stone into her pocket, Eisha climbed onto the deck and walked toward the front of the ship. As she neared the bow, she uttered a cry of joyful surprise. The huge head of a lion was carved on the prow of the ship! Climbing up onto a little bench that gave her access to it, Eisha put her hands on the lion's head. Was it her imagination, or did the wood feel strangely warm? Next, she put her arms around the lion's neck, and thought she felt the slightest possible vibration in the lion's throat—nothing more. Eisha waited, and listened, and listened, and waited, without sensing or hearing anything else.

Finally, she decided to go on exploring the ship. As long as the Lion was there, even in the form of a carving, it seemed like a good place to be. So she walked the deck towards the back end of the ship. Near the stern, she came across a small ladder leading down into the hold. With mounting excitement, she descended the steps and looked about her. On her right was a small room with a bunk under a large porthole on the left, and a hammock filled with books slung under another porthole on the right. Beneath the hammock was an old yellow sea chest, painted with pictures of various kinds of fish. Across the back of the cabin, opposite from where she stood, a shelf ran the entire length of the wall. Above it was a large chart of the stars. On the left side of the shelf stood a small telescope and a compass. In the middle was an open ship's log with blank pages inviting entries, and a quill pen set in an ink well. On the right was an ancient book, bound in blue leather, written in calligraphy, and illustrated with marvelous multi-colored round pictures. Eisha leafed through a few of the book's pages, lingering over the mysterious mandalas. What could these beautifully written words and entrancing round pictures mean? They seemed to draw her in.

But her curiosity about the cabin was even stronger than her interest in the book, and she decided to look inside the sea chest. The lid opened easily. Inside were several brightly colored pants with matching tunics in bright colors embroidered with designs of flowers and leaves, a warm, heavy cloak, and a nightgown. They all looked as if they would fit her perfectly! With growing wonder, Eisha walked across the cabin to the bunk, sat on its beautifully embroidered bedspread, and leaned against a few of the many pillows propped against the side of the ship. Nothing could have been more comfortable.

Then she got up and went out into the little hallway that led to the forward part of the ship. There, she found another room. A counter ran along the wall opposite her, and above it was a large porthole that looked out toward the front deck and prow. She could see the back of the lion's mane through it, and on either side of the ship, the blue-green water of the sea. Beneath the porthole was a sunken bowl set in the counter, with a small, carved fish above it. She found that when she pressed the fin on the fish's back, it released fresh water through its mouth into the bowl. "What fun!" she thought as she let the water splash over her hands. "I wonder who made this ship and all its clever furnishings?"

Next, she turned her attention to maps that were on the wall on either side of the porthole. They showed the sea and numerous islands in it, with names and pictures of fruits, nuts, and plants found in these places, and little notes of what uses they had for nourishment and healing. After studying them for a little while, Eisha opened some cupboards below the counter, and found a few wooden goblets, bowls, and plates, a pot or two, and some neatly folded napkins embroidered with human figures. As she looked admiringly at the handiwork, she felt a shock of recognition as she looked at the figures more closely. All of them were her own face and figure, though dressed in gowns of a kind she had never worn!

Amazement filled her as she continued to look about. In a cupboard to the right of the door of the cabin she found a clear crystal bowl filled with round, thin white wafers, a crystal decanter of wine, and a crystal goblet. Piles of white linen cloths embroidered with grapes, wheat, and vines surrounded them. In a small drawer were bars of fragrant soap in flowered shapes, a pumice-stone for scrubbing, and small jars of various ointments and powders, labeled in beautiful letters according to their various uses. In a small enclosure to the left of the door she found a basin and pitcher of engraved metal for washing, and a chamber pot and cover of the same metal. It rested in a little hollow in a low wood platform. Next to it was a covered container filled with large, soft leaves with a mint-like fragrance.

"Well!" thought Eisha. "Someone seems to have thought of everything!" It seemed clear to her by now that this ship was for her, and that in this ship she would be taken on the journey that would bring her to her heart's desire.

She went back into the hallway and turned to go up the ladder to the upper deck when she heard a voice.

"Come further down, Eisha."

Startled, she looked down near her feet, for the voice seemed to come from beneath her. She was standing on a trapdoor! Eisha opened it, and saw another ladder, made of rope, hung on hooks, descending into the lowest part of the ship. She began at once to climb down the ladder. As it swayed slightly beneath her feet, she flashed back to her climb down a rainbow ladder long ago into the cave where she had met the Lion, and the Lady, and watched over the Child cradled in light. A great longing arose, and ached inside her. Unexpected tears welled in her eyes. Would she ever see them again?

"Yes," said the Lion, as her foot touched the very bottom of the ship. "You will see them again, for as I chased and lured you there to begin with, and called you to my side after you left the Child, so I will guide you back to the Child—and the Lady too, for I am the Lady's Lion, you know. And this ship has been lovingly prepared especially for you. Many a night I have sailed down the paths of star shine and moon gold, waiting and hoping you would come out of the castle and climb on board."

Eisha stared at the Lion in open-mouthed astonishment. How did it get down here? And what was this about waiting for her? Aloud, she simply blurted, "I thought I was only in the castle for a little while."

"It was far longer than you realize," said the Lion. "But that is in the past, and we are here and now. Look about you."

Eisha did, and saw that the ship's walls around her in this deepest hold were transparent like glass, yet strong and flexible. The hold was filled with the blue-green light of the waves that shone through its walls. She could see into the water on all sides, and straight down as well, for the floor was also transparent. "The ship must have moved into deeper water!" she exclaimed as she caught glimpses of orange, yellow, blue, and purple fish swimming among gracefully waving sea plants of deep green and wine red. Eisha gazed in fascination at the life of the sea around her. Finally, she looked up, and noticed a single hammock, woven in rainbow colors, hanging suspended across the width of the hold. "Is this for me?" she asked, looking at the Lion.

"Yes indeed," replied the Lion. "There will be times when you will need to come here, where you feel more at one with the sea. During storms, you will be held here in this hammock, far below the turmoil, and not be overwhelmed. When it is calm, and there is no wind, you can simply BE here, basking in the beauty of the sea, listening as it murmurs its secrets to you, and watching as it reveals its mysteries. Should you need to hide, here no one will find you. And here I will wait for you whenever there is need."

Eisha looked about and her eyes sparkled. "Is there anything else you want to ask?" said the Lion gently. She thought for a moment.

"Yes," she replied. "Is this voyage one I must take alone—I mean, without other people?"

"Yes," replied the Lion. "And there are few who dare do it. It will take great courage."

"I know I will be afraid sometimes," replied Eisha. "But as long as you are with me, I can do it." She paused and looked intently into the Lion's face, as if to gather the courage she would need from its eyes. They shone with loving encouragement. Eisha took a deep breath and straightened her shoulders. "When do we set sail, and where are we going?"

"We begin very soon—if you are ready. We sail toward the setting sun. If you go with the wind, and set your sail in the direction it takes you each day, you will come at last to the land that lies east of the sun and west of the moon, where the Child and Lady dwell."

"Then that is the place I want to go!" cried Eisha. "I am ready, dear Lion, I am indeed ready."

With these words, Eisha turned and climbed up the ladder from the deepest hold, and then on up the next ladder onto the forward deck. She walked over to the carved head of the lion, and looked about her. The sun was midway toward the top of the blazing blue sky dome. A brisk breeze blew over the water, lacing the blue and green waves with white foam. A flock of sea gulls circled the ship, squawking as if to urge her on her way. The wind had shifted while she was below deck, and the waves and currents of the outgoing tide had combined to take the ship out from shore into fairly deep water.

With another deep breath, Eisha walked over to the mainsail, and began pulling at the ropes that hoisted it. The sail went up smoothly and quickly, its silky folds catching the wind and billowing out in a burst of blue beauty. The ship began moving with increasing speed, and Eisha sprang to the tiller and steered the ship out toward the west and the open sea. The prow cut into the waves, and the land quickly receded, until it was only a shadowy blur of mauve mountain-shapes against the sky. After some struggle and experimenting, Eisha caught on to the trick of setting the sail and using the tiller to take advantage of the wind, while maintaining a westward direction. She had learned to sail as a girl, and her skills came back as if her muscles as well as her mind had memorized the judgments and motions made long ago.

When the ship had gone so far out to sea that the land had dropped beneath the blue horizon, Eisha went below deck for a little while to inspect the wall maps she had seen in the forward cabin. She looked for a long time at the various islands drawn on the map. None of them were labeled, and since she did not know which of them was the land she had just left, she could not figure out where she was. She realized she would have to head into the unknown in trust, and let the wind blow her wherever she needed to go.

All that day Eisha sailed, recalling and using more and more of her childhood skills. She delighted in the tug of the sail, the swing of the tiller, the spray of seawater in her face, and the surges of speed as the wind filled the sail, until the sun began sinking into the sea. Straight into the sunset she sailed, watching the fiery ball flatten and melt like liquid fire into a sea of violet, scarlet, and coral, until it was nothing more than a shining, thin line of red light on the horizon. Then it slipped and was gone to rise somewhere over a sea on the other side of the world—perhaps over the land for which she was bound that lay east of the sun and west of the moon.

Ever so slowly, the sky began to turn from fiery shades of color to cool blues and purples. High above her, a star shone out in the deepest blue at the peak of the sky dome. As she watched, it grew brighter and brighter, until it was a brilliant silver swirl in the sky. It was the Star that had lured her into the forest and led her on her way with the Lion! Its presence comforted Eisha, and she gazed at it for a long while. Then she went below deck, feeling that somehow, because the Star was there, swirling in the sky above the ship, she could take her rest, and know that the Star and the Lion would somehow keep the ship safe and on course while she slept.

With this thought, Eisha let down the sail and went below deck to her cabin. She undressed and put on the nightgown that lay in the sea chest. It was midnight blue, and embroidered with silver stars all over it, as if it were a piece of the night sky. She put it on with delight, and was about to crawl into her bed, when a growl in her stomach made her realize that she needed something to eat. She remembered the wafers and wine in the cupboard in the forward cabin. They were the only food on board that she could find, so she drank a little of the wine, and ate a few of the wafers. The wine warmed her and refreshed her with its lively, fruity fragrance and flavor. The wafers tasted like milk and honey, melting in her mouth and completely satisfying her hunger. After washing up, she returned to the stern cabin, and climbed into the bed that lay beneath the porthole. The ship had stopped moving, except for a slight swaying motion. The waves slapped softly against the side of the ship, and the night breeze blew gently through the porthole when she cranked it open part way. Eisha laid back and her head rested on a pillow as soft as the fur of a kitten. The last thing she saw through the porthole before her eyes closed was the Star, and the last thing she heard, far below, from the bottom of the ship, was the ever-so-faint purring song of the Lion...

"Back and forth the sailship tacked, crisscrossing the golden moon-path, growing bigger ands bigger as it came towards her."

CHAPTER SEVEN:

THE ISLAND OF THE HORSES

The next thing Eisha knew, the ship was beginning to move. Outside the porthole, the waves of the ocean, a bit bigger than the day before, were slapping against the ship vigorously, as if to wake her up. Quickly, she changed into a green pants and tunic that lay in the open sea chest, made the bed, washed her hands and face, and climbed up on deck.

The wind was tugging at the sail. The ship was turned northward. Eisha adjusted the sail until it was taking the wind more directly. She saw that the wind was now blowing the ship in a north- westerly direction. As she sailed on, the waves grew bigger, and after awhile the ship was beginning to go up and down as if it were going over small hills and down into valleys. Still the wind grew stronger, and soon it seemed to her that the ship was almost flying. The wind whistled in her face and blew her long brown hair behind her in streamers. The spray of the waves broke over the prow and splashed her with salty spray until she was thoroughly wet.

After a few hours, clouds began to loom on the western horizon, and grew until they covered the whole sky. Eisha had to put on the warm cloak from the sea chest to keep from getting chilled. The wind continued to blow strong, and the ship flew along at great speed, as if in a hurry to get somewhere.

That "somewhere" presently appeared ahead on the left side of the ship. It was obviously an island. From a distance, it looked rather flat, but as the ship drew closer, Eisha could see that it was covered on its western side with gently rolling hills. The wind carried the ship straight toward the hilly end of the island, and soon, with a little direction from her, it headed into a small cove.

Eisha dropped anchor and surveyed the scene. To her left the curves of the hills sloped down toward the stony shore. They were covered with long, silvery-green grass that moved in a wave-like motion as the wind blew through it. To her right, a flat plain, covered with the same sort of grass, stretched away from the shore toward the sky. Straight ahead of her, a herd of horses grazed quietly in the long grass at the edge of the beach. Eisha stared at them in amazement. She had seen brown and black and gray and white horses, but never horses like these—purple and blue, green and gold, rose and turquoise! Each horse's hide was a mottled mixture of a pair of colors. Their manes and tails were a glossy, jet-black, as were their hooves and eyes.

"I wonder if they're wild or tame?" thought Eisha. She suddenly felt a strong impulse to ride one of them. She was about to climb out of the ship when she remembered her Heart-Stone. It was in her cabin beneath her pillow. She took it from its resting place and gazed at it as it lay in her hand. It felt heavy and glowed a brilliant blue-and-green beauty. She smiled, put it in her pocket, dropped the rope ladder from the side of the ship, and climbed down it into the water. It was only knee-deep, and a few minutes of wading brought her to shore.

Now she was only a few yards from the herd of horses. As she stood there staring at them, the smallest of the horses, a turquoise and rose one, looked up and stared directly back at her. Eisha slowly advanced towards the horse. It did not move. When she was within reach, she stretched out her hand towards its head, palm upward. The horse sniffed it. Then she noticed it was looking at something over her shoulder. She whirled around and saw the Lion standing on the sand.

"Go ahead," she heard the Lion say, "Ride it, it if lets you, Eisha. It will take you where you need to go. But do not presume to direct it. The horse knows better than you the ways of this land."

Eisha paused. It had been quite a while since she rode a horse. Could she stay on its back without the saddle she had been used to? Could she hang on without reins? How long would she be gone from the ship, if she could not control where the horse took her, or where? And what about provisions?

"Go!" she heard the Lion growl as she hesitated. "Time is precious. Trust is of the essence."

Eisha stepped forward, laid her hands on the horse's mane, and hoisted herself up and onto its back. She was barely seated when it began to trot toward the hills on the western part of the island. Eisha looked back and saw the Lion standing on the shore with the ship behind it, both rapidly dwindling into the distance. The afternoon sun, breaking out from behind the clouds, sent a shaft of light falling on the grass around her, touching her head with warmth as if in blessing.

Soon, she was surrounded on all sides by grassy slopes. The horse trotted steadily upward into the hills. A fragrance like that of thyme and sage rose from the grass. Eisha breathed deeply, her knees gripping the sides of the horse, her hands holding tightly to its mane. But after awhile, she relaxed her grip as she grew used to its motion. She settled into a steady, balanced position on the horse, and let herself enjoy the scent of the grasses and wild herbs around her, the wind in her face and hair, and the warmth of the sun on her shoulders. The horse slowed from a trot to a walk, and stopped now and then to crop the grass. Presently, it came to the top of a hill and stood still. The slope had been so gentle Eisha did not realize how high she was. The view was breathtaking. Far below on her left, she could see the blue-green sea shimmering in the sunlight and wrinkled with waves. To her right stretched the grassy plain, its surface rippling in the wind that blew steadily from the north.

At that moment, without warning, the horse lay down so suddenly that Eisha lost her balance and tumbled off, falling face forward onto the grass. She was startled for a moment, but not hurt. Gaining her composure, she moved into a sitting position and looked about. Nearby, at the crown of the hill, was a single tree, huge and ancient, its gnarled branches reaching out in all directions, its leaves like a great green pile of cloud.

Eisha loved trees, especially old ones, and wanted to see it more closely. She got up and walked to it. It was not like any tree she had ever seen. Its bark was smooth, and pale purple. Its branches began so low down on the truck that she could easily step up onto them. They were broad, with an almost flat surface, as if made for climbing. Eisha remembered how much she loved to climb trees when she was a little girl. Now, here she was, standing a step away from the most perfect climbing tree she had ever seen. With a big smile, she put her foot on the bottom branch, held on to the one above her, and started climbing until she was high up in the tree. The branches were thinner when she got near the top, but still sturdy enough to hold her. She found one that was angled so that she could sit astride it with her back leaning against the trunk, and rested for a moment. About her, the silvery green leaves of the tree, moved by the wind, sounded like a hundred tiny hands softly clapping.

Then Eisha noticed that there were long, green, bean-shaped pods hanging from some of the branches around her. She picked one, and slit it open. Inside were purple peas. "I wonder if I could eat these?" she thought. Once again, she remembered her Stone. She pulled it out and looked at it. It lay lightly in her palm, and was a dull green color. "It must be mistaken," thought Eisha. "It probably doesn't mean anything when it comes to something as ordinary as eating. Anyway, they look good, and I am so hungry I can hardly stand it!"

So saying, she popped some purple peas in her mouth. They spurted sweet juice on her tongue and crunched nicely between her teeth. She liked them so well, she picked and ate the purple peas in another pod, and then another, until she had eaten more than she should have. Before long, she began to feel heavy and drowsy. She could not keep her grip on the branch on which she sat. Things began to get blurry. Then, with a crash, she fell down from one branch to another, and landed at the foot of the tree with such force that it knocked her unconscious.

When Eisha came to, the horse was nowhere to be seen, and the sun had already set behind the hills. Pain throbbed in her head like a drum. Her hands and arms were badly scraped, and covered with blotches of dried blood. The wind had turned cold. Shadows covered the ground. She struggled to her feet and swayed unsteadily. A sharp pain went through her stomach. "Ooooh! Never again will I eat so carelessly," groaned Eisha. But try as she could, she was unable to walk more than a few steps before the world began reeling around her. Finally, she gave up all effort, sank to the ground at the foot of the great tree, curled up into a tight little ball of misery, and fell asleep.

She awoke, shivering. It was a dark, starless night. She felt that something or someone was near, but could see nothing. She lay very, very still, every muscle tense. A man's low voice spoke in the dark.

"I have been watching this stranger since she came onto our shores. She has ridden one of the Sacred Horses without permission. She has climbed the Sacred Tree without reverence. She has eaten its sacred fruit without restraint. She must be punished."

"Wait!" came another voice, higher and sweeter like that of a woman. "She rode the Sacred Horse with trust. She climbed the

Sacred Tree like a carefree child. She ate in hunger and with delight. Do these things not balance her fault?"

"There is only one way to decide," replied the first voice. "We must take her to the Council Circle." With these words, Eisha felt a large blanket being thrown over her. Too weak to struggle, she decided the best thing to do would be to act as if she were still unconscious. She felt large hands hoist her, wrapped in the blanket, onto a hard wooden surface. Then, with a creak and a jolt, the surface moved, and she realized she was on a wagon or cart of some sort.

It jerked along for a long time before it came to a halt. Once again, Eisha felt large hands removing her from the cart, and carrying her by her hands and feet. Then she felt herself being lowered—none too gently—onto the ground. The blanket was removed from her head, but remained wrapped tightly around her body, so that she could not move her arms or legs. She was grateful for its protection from the cold, but hated the tied up feeling. From the feel and smell of the wall next to which she had been put down, she guessed it was of thatched grass. It was too dark to see anything. She hardly dared move, not knowing who might be watching, and what they might do if they noticed her movements. All she could do was lie there in the dark, berating herself for her unwise eating, wondering where the wonderful turquoise and rose horse was, and why the Lion had brought her to this island.

"So, she put her foot onto the bottom branch, held on to the one above her, and started climbing until she was high up in the tree."

CHAPTER EIGHT:

THE TRIAL

Eisha lay for a long time in the dark, unable to sleep because she was worrying and wondering what would happen to her next. As early morning light began to filter into the grass hut, she heard voices, and then saw human figures standing in the doorway.

"It's time to bring her out into the light of day," said a voice she recognized as the same one that had defended her a few hours earlier. Then she saw the face of a woman bending over her, and a tall man standing behind her.

Eisha could tell that the woman was as tall as the man, and that both were big-boned. They had pale, yellowish-tinged skin, slanted eyes of green, and long red hair. The man's hair was in a braid down his back, and woven with strips of leather of the same colors as the horses Eisha had seen the day before. The woman's hair was coiled in braids on each side of her head, and woven through with the same sort of leather strips. Both wore leather pants and tunics of the same hues as the leather strips in their hair. The man was dressed in green and gold, and the woman in turquoise and rose.

"The Council of the Keepers of the Horses is ready for your trial," said the man sternly. "Arise! Come!" The woman reached out her hand to help Eisha up, and her eyes were kind. Eisha grasped her hand and walked slowly with her out of the hut behind the man.

In a grassy clearing ahead of her, surrounded by round thatch-roofed huts, sat a circle of men and women very much like the pair who accompanied her, both in dress and size and general appearance. In the distance, between a couple of the huts, Eisha glimpsed a herd of horses like the one she had seen cropping grass near the beach. Only the sound of their munching and occasional soft whinnying broke the silence.

She was led to the center of the circle. Then her escorts joined the circle of strange women and men who surrounded her. The man began, saying, "This is the person of whom you have been told. She is the one who rode a Sacred Horses without permission, climbed the Sacred Tree without reverence, and ate its sacred fruit without restraint."

Then the woman stood to speak. "Nevertheless," she said, "she rode the Horse with trust; she climbed the Tree with a child's carefree spirit; and she ate the fruit of the Tree out of hunger and thirst, and with delight." Neither of them said anything more to try to persuade the others. There was a long silence as the gathered women and men pondered the words they heard and gazed solemnly at Eisha, who was feeling bewildered, ashamed, and defensive.

All at once, the men spoke in unison. "Justice demands that this woman be given a fitting punishment for her careless riding of the Sacred Horse, her irreverence for the Sacred Tree, and her lack of restraint in eating its sacred fruit." Eisha's heart sank.

Then the women spoke with one voice. "Yet, mercy requires that she be allowed her freedom. She has, perhaps, not been taught well, and is a stranger here, and quite defenseless. And she also acted with trust, child-likeness, and in need and delight." Eisha looked up with a spark of hope in her heart.

"I wish to speak," she said boldly. The women and men fell silent, and then, one by one, nodded their assent.

"I was blown here by the wind in a ship prepared for me by the Lion," she said. "And the Lion told me to mount the horse and go where it would take me."

"The Lion!" exclaimed several. "It has been a long time since the Lion visited our shores."

"Something special must be afoot in these islands!" said the woman with the kind eyes. "And you must be a part of it, somehow."

She and the others gazed at Eisha with new interest and respect. At that moment, Eisha remembered her Heart-Stone. She reached for it in her pocket, hoping against hope that it had not fallen out when she fell from the Sacred Tree. Her fingers closed around it, and she let out a great sigh of relief. Then she slowly took it out of her pocket and looked at it. All eyes followed her motion, and with her, caught a glimpse of the flash of red and purple that sprang from the stone as it lay, heavy, in Eisha's open, outstretched palm.

"This Stone is the heart of the heart of the mountains in the land from which I began my journey," said Eisha slowly, her eyes fixed on her Heart-Stone. "Even now, it speaks to me and tells me that I am in the right place here among you."

The women and men all nodded and made approving noises, as if they understood what she meant. The man who had brought her for trial rose and stood opposite her, his red hair gleaming like fire in the morning sun, his bright green eyes flashing.

"I see that the Stone and the Lion have guided you here among us, that we might help you learn something of great importance," he said. "It is clear that your very trespasses are the means for your learning." He paused and looked about the circle. "Mercy and justice may meet here today, if we are wise. Let us sit for a time in silence, and listen within, so that we may discern how best to respond."

With that, the circle of red-haired people fell into silence, sitting with closed eyes and crossed legs on the ground, their hands crossed over their hearts. Eisha decided to do as they did. Surely, it could do no harm. She sat down with them in the circle, closed her eyes, and crossed her legs. As she crossed her arms and hand over her heart and breathed a deep breath, she felt herself drawn into the common silence of her captors. She realized that by giving herself to the shared silence, she was being woven, deep in her spirit, like a thread, in and out of their spirits.

A glance at the Stone reassured her that it was all right, and she let herself go into the silence without further hesitation. As she did so, vivid images rose in her mind's eye: images of herself running alongside a herd of horses; of breathing deeply into the nostrils of a horse, and receiving its warm breath in return; of being carried like the wind on one of them over a flat, grassy plain; of sitting in the shade of the Sacred Tree, a horse kneeling beside her, a great thirst in her throat, and a gnawing hunger in her stomach.

The sound of a high, silver note ringing in the silence broke into her visions, and her eyes flew open.

"Arise," commanded the spokesman who had found Eisha the day before. "We will speak out of our hearts. You must listen with yours!"

Eisha rose to her feet. She looked about her at the faces that gazed so solemnly at her, then at the circle of huts beyond them and the herd of horses in the distance. For a split second, she thought she saw the sun gleaming on a great, tawny Lion's hide. But a horse moved into her line of vision, and the gleam was gone.

She turned her attention to the spokesman, who was saying, "It is clear to us that you have much to learn, O child of the mountain's Heart-Stone. It has come to us that you must live and run with our herd of horses until you learn to regard them as one with yourself. Your breath and theirs, your movement and theirs, your eating and drinking and theirs must be as one. In this way you will come to that care and regard which fits you to ride the Sacred Horse. When you see it, not as a beast of burden, or even a servant, but as your partner, you will be ready to ride it aright."

A brief silence followed the spokesman's words. Then the spokeswoman rose and said, "When this regard has rooted itself within you, you must go with your horse and keep vigil at the roots of the Sacred Tree. You may not climb it, or eat of its fruit, until you have learned its secret, and have surrendered your clamoring thoughts, your greedy hunger, and your demanding thirst to the whisper of the Holy Wind in its branches. When the sacred silence has rooted you in reverence, and the noise of your needs has faded away, the Tree will lift you up into its branches, and a small taste of its fruit will be enough to satisfy you until you reach the ship which will bear you away from our shores at the right time."

Eisha listened with a mixture of dismay and anticipation. What a strange sentence she had received for her unknowing, careless acts!

"I am willing to do as you say," said Eisha simply. "I only ask that you give me the help I will need, for your directions seem hard to me."

"Yes, it will be hard for you," answered the woman who had spoken. "But we will be watching, and waiting, and help when there is need."

"You must begin now, by joining the horses," added the man, and pointed toward the herd.

The circle of people rose, parted, and made a path for Eisha that led directly to the horses that grazed quietly in the grass behind the huts on the east side of the circle. Slowly, with wonder, and a little fear as well, Eisha walked toward the horses.

"The woman reached out her hand to help Eisha up, and her eyes were kind."

CHAPTER NINE:

THE SACRED HORSE-HERD

As Eisha approached the horses, one of them came trotting out to meet her, whinnying as if in welcome. It was the horse that had carried her from the beach up to the Sacred Tree! Eisha impulsively reached out her arms and as they met, she put them around the horse's neck. When she let go, the horse stood looking at her, and she felt there was something she was supposed to do. What was it? She stood there dumbly, at a loss, waiting for some clue.

Then the words of the spokesman came to mind. "Your breath and theirs…must be one." Ah! That was it!

Eisha took the horse's head in her hands, and as she looked into its eyes, she put her nose next to its nose, and inhaled deeply, so that she could feel the breath from its nostrils enter into her nostrils. Then she exhaled, so that the breath from her nostrils entered into the horse's nostrils. It seemed to assent, and for several long moments they stood there exchanging breaths. The other horses watched attentively as they did so, and when Eisha stepped back from the horse, they all whinnied at once, and shook their manes, as if in approval.

Eisha felt that now she shared a special bond with the Sacred Horse. Somehow, she could feel its vigor coursing through her own body, and when it began to move, she felt the muscles in her own body demanding motion. For a moment, she felt so at one with the horse that she looked at her body, almost expecting to find herself having turned into a horse. But of course, she hadn't. Still, something in her had changed —she was sure of that!

The horse began to trot, and then broke into a full gallop. Eisha began to run with it, and found, to her surprise, that she could keep up with its pace, as long as she watched it rather than herself. She ran and ran alongside the Sacred Horse, with the rest of the herd just behind them. Her feet flew with their hoofs over the grassy plain. The wind blew through their manes and her hair, and she laughed as they whinnied with the pure joy of running swift and sure, fast and free, through the fragrant and sunlit grasses.

After awhile, however, Eisha began to tire. She slowed to a walk, and so did the herd. Several of them lay down on the grass, and so did she. They began munching the grass—and she wondered what she would eat. She could chew on a stem of grass, or one of the fragrant herbs that grew among the grasses, but that was hardly a meal! And after all the running, she was sweaty and thirsty too. But there was no water and no food fit for a human being anywhere in sight.

By now the sun was at its noonday zenith in the sky. Fortunately, it was not too hot, and Eisha began to enjoy its warmth once she had cooled down. The horses seemed to have decided to stay where they were for a while, so she wandered about a bit, always keeping close to them, while she looked out at the plains and the distant hills. She could just see the peaked tops of the village houses where she had been on trial early in the morning, at the place where the plains and hills met. How far away it seemed! Had she come such a distance in such a short time? She wondered if the red-haired people ever ran with the horses as she had done. She suspected they did.

As Eisha mulled these thoughts over in her mind, she lay down on the grass, flat on her back, and fell to gazing at the sky overhead. It was a vivid, tender blue, with a wind chasing cloud-shapes across it with even greater speed than she had run with the horses. A few butterflies—yellow, white, and orange — flitted across her line of vision, flying in playful circles through the tall grasses that surrounded Eisha. A cricket chirped from somewhere nearby. A faint breeze brushed her face with coolness. She closed her eyes...

A cool, snuffly nuzzle in her neck wakened her. The Sacred Horse was trying to get her attention! Eisha jumped up, rubbing the sleep from her eyes. The horses were starting to move again, and she must move with them. They walked this time, and Eisha was grateful, for her muscles were sore, and her mouth was dry with thirst. If only the horses would go somewhere to drink! Didn't they get thirsty too? Unfortunately, there was nothing to do but go along with them, bearing the hunger and thirst.

Soon, Eisha noticed that the land was sloping gently downward. A few bushes began to appear among the grasses, and then, far ahead and below them, she saw the gleam of a river! Water! She almost broke into a run at the sight. But the horses were in no hurry. Slowly, munching here and there as they went, they walked down the long, gentle slope toward the river. The air grew cooler, and the shadows lengthened as the sinking sun gilded the hilltops and grasslands with a layer of mellow golden light.

Eisha grew more and more hungry and thirsty and tired. The Sacred Horse seemed to sense it, and drew alongside her, whinnying encouragement whenever she faltered. It did not occur to Eisha to mount the horse. She felt herself to be its companion, and somehow, simply climbing onto it would have seemed unthinkably presumptuous—as if she were its master.

After what seemed like an interminable trek, the horses drew near the river. It was a broad one, and it curved away on both sides from the place where they approached it, as if it ran in a circular bed.

"That would be a strange shape for a river," thought Eisha. But she was more interested in the foaming water that swirled over rocks and logs only a few feet away. As soon as the Sacred Horse planted its front hoofs in the water's edge, and put its mouth in the water to drink, Eisha knelt beside it, and eagerly scooped the fresh, clean water into her hands, lapping it up like a puppy. Never had she so keenly tasted the goodness of fresh water, or so much enjoyed the feel of its cool wetness as she splashed it on her perspiring face and neck.

When all the horses had drunk their fill, they began to wade into the water. Eisha waited, afraid that they would lead her into water too deep and swift for her to keep her footing. She could swim, but the current was too strong for any human swimmer, though not for strong horses. As she feared, the horses kept going on into the water, and the Sacred Horse waited at her side for her to go in too. "Well, if worse comes to worse, I'll hang onto my horse-friend's neck," she thought, and plunged in.

The opposite bank of the river towards which the horses were leading her was lined with huge willow trees, their long, leafy branches draped gracefully over the water in shapes very much like the long tails of the horses. The willows were so evenly spaced, it looked as if they had been deliberately planted in their places to hide and guard whatever lay behind them.

All this Eisha took in while the water swirled higher and higher around her body as she followed the horses across the river. When the water reached her neck, she grew afraid, and reached for the Sacred Horse's neck. It moved closer, as if to help, and she clung to it as the water reached her chin. She could barely keep her feet on the rocks at the bottom of the river, for the current was deep and swift.

As they neared the opposite bank, and the water grew shallower, Eisha relaxed her hold on the Horse. A moment later, her foot went down into a hole in the riverbed, she lost her grip altogether, and was swept off her feet and down river by the current. Her mouth and nose filled with river-water, and she choked and spluttered as she flailed at the water with her hands and feet, trying to stay afloat.

"I mustn't panic," Eisha thought to herself, "or I'm done for!" She held her head above the water and saw, just ahead, the branch of a willow tree hanging low over the water. She grabbed at it as the current swept her along, and was able to haul herself up out of the water onto the branch. There she hung, too weak from the effort to move, and feeling as if she might faint at any moment.

Just then, Eisha felt the strong back of the Sacred Horse moving under her feet. Slowly and carefully, she lowered herself down onto the Horse and clung to its neck with all her might. It carried her up the bank and under the willows, where the other horses stood waiting. Shaking the water from their manes and tails, the herd trotted after the Sacred Horse through the great, drooping green willow-branches toward whatever lay beyond.

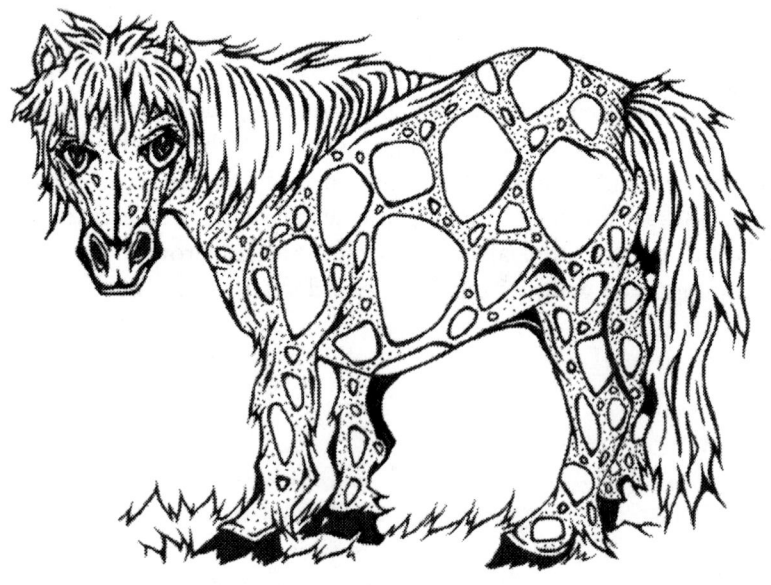

"When she let go, the horse stood looking at her, and she felt as if there was something she was supposed to do."

CHAPTER TEN:

THE WILLOW GROVE

By now, the sun was gone, and the sky was deepening into night-blue. The willow-trees' shadows mingled with their leaves, branches, and trunks to create a moving wall of dark shapes that confused Eisha's sense of direction. Had the Sacred Horse not been carrying her among and through the willows, Eisha felt she could have wandered among them, lost, all night—if not longer. As it was, however, she felt quite secure as the horses wove in and out of the willowy shadows until they emerged into a large, circular clearing. Eisha slipped off the Horse and surveyed the scene with wonder.

The clearing was ringed all around with huge old willow trees. The ground was thickly covered with daisy-starred grass. At the center of the clearing, a hedge of primroses formed an inner circle. In the twilight, the little blossoms still glowed a pale pink, and Eisha could smell their fragrance, faintly, on the evening breeze. It was a serene and magical place. Only the faint sound of the river's waters that circled the ring of willows, and the whisper of the breeze in their gracefully draped branches broke the quietness.

The Sacred Horse paused too, as if sensing the same silence and peace. Then it walked slowly toward an open archway in the primrose hedge, looking over its shoulder as if beckoning her to follow.

"What mystery lies through that opening?" Eisha wondered as she followed the horse through the archway in the hedge. Then the Horse stood aside, and Eisha saw a small pool of dark, quiet water. On its surface floated a number of lily-white lotus blossoms. The water was very still, and as Eisha gazed into it, the reflection of a single brilliant star shone out from its depths. A string of words came into her mind, as if from a long-lost memory, and as she said the words aloud, they sounded like a chant: "In the daisy-starred grasses by the still and silent pool," murmured Eisha to herself, and wondered where the words came from. "It feels as if this is where I have been meant to come since before I was born," she continued, "and this is where I am going to be born all over." She shook her head and exclaimed, "What strange words and thoughts! I feel as if I am in a dream. I wonder what is going on?" But her wonderings and questionings met only with the profound silence of the place.

It seemed the next natural thing to do to was to kneel down and feel the water. It was warm as bathwater. Little curls of steam rose into the cool evening air. She felt a strong desire to bathe in this beautiful, mysterious pool. But before she took off her clothes, she pulled her Heart-Stone from her pocket. It lay in her palm, heavier than she had ever felt it before, and glowing with the same silvery brilliance as the star's reflection in the pool.

Eisha smiled, and stripping off everything, slipped into the water. Beneath the surface, a million moving bubbles tingled against her skin in the most delightful way. The water felt alive, massaging every inch of her tired, aching body with tiny, tender fingers. She floated out into the middle of the pool. Taking a deep breath, she lay on her back among the lotus blossoms, looking up at the sky. One huge star blazed above her, and when she closed her eyes, she could feel its light pouring down into her body.

"It's the Morning Star again," she exclaimed! "I wonder if it led me here or found me here?" Then she let go of the question, and all questions, and simply lay there, floating quietly in the pool. All her hunger and soreness and weariness seeped out of her. She found that if she breathed deeply, yet gently, in a regular rhythm, she could stay afloat in the water with no other effort. She was held up by her breath and trust in the water...

How long Eisha continued lying there on the water she could not say, for it seemed that time stood still in this still, sacred place that felt like the center of everything. Finally, the Star began to fade, the sky began to turn light blue and pink with the coming of dawn, and Eisha moved again. She looked at a large lotus blossom near her, and was about to pick it to take with her, when something inside her stopped her. Instead, she gently kissed the lotus in the center of its blossom.

At that moment, a bird-song rang out joyfully, breaking the dawn stillness. As Eisha climbed out of the water, the air was filled with the chirps and songs of other birds as they wakened the new day. Her clothes had dried out during the night, and as she put them on, she saw the Sacred Horse standing in the open archway of the primrose hedge. Although she had not really slept, Eisha felt refreshed and renewed. Her head was clear, her body clean and strong, and her heart filled with peace. She could not tell what mystery she had experienced in the water of the lotus pool, but she felt she was somehow a new creature, and that whatever happened to her in the future, the memory of this night in the healing waters of the still and silent pool would always sustain and renew her.

"I feel ready for whatever lies ahead!" Eisha thought to herself. Then she walked slowly towards the Sacred Horse, looking steadily into its eyes as she approached it. As they met, Eisha sank to her knees, and so did the horse. Very gently, she kissed the horse between the eyes, and knew that it was time and it was right that she should let it carry her to the Sacred Tree.

"She looked at a large lotus blossom near her, and was about to pick it to take with her, when something inside her stopped her."

CHAPTER ELEVEN:

THE SACRED TREE

Feeling its permission, Eisha climbed onto the Sacred Horse's bare, glossy back. She could feel its breath moving its sides in and out beneath her legs. She sat tall, straight, and still, remembering that the Lion had said it needed no direction, but would take her wherever she needed to go. The Horse walked through the willows, splashed across a shallow ford in the river, and began to trot vigorously away from the willow-ringed clearing, with the rest of the herd following close behind.

All day long, Eisha rode the Sacred Horse as it carried her over the plains and back toward the hills. Once, in the distance, she thought she glimpsed the red hair of one of the horse-people just above the tall grasses that covered the ground. In a flash, it disappeared, and there was nothing to be seen in all directions but green plains and hills, horses, and the herbs and brightly colored wild flowers that grew profusely among the grasses.

By late afternoon, the Horse was well into the hills. As it carried her up one of them, Eisha looked about her and thought, "This seems familiar, somehow." A moment later, at the crown of the hill above her, she saw the towering shape of the Sacred Tree silhouetted against the sunset-stained sky. At the same moment, the herd of horses halted, and stood waiting while the Sacred Horse proceeded with her alone up the hill toward the Tree.

As they entered its deep shadows, the Horse stopped, and Eisha dismounted. Once again, she walked toward the Sacred Tree. But this time she did so slowly, fully aware of its magnificence and mystery. Instead of climbing it, she found a wide hollow between two huge roots that rose above ground level, and nestled into it like a little bird returning to its nest at eventide. With her back against the smooth trunk of the Tree, Eisha crossed her legs, folded her hands between them, and watched the coral, orange, and red rays of sunset-light fade from the sky, and the stars come out, one by one, in the deepening violet-blue dome above her. High above, among the branches of the Tree, she could hear the sleepy chirps of birds settling in for the night. She wondered if mother birds were feeding their young a juicy worm or bug.

The thought awakened a ravenous hunger in Eisha. She heard her stomach growl, and its emptiness became a strong and demanding ache. She remembered how good the Sacred Tree's fruit had tasted. The memory awakened her thirst as she recalled how juicy and refreshing the little purple peas had been. How she longed to climb the Tree and pick and eat its fruit! But the warning words of the spokeswoman rang loud in her mind. "You may not climb it or eat of its fruit until you have learned its secret..." So she folded her arms over her stomach to ease the hunger-ache, and continued to sit silently between the roots of the Tree.

Presently, she became aware of the sound of the evening breeze whispering through the leafy branches above her head. For the first time in her life, she listened really intently to the wind. As she did, words formed in her heart and mind.

"Eisha, my love, let go. Let go of your hunger and thirst. Eisha, my dear, let be. Trust in Me, and in the Tree. Rest in its roots, and be still."

All night long, as the fiery stars slowly danced in a great circle across the sky, Eisha pondered the wind-born words. Nor did she fall asleep even once, for the hunger and thirst she continued to feel kept her wide-awake. A moment came, during those hours, when she stretched out her hands toward the branches above her, and said aloud, "Here! I am letting go of my hunger and thirst!" After that, she still felt hungry and thirsty, but the sharp, demanding edge was gone, and she felt a sense of peace which was deeper and stronger than her hunger and thirst.

When the stars finally began to fade from the sky with the coming of dawn, Eisha rose to her feet, stretched, and walked through the tall, dew-wet grass to the place where the Sacred Horse stood. Once again, she stood face to face with it, breathed into its nostrils, and received its breath in return into her own. Somehow, she felt strengthened and refreshed, though she was weak with hunger and thirst. With her arms about the Sacred Horse's neck, she stood and watched the fiery rim of the sun slip up from behind the eastern horizon.

When it was too bright to look at any longer, Eisha knelt down in the grass, and licked the shining dewdrops from its stems and blades to moisten her mouth and tongue. She savored every dewdrop, realizing how each one was far more precious and important for life than the diamond it so closely resembled. With her cool, dew-dampened hands, she rubbed her face and throat and arms. Then she walked quietly around the hilltop, pausing to look long in each of the four directions. To the north lay more hills, gradually sloping upward to ranges of greater heights, all blue and hazy in the distance. To the east the land stretched downward towards the plains where she had run with the horses. Far off, she caught a glimpse of the river she had crossed, bordered by a wavy blur of trees. To the west and south, where the land shrunk down into smaller hills, she could see the blue shining of the wrinkled sea that surrounded the island.

Finally, Eisha returned from her meditative gazing at the surrounding countryside to sit once again between the roots of the Sacred Tree. She felt a centeredness and groundedness that was new to her, and she savored its deep peace. But after awhile, her hunger and thirst returned to trouble her. Her stomach growled and rumbled and ached. Her throat became dry and itchy. To make matters worse, hundreds of thoughts came buzzing into her head like a swarm of flies. Sometimes she would shake her head and wave her hands about as if to brush them away. But they would not leave her alone. Bad memories and worries of all kinds pestered and stung her mind.

The day grew hot and still. No breeze moved in grass or tree. Eisha was miserable. Her only comfort was the memory of the Wind-borne words she had heard the night before. But somehow, she was not able to let go, or let be, or rest, or trust enough to simply be still. She stood up. She sat down. She shifted about. She walked around the Sacred Tree. She sat down again.

"I just don't get it!" she finally said aloud. "I know I'm supposed to keep vigil here. But I can't seem to do what the Wind said. If only someone were here to help me!"

As she said these words, she remembered that the red-haired spokeswoman had promised her help when she needed it—and she needed it now. Not knowing what else to do, Eisha called out, "Help! Help! Help!" Her voice rang out over the grassy hills in the hot afternoon air, and vanished into the sultry silence. Then, feeling foolish, lonely, and helpless, she threw herself on the ground and let herself wail and moan to release her pent-up frustration. She wailed and moaned, and moaned and wailed, until a sharp, sudden whinny from the Sacred Horse made Eisha stop and look. Coming up the slope of the hill to her right was the tall, red-haired figure of her friend the spokeswoman!

"Ah, my sister—your crying called me to you," she said, as she knelt next to Eisha and gently wiped the tears off her face with a small square of soft cloth.

"Oh, I'm so glad you've come," cried Eisha, throwing her arms around the woman's neck. "I tried to do as you said, but I can't seem to let go and be still the way I need to."

The woman sat down in the hollow between the two largest roots of the Tree, and motioned to Eisha to sit down next to her. Then she leaned her back and head against the Tree, looked up into its beautiful green branches, and began to sing. It was a simple chant, with a melody and words that repeated themselves over and over:

> "Ruah, Shaddai, Eemah.
> Ruah, Shaddai, Eemah.
> Ruah, Shaddai, Eemah."

After awhile, Eisha started chanting along with her. The simple melody and the repetition of the words began to quiet her inside. The thoughts that had been buzzing about in her head fled, leaving a lovely quietness in their place. Eisha kept chanting softly, and whenever she became aware of hunger or thirst, she lifted her hands and opened them in a gesture of letting go. Gradually, she relaxed more and more. Beside her, the red-haired woman continued her gentle, melodious chanting, and the whisper of a breeze began to blow through the grasses nearby and the leaves overhead. Eisha closed her eyes, and felt the breeze cool on her skin. By now the chant felt as if it had soaked into her soul. It sang itself through her relaxed jaw and open lips without effort on her part. She felt that she was resting in the heart of a sacred Silence...

When Eisha next opened her eyes, she was slowly rising into the air, and saw that she was surrounded on all sides, above, and below, by leaves and branches! She gasped, and began to squirm, but immediately the words, "be still," welled up inside her. From far below, she heard the faint melody of her friend's chanting. She joined in the chant again, relaxing as she did so. Then the upward movement of her body stopped, and she came to rest on a broad, smooth branch that easily and comfortably supported her whole body. A gentle breeze was still blowing through the branches, and the golden light of the late afternoon sun played among the leaves all about her, immersing her in a beautiful pattern of shimmering light and shadow.

For many long moments, Eisha let herself delight in the play of the pattern in which she sat. Then, right in front of her, she saw a single long green bean-pod that she knew enclosed the sacred fruit. How beautiful it looked! And how delicious! Her mouth watered as she remembered the taste of the purple peas hidden inside the pod. She reached out her hand to pick it. Then she remembered. Putting her hand in her pocket, she pulled out her Heart- Stone. It lay in her hand, glowing deep green and gold, and grew heavier as she held it.

With a quiet smile, Eisha replaced the Stone. She picked the fruit-pod, opened it, and very slowly, put one little purple berry at a time into her mouth, savoring its crunchy sweetness on her tongue, and its fragrant juice as it slipped down her dry throat. It was even more delicious than she had remembered! She took a long time to slowly savor and eat the seven berries in the pod. Before she ate each one, she smelled its fruity fragrance, and rolled it around in her palm, admiring its beautiful purple color. Then, with a silent "thank-you" in her heart, she ate it.

Finally, feeling refreshed and well nourished, Eisha leaned back on the branch and looked up through the leafy branches at the sky. All her hunger and thirst were gone. She felt completely at rest. The quiet within her matched the quiet around her. She was in no hurry to do anything. She was just being, and that was enough.

As the golden afternoon light dimmed into the lavender-blue of twilight, she noticed a nest near her, and in it, four tiny baby birds, opening their beaks and uttering little squawks of hunger. A few moments later, the mother bird flew down to the nest, a long worm dangling from her beak. Though Eisha was hardly more than an arms length away from them, the birds took no notice of her. She sat perfectly still, watching them closely, noticing the lovely, intricate design of yellow and black on the mother bird's wings and throat. Eventually the baby birds were fed and satisfied, and the mother bird nestled over her young ones, enfolding them with her protecting wings.

Slowly and silently, Eisha climbed down from the Sacred Tree. When she reached the hollow between the roots where she had kept long vigil, she saw that her friend was gone. So was the Sacred Horse. She was alone on the hilltop. Above her, a few stars were already sparkling in the evening sky. A faint line of scarlet light to the west was all that was left of the sunset. She yawned and stretched out full length on the soft grass beneath the Tree, and before long, she was as fast asleep as the birds above.

"A few moments later, the mother bird flew sown into the nest, a long worm dangling from her beak."

CHAPTER TWELVE:

THE STORM

At the same time that a bird in the Tree above began its morning wake-up song, a bright beam of sun struck Eisha's face. Her eyes flew open. Was it morning already? She yawned and stretched. Her body felt refreshed and rested. As she sprang to her feet, she felt an incredible new lightness of being, and a surge of joyful energy in every limb.

"This is how I remember feeling when I was little!" she exclaimed to herself. "I wonder if it's because of the Sacred Tree's fruit, or the chanting, or the waiting and resting..." Her voice trailed off as she realized it was all of these, and more, and that there was a mystery about it that she could not explain.

Eisha looked about and saw that she was completely alone on the hilltop. There was no sign of the Sacred Horse or her woman friend. Slowly, she turned to look in all four directions. When she turned to the south, she saw the tiny triangular shape of a sail at the edge of the sea. Eisha's heart leaped at the sight, and she knew it was time to return to the ship and the Lion. Just to be sure, she checked the Stone in her pocket. Its solid weight and glowing color said "yes" to her heart, and she set off southward, walking downward toward the sea through grass almost as tall as her head.

It was hard going. "It will take me all day to get to the shore at this rate," Eisha thought as she trudged along, pushing the tall grass aside in front of her. After an hour or so, she was relieved to notice the faint beginnings of a path in the grass. It was overgrown, as if no one had used it for a long time. But she could follow it if she paid close attention. Fortunately, the path became clearer and clearer as it led her downward from the hills into the flat land that bordered the beach. Though the path made many turns, and sometimes seemed to double back on itself, its over-all direction was clearly southward. As Eisha walked along, the grasses that grew at the path side became shorter, and she could see the ship in the bay ahead of her growing bigger and closer with every mile.

When she finally emerged onto the beach, it was noon, and the sun was hot and high overhead. Except for the ship that still lay anchored a little way from shore, the beach was deserted. Eisha's steps quickened as she neared the ship. It already felt like a "home away from home," and she was eager to board it and set sail again. Heaving a sign of relief, she waded through the water to the ship, climbed up the rope ladder that still hung from its side, and pulled it up behind her. Then she raised the anchor, adjusted the sail, and waited for the wind to blow as she stood next to the carved lion's head on the prow of the ship.

She did not have long to wait. As if on cue, a stiff breeze sprang up and carried the ship away from the island in a southerly direction. The sky-blue sail billowed out and the ship ran swiftly before the wind. The Island of the Horses disappeared over the northern horizon, and once again Eisha was on the open sea, headed for another strange place in her search for the Lady and the Child.

Then, out of the north, a great, dark bank of clouds began to tower ever higher into the sky. Flashes of lightening darted in and out of the darkest parts of the clouds, and thunder growled in the distance. Gradually, it grew into a roar, and the wind blew wildly. The waves became huge hills of foaming water that tossed the ship about like a cork. Eisha's heart raced, for her childhood experience in sailing did not include being on the open sea in a storm, and she had no idea how to handle it.

By now, it was almost impossible to walk on the heaving surfaces of the ship. Eisha clung to the railings and the mast as she went along, while the rain and the wind soaked her to the skin. It was a torrential rain that rushed from the sky like a river flowing earthward. Eisha finally got on her hands and knees and crawled, gasping, to the hatch that led into the rooms below the deck. She shut the hatch over her head, scrambled down the ladder, and sank to the ground. At least she was no longer deluged by rain and wind. But the ship's tossing seemed even worse in the dim passageway where she sat. She began to feel seasick. She groaned, and held her stomach. Once again, she cried out in desperation, "Help! Help! Help!" Even as the cry left her lips, she remembered what the Lion had said when she first boarded the ship that had so mysteriously been prepared for her.

"There will be times when you will need to come down here ...When it storms, you will be held in safety and not be overwhelmed..."

A few feet from where she sat, Eisha saw the hatch that led down into the bottom of the ship. Eagerly, she crawled to it, lifted it up, and went down the ladder. The hatch slammed shut above her. She clung tightly to the sides of the rope ladder, feeling each rung bend beneath her anxious feet. As she climbed downward, she became aware of three things: she heard the sound of the Lion's purring song surrounding her; she felt no more violent, rocking motion; and she saw, instead of the stormy darkness of the sea above, a calm green-blue light that came through the transparent sides of the deep hold.

When she gained the floor at the bottom of the ladder, Eisha found that she could once again stand easily and firmly, and walk without difficulty. She looked around for the Lion, but though its song filled the space in which she stood, it was nowhere to be seen. The sick feeling in Eisha's stomach subsided. Then she felt her legs go weak with relief, and she quickly stepped over to the beautifully woven rainbow-colored hammock that stretched across the width of the hold. Sinking gratefully into its strong support, she settled quietly onto her back.

From her place in the hammock, she could see waving sea plants and schools of fish swimming by. The water at this depth seemed unaffected by the storm raging on its surface. Eisha knew enough about ships to realize that what she was experiencing was most unlikely. No ship had a hold so heavy and deep that it could keep the ship steady and provide a place of such calm in the midst of such a storm! But there she was, and there was no denying her experience, however unlikely and mysterious it was. With this thought, Eisha happened to look upward, and there, almost directly above her, lay the Lion, curled up comfortably on top of the roof's rafters!

"Are you still afraid, Eisha?" asked the Lion softly as its great golden eyes gazed into hers. Eisha listened to her body and her heart.

"I'm still a little tense," she said honestly, "but no, I'm not afraid now that I'm down here with you."

"That's good!" replied the Lion. "You have grown in courage and wisdom."

Eisha was silent for a while, as was the Lion. Then she said simply, "I think my body finally caught up with my soul, and we're better partners now."

The Lion nodded and remained silent. Eisha closed her eyes, and memories of her Island experience came flooding into her mind. She sensed that the Lion was sharing them with her, and that its Presence in the process of remembering and reflecting on her experience made an important difference. The memory she returned to most often was of the night in the pool among the lotus blossoms beneath the shining, swirling Star. It filled her with a deep peace and sense of healing. She rested in the hammock in that peace until she fell asleep, rocked ever so gently in the cradle of the deep.

"From her place in the hammock, she could see waving sea plants and schools of fish swimming by."

CHAPTER THIRTEEN:

THE SECRET ENTRANCE

When Eisha awoke, the hold was perfectly still. The Lion had disappeared again. She climbed out of the hammock, stretched herself like a cat after a nap, and climbed back up the ladder to the forward cabin. There, she washed up, and changed into a fresh, dry tunic and pants of creamy white, with yellow sunflowers embroidered around the neckline and sleeve edges. Then she had some wine and wafers for breakfast. The rich, sweet milk-and-honey taste of the wafers, along with the fruity, tangy taste of the wine was most welcome. When she had finished eating, Eisha looked again at the colored maps of the islands on the wall over the washbowl in front of her. One of the islands, she noted, had a picture of a rose and turquoise horse, and a great tree. "That's it! That's where I was!" she exclaimed. "I wonder where I am now! Probably way south if the wind has kept blowing the way it was. I better go up on deck and see."

With these words, Eisha climbed swiftly up the ladder and went to the prow of the ship. She followed the straight-ahead gaze of the carved lion's head, and saw a faint shape on the horizon. Could it be land? She looked about and noticed that the sea-waves were now a comfortable size for sailing on an even keel. The wind was blowing strong and steady in a southerly direction. She didn't even need to steer, for the ship was heading straight for the faint patch on the horizon. The patch grew rapidly, until it became a dark range of jagged peaks against a hot blue sky.

As the ship drew near land, all Eisha could see were sheer, rocky cliffs, barren of any vegetation, with the waves of the sea dashing themselves into foaming white pieces against their granite walls.

"Oh my!" thought Eisha in dismay. "How can I possibly land here?" As if reading her mind, the wind suddenly died down as the ship entered the shadow of the cliffs. Not knowing what else to do, Eisha dropped anchor. It took a great deal of rope to let it down, for the water was deep even as close as she was to shore.

"I could swim to shore," she thought as she surveyed the island from the deck. "But then what would I do? There doesn't seem to be any break in the cliff's walls where I could go further in."

A moment later, an idea occurred to her. Perhaps there was a dinghy somewhere on the ship. Most ships of this one's size had them on board. Eisha searched for a few minutes, and to her delight, found a dinghy stashed on deck at the rear of the ship. Fortunately, she was strong, and the dinghy was small enough that she could lift and haul it where she wanted it—over the side of the deck and down into the water. Then she climbed down the rope ladder which she hung from the side of the ship, got into the dinghy, and set off rowing away from the ship toward the island, her heart pounding with excitement as she wondered what adventure would befall her next.

"I think I'll row slowly around the island," said Eisha to herself. "Perhaps I'll find a place where I can land the ship and go inland. I just hope the island isn't too big to row around before night comes." Cautiously, she rowed the dinghy as close to shore as she could without getting caught in the surge of the waves that smashed against the rocky cliffs. Turning the small craft left, she rowed steadily for several hours in the hot sun. Her arms, shoulders and back began to ache so that she could hardly keep going, and her mouth was so dry she was tempted to drink the salt water in which she rode. But she knew how sick that would make her! Instead, she put down her oars and stretched out in the ship for a brief rest. As she lay there in the sun, she wondered whether or not to keep going or give up and return to the ship.

Suddenly she sat bolt upright! Of course! The Stone would help her decide! She took it out of her pocket and laid it in her lap. Then she headed the dinghy towards the ship. The Stone grew a dull brown in color. She turned the dinghy back toward the coastline. The Stone began to glow a brilliant golden color.

"Well, that's my answer," thought Eisha. "I hope I don't have to row too much further."

She sighed, put the Stone in her pants pocket, and took the oars into her blistered hands. By now the sun was getting low in the sky, and Eisha was worried that she would find no place to land before dark. As she rounded a curve in the coast, she guessed by the sun's direction that she was now on the west side of the island. The towering cliffs that surrounded the island still rose straight up from the sea without any visible break.

The sun began to set into the rim of the sea to Eisha's left. She looked anxiously at her Heart-Stone once more. Should she continue on? The Stone glowed bright as before, and weighed heavy in her hand. Shaking her head, Eisha continued to row. By now, she was far out of sight of the ship anyway. And if night came—well, she could just keep rowing. Of course, by now she was very thirsty, hungry, and tired. But she was able to press on, for she had grown stronger and learned to live with hardship on the Island of the Horses.

The sky grew dark, and the stars of the southern constellations shone like diamonds on black velvet. Eisha let herself rest on her back for a while in the dinghy, and gaze in awe at the strange star-patterns in the sky. She had never seen them before, and she wondered if there were people who lived under these stars and gave them names. The breeze died away, and the waves lapped softly against the nearby cliffs. Once again, Eisha felt as if she were keeping vigil, and she began to softly chant the words and tune her red-haired friend had taught her under the Sacred Tree.

"Ruah, Shaddai, Eemah," she repeated over and over. Finally, the tension drained from her body as she chanted in rhythm with the waves. She let her hot, blistered hands trail in the cool water. She closed her eyes…

When she opened them, the stars had moved to new positions in their eternal dance in the sky. And straight above her was a brilliant star that began to swirl as she gazed intently at it. Eisha sat up in a shock of delight. It was the Morning Star—her guiding Star! She must be where she needed to be—wherever that was! Eisha peered into the darkness on her right, where she had last seen land. The dark shadows of the all-too-familiar cliffs rose forbiddingly against the starlit sky. As she gazed intently at them, she noticed a gap in the cliffs shaped like a huge "V". Below the bottom of the "V," at the foot of the cliffs, the light of a fire shone on the shore! With renewed hope, Eisha rowed towards the fire, sure that there she would find some sign to guide her on her journey. Before long, she was on land. A small cove, only a few feet wide and deep, offered a place to beach the dingy. Eisha climbed out and walked toward the fire. It burned at the mouth of a cave. There was no one in sight.

"Who lit this fire?" wondered Eisha as she sat down in the sand next to it. She peered into the black depths of the cave behind the fire. "I wonder what's in the cave?" she thought. "I'm not going to find out right now! I'll just stay here by the fire tonight, and see if tomorrow brings any answers to my questions." With these words, Eisha stretched out in the sand, bone-weary with the day's searching and rowing and skin-sore from hours in the blazing tropical sun. Her eyes grew heavy with sleep...

A flash of lightening jolted Eisha awake as night was moving toward morning. It was followed by a loud clap of thunder, and a sudden torrent of rain. In an instant, Eisha was soaked, and the fire was drowned out. Quickly, she moved into the mouth of the cave for shelter. She sat with her back against one of its sides, where she could see out to the sea in one direction, and into the cave in the other. "I don't want anything sneaking up behind me," she thought as she sat there, wide awake, waiting for morning to come.

Then, in the darkness of the cave, she saw one small, twinkling light after another appear. It was as if the cloud-covered stars had flown into the cave and were playing together in the dark!

"Fireflies!" exclaimed Eisha with delight. "Aren't they beautiful?" All at once, for the first time on her voyage, she was overwhelmed with a feeling of loneliness. It would be so nice to have someone with whom to share this beautiful sight. She sighed, and shifted her position so that she faced into the cave's depths and could see the fireflies more fully. As she watched, they disappeared into the dark depths, one by one—except for a single particularly bright firefly, which approached her until it was no more than an arm's length away, and then flitted back into the darkness. It repeated this pattern several times, until Eisha began to think it was deliberate—almost as if it were inviting her to follow it deeper into the cave.

Eisha considered. A curtain of rain fell outside of the cave. She had found no other landing place on the island. The Stone and the Star seemed to have led her here. Perhaps this was the one way into the island. Of course, there was no way of knowing where the cave might lead, or what was in its dark interior. As Eisha hesitated, the memory of the cave in which she had found the Lady and the Child came flooding back. Something about the firefly reminded her of the glow that cradled the sleeping Child.

"I'll do it!" she exclaimed to herself. "I'll go on in!"

Eisha stood up and began to follow the firefly, which danced and winked ahead of her. Slowly, step by step, into ever blacker depths of darkness, she walked onward, until the faint light of the cave's opening, which she frequently glanced backward to see, disappeared. On and on the firefly led her, turning one way and then another. "If it should leave me, I would never find my way out," worried Eisha, and her hands turned cold and clammy. She felt a sense of panic creeping up into her throat, and was about to scream, when she remembered that she didn't want to attract unwanted attention! So, she swallowed her fear as best she could, and kept following the firefly. She could see absolutely nothing but its tiny light. The ground was rocky, but fairly level beneath her feet, and she walked slowly and carefully so that she would not trip and fall.

Finally, when Eisha was feeling she could not take another step without collapsing into a weary heap, she saw light—a small glimmer far ahead and high up. The firefly flew faster, leading her toward it, until she stood at the bottom of a steep slope, with an opening at its summit, through which the dim light of pre-dawn poured into the darkness. To her surprise, Eisha saw that a set of stone steps angled their way up the slope to the opening.

"Who made these steps?" she wondered aloud. "And how long ago? And why?" The firefly flew up towards the opening and disappeared into the light. With a deep breath, Eisha climbed up the steps, and squeezed through the opening, which was just big enough to let a human body through.

Before her stretched a strange sight indeed! She was on the side of a steep hill, on a rocky ledge. Below her stretched a tropical jungle of brilliant green hues, with bright splashes of color visible even from a distance. Far off to the east, beyond the jungle, lay an expanse of desert in which nothing seemed to be growing. On all sides, the jungle and desert landscapes were ringed with high, jagged cliffs. To the left she could see the "V" shaped opening in the cliff wall that marked the place where she had found the fire and entered the cave. There were no other breaks in the cliffs anywhere. They towered all around and behind her, shutting out the sight of the sea. Near the ledge on which she stood, a small waterfall tumbled down over the rocks. It was bordered by a thick bed of ferns. Tropical trees of various kinds clung to the hillsides. A brilliant red and purple bird flashed by.

Eisha drank at the waterfall, and then looked for something to eat. A few yards down the hill from the waterfall, she found a grove of orange, banana, and mango trees, filled with ripe fruit. Eagerly, yet slowly, Eisha ate one of each kind of fruit, savoring its unique flavor, texture, and fragrance. Once her hunger and thirst were satisfied, she began exploring the grove of fruit trees, and came upon a small foot-path on the south side of the grove, at its lowest point on the hillside. It led toward the heart of the jungle below.

"Eisha saw that a set of stone steps angled their way up the slope to the opening."

CHAPTER FOURTEEN:

THE GOLDEN GROVE

It seemed the obvious thing to do, so Eisha took the path downward. Before long, she found herself beneath huge, vine-covered trees of kinds she had never seen before. Blossoms big and small, in all the colors of the rainbow, filled their branches with brilliant beauty. Birds with feathers that matched the flowers flickered in and out of sight as they hunted their food and warned of her coming with musical cries.

As Eisha kept walking, the shadows of the jungle thickened and deepened, and she sensed she was being watched. The feeling grew as she proceeded, and every now and then a swift, rustling movement in the thick undergrowth that bordered the path would make her stop and look about. But only the birds revealed their presence to her. The path led ever deeper into the jungle, curving like a huge Island Snake through the towering trees and trailing vines.

A wave of loneliness swept over Eisha. She longed for the sight of another human face, however strange. Surely, there must be someone on this island. Someone started that fire on the shore. Someone who, perhaps, was watching her from within the jungle's deep green shadows even now! She stopped suddenly in her tracks and looked sharply about her in every direction. For a moment, the jungle grew strangely silent, as if holding its breath with Eisha.

Then, as she resumed walking, a flock of blue and yellow parrots flew overhead, squawking loudly. They flew ahead of her along the line of the path, and every now and then, they would all stop at the same time, and settle overhead in the trees until Eisha had caught up with them. Then on they flew, as if to entice her further along the path, deeper into the jungle.

"How strange," thought Eisha as she trudged along. Still, she was glad for their company. So glad that she began to talk to the parrots.

"Hello," she called out. "My name is Eisha."

"EEesha! EEesha!" squawked a couple of the parrots in reply.

"I'm looking for the Lady and the Child, and the Lion is helping me," called Eisha.

"EEesha! EEesha!" squawked the parrots louder than ever. They kept flying ahead and waiting for her, calling her by name as they did so, until Eisha was sure the whole jungle and everyone in it knew her name and where she was.

By now, many hours had gone by, and Eisha was growing hot and tired. "I need a rest," she said out loud, and looked about for a place to sit down. As if they sensed her intent, several parrots circled around her head, just out of reach, and then darted away from the path toward the right. Eisha noticed that the tangle of plants and bushes thinned out under their flight-path. She decided to follow their leading.

A few moments and not too many steps later, Eisha was under a canopy of golden-flowered trees. Their blossoms filled the air with a tangy-sweet fragrance, and covered the ground with a golden-yellow carpet of petals. The very light in the grove was golden. Ahead of her, Eisha saw a circle of gray stones, each of them a comfortable size and shape for sitting. In the center of the stone circle were the charred remains of a fire.

"How long ago was it burning?" wondered Eisha as she approached the stones. "And is there anyone who sits on these stones?"

There were no ready answers to her questions, and with a sigh of both relief and weariness, Eisha sank down on one of the stones. It felt good to just sit there, soaking in the golden beauty of the grove that surrounded her.

"What a beautiful place this is," she thought. "I wouldn't mind staying here for quite a while." But soon she was not thinking, or looking, or wondering. She was slipping into sleepiness. She did not fight it, but lay down on the bed of golden blossoms that covered the ground, and entered the mysterious world of dreams.

While she napped, one of the jungle's inhabitants who had been watching her crept closer and closer to her sleeping form.

"EEesha! EEesha!" shrieked the blue and yellow parrots overhead.

Eisha's eyes flew open. She was lying on her back, with a canopy of yellow flowers above her. Suddenly she screamed! A huge Snake lay coiled at her feet, with its head not far from hers.

"It's the Snake that lured me out of the cave and away from the Child!" thought Eisha. "What is it doing here? What does it want?"

But a second scared look revealed a very different Snake than the one Eisha had first encountered. This one was a deep and brilliant ocean blue, with large green spots outlined with crimson. They looked rather like islands in a sinuous sea. Its eyes were golden, like the blossoms above and below.

"Who-who are you?" stammered Eisha in a frightened voice. "What do you want from me?"

"I am the guardian of the jungle," replied the Island Snake in a golden and melodious voice. "Who are **you**? And what do **you** want?"

Eisha sat up to face the talking Island Snake. It didn't seem **un**friendly. Still, how could she tell whether to go on speaking with it or trust it? Her last conversation with a Snake had not turned out very well! She instinctively put her hand in her pockets, and in one of them, felt the Stone! She had forgotten about it again! How **could** she? Eisha shook her head remorsefully and pulled it out. It weighed heavy and flashed gold and blue in her palm. She breathed a sigh of relief, and looked the Island Snake straight in the eyes.

"I am Eisha, and with the help of my Heart-Stone, the Morning Star, and the Lion, I am searching for the Lady and the Child I found and lost in a cave long ago," she replied.

To her surprise, the Island Snake bowed its head low before her, and then raised it saying, "You are most welcome here in the jungle, O keeper of the Heart-Stone. I know the Lion well. It told me of your coming!"

Eisha was dumbfounded! Her mind whirled with questions. The Island Snake waited in silence for a while, sensing her confusion and distraction. Then it spoke again.

"If you remain here at the circle of stones until nightfall, Eisha, your loneliness will be lessened, and at least some of your questions answered. And—most important—you will have the chance to find out more clearly, and know more deeply, who you are and why you are here."

With these mysterious words, the Island Snake slipped swiftly and silently through the golden petals covering the ground, and disappeared into the jungle.

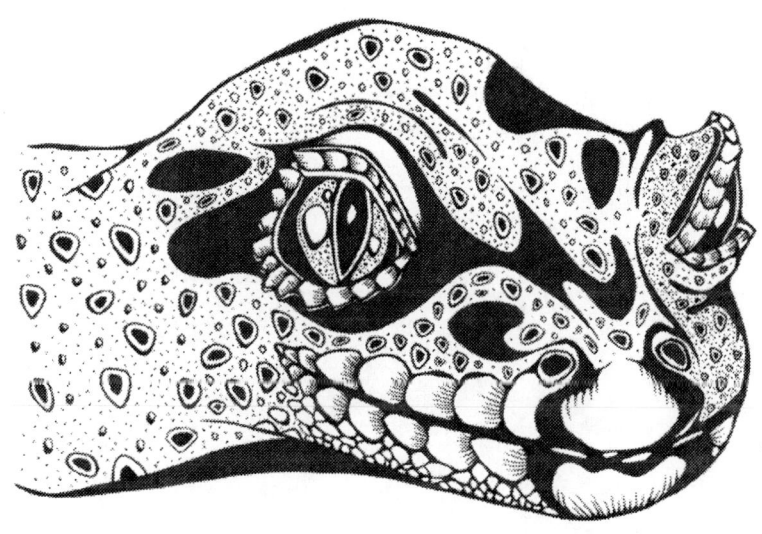

"But a second look revealed a very different Snake than the one Eisha had first encountered."

CHAPTER FIFTEEN:

THE STONE CIRCLE

Once again, Eisha was alone with plenty to ponder—and that is just what she did, all through the long afternoon hours. The golden grove in which she sat was still and silent. There was no breeze, no rustle of leaves, no parrot-squawks, and no creature-sound of any kind. A breathless hush filled the air, as if the whole jungle were waiting along with Eisha for something to happen. Eisha realized that her times of waiting and vigil on the Island of the Horses had not only made her stronger, wiser, and hardier, but also trained her in the art of patient waiting and watching. Patience and stillness, she could sense, were becoming a habit of her being, and she knew that was good.

The afternoon wore on towards evening as Eisha sat on one of the stones in the circle, her mind full of questions, and her heart full of anticipation. Now and then, she felt a twinge of anxiety, but she clung to her trust in the Stone's assurance, based on the Lion's promise, and supported by the Island Snake's words, that she was where she needed to be.

Then, as the golden light was fading into dusky gray, Eisha saw the flicker of moving firelight in the distance. The far-off flames looked almost like the fireflies that had led her into the cave on the beach of this strange island. As they moved closer, she saw that they formed a long, curving line at about the level of her eyes when she stood up.

"There must be people carrying them!" she said to herself. She was right. A line of dark-skinned women, each one bearing a torch, emerged one by one from the jungle shadows surrounding the clearing in which Eisha sat. All had thick halos of curly blue-black hair with multi-colored flowers woven skillfully through the tiny curls. Their dark skins glistened in the firelight, and they were dressed in short, sleeveless shifts made from various kinds of large feathers of the same colors as the flowers in their hair. Silently, they stood before Eisha, one by one, and bowed their heads in welcome. Silently they took their places in the circle of stones.

When the circle of women was complete, with Eisha included, they each placed a piece of wood that they had been carrying on the ashes of the old fire. Then, all at the same time, they lit the new fire with their torches. As the flames leaped into life, each one extinguished her own torch. One of the women, who looked like the oldest in the group, pointed a finger upward to the sky. Eisha followed its direction with her eyes, and saw, directly above their heads, the crescent of a new moon, as golden as the grove by daylight.

"Eisha, you have come at an auspicious time," said the woman. "Our friend and guardian, the Island Snake, told us of your coming. Our friends the fireflies and parrots led you to our circle of meeting, and we welcome you among us with joy."

Eisha was speechless with wonder. But she needed no words, for the women around her joined hands, and began to sing a beautiful song that somehow reminded her of the chant taught her by the red-haired woman under the Sacred Tree. It was far more complex, however, and Eisha listened with delight to the haunting melodies that wove through each other. The beauty of the women's sweet, strong voices singing together around the fire beneath the new moon moved her deeply. Each of her hands was warmly held by the two women on either side of her, and Eisha felt a rush of relief from her loneliness that brought tears to her eyes. The women noticed, and their song faded away.

"Eisha," said a woman who sat across the circle from her, "tell us your story. We know only that you came here on the Lion's ship. The Lion watches over us too, and we are eager to hear of your experience, and how it is that you come to us in this place. For we must tell you that it has been many years since anyone found their way through the secret entrance into the jungle."

Eisha had questions of her own about these women and how they knew the Lion. But she was their guest, and they seemed so kind and genuinely interested in her that she found it easy to comply with their request.

"I first met the Lion in the desert," she began. "I ran from it in fear. I did not know better back then."

The women nodded silently in sympathy, as if they understood the fear. Eisha went on.

"I was in the desert because the castle in which I grew up was destroyed by an earthquake. My grandmother had told me once, when I was a little girl, that if I ever had to leave the castle for any reason, I should go into the desert, and there I would find help." Eisha paused and reflected. "Now that I think about it, she must have had a premonition about the earthquake. And maybe she even knew the Lion!" Her voice filled with surprise as she realized what she was saying. The women in the circle smiled knowingly, but said nothing, waiting to hear more.

"My father, the king, told me stories about the wild and dangerous beasts that dwelt in the desert. But I trusted my grandmother, and did as she advised when the castle crumbled. After a few days, the food and water which I had taken along for the journey was gone, and I had no idea of which way to go. There was no path to follow, and I had begun to believe that I would not survive. I remember now that I was wondering why my grandmother told me to go to the desert, and why I had listened to her advice, when I first saw the Lion running behind me as if chasing me..."

With these words, and many others, Eisha told her story while the new moon sank slowly behind the trees. The women listened with the closest attention, and Eisha felt as if they were hearing her into speech, calling forth her story, and evoking whole new meanings in the story by their listening. No one had ever listened to her so long and so lovingly!

Then they asked her questions that helped her remember more about her lonely childhood as an only child, the loss of her mother, the stories her grandmother told her, and what she had learned by acting them out as a girl. By the time she finished, Eisha realized that the Island Snake's words had come true. She did know more clearly and deeply who she was. But she still did not know why she had come to this island. In the silence that followed her story, Eisha waited, and wondered.

Then the woman on her right spoke. "Eisha, my sister," she said. "You have great courage! You are on a vital, even crucial journey. It will affect us all in ways we cannot know now. When you speak of the Lady and the Child, I feel joy leap in my womb, and yearning fill my heart." All the other women nodded their agreement. There was a long pause.

The woman on Eisha's left broke the silence. "Do you have questions for us?"

"Oh, yes!" Eisha blurted eagerly. "I want to know—oh, so much! Have you always lived in the jungle? How do you do it? When did you meet the Lion? What about the Island Snake who scared me so, yet spoke so wisely? And who, if anyone, lives in the desert I saw beyond this jungle? And who lit the fire on the beach and built the steps of stone that lead out of the cave-passages to the secret entrance into this land?"

"Eisha, you have come at an auspicious time," said the woman.

CHAPTER SIXTEEN:

THE WOMEN'S STORY

The oldest woman laughed and held up her hand to stop the impulsive flow of Eisha's questions. "Let us see if there is enough time before sunrise to answer some of your many questions, my sister," she said. "But first, we need to move and dance, laugh and sing, eat and drink. Come, let us celebrate being together before the night of the new moon is over, and she sets beyond the invisible sea."

As if the words signaled the beginning of a familiar ritual, the dark-skinned women rose and began to dance in a circle, moving in graceful rhythm with the chant they began to sing. One of them produced a small drum, and with its help, Eisha was able to join in the rhythm of the dance. The movement and music caught her up in a strong feeling of unity with the other women in the circle, and she lost all traces of her loneliness as the drum beat out the rhythm of her heart and theirs. The words the women sang over and over soon rang from her lips too:

> When the people live their life
> As if it were a song for singing out the light,
> It creates the music for the stars
> To be dancing circles in the night.

As Eisha sang, she happened to look up at the sky above, and there, where the new moon had been, a familiar Star shone brightly upon the dancing circle of women, and its silvery swirling seemed to be a part of their dance.

"The Morning Star! My guiding Star!" cried Eisha excitedly, pointing up at it. The women stopped singing and dancing and stared at the Star with Eisha.

"Ahhh—it is beautiful!" breathed one of them. "Where did it come from? I've never seen it before, and I thought I knew the stars well, for I watch them often in the sleepless hours of the night."

"It led me here," replied Eisha. "It is the Star I told you about in my story, that watches over me and leads me."

"I think it must be the Lady's special sign of love and care for you as you search for Her," said the star-loving woman softly. Eisha remembered how the Lady's kiss on her forehead had felt as if a star had been imprinted there forever, and she nodded her head in agreement.

Then all the women sat down again, and under the streaming radiance of the Star, told Eisha their story. The oldest woman told most of it, with the others joining in from time to time. Eisha listened intently.

"We have lived here in the jungle for many years," began the oldest woman. "We used to live in the desert you saw, with men who were our fathers, uncles, husbands, brothers, sons, and friends. For many ages, we lived in peace and happiness together. The men respected us as the bearers of life, and for our knowledge of the stones and plants and their uses for food and medicine. The desert was a fertile land then, and we never lacked for food or water or any good thing.

But one day a white-skinned man with brown hair, like yours, somehow found his way into our land. He planted strange ideas in the men's minds, which he said were the revealed will of his thunder-god, who was above all other gods. "Men," he said, "were made to rule women, who are by nature weaker and inferior." He also insisted that the Great Lion and the Island Snake, who had always lived among us, guiding and guarding us, were demons, and that we must not heed them. I do not think that his ideas would have won the men over if it had not been for the fact that at about that time, the rains stopped. There was a long and terrible drought. Then a mighty earthquake struck the island, and changed the course of the river that watered the farmlands. Gradually, much of the land began to turn into desert. "This is the thunder-god's punishment," the white man said. "He is angry because you have allowed women to usurp the power that is rightfully yours, and because you honor the Lion and the Island Snake rather than himself."

Many of the men believed him. They became unkind and disrespectful of us. Though we had taught them much about the arts of farming and healing, weaving and pottery, writing and music, they refused to even let us do these things anymore. "Your job is to bear and care for children, the more the better," they said, "and to serve us and make us happy." They stopped consulting us, or even listening to our wisdom and experience. They refused to share in the care of the children as they once did. Instead of being their partners, we became their servants. Women who protested—and many did—were derided, beaten, or even shamed and raped by the cruelest men. Because most of the men were bigger and stronger than us, they could do this. During this time, the white man became their chief, and the high priest of the religion he had introduced.

Finally, a number of us women met in secret desperation. Our deliberations led us to realize that the only way we could survive with dignity and keep women's ways alive for the future was to leave the men. The only place we could go was the jungle. It had always been a dark, mysterious, impenetrable place, where neither men nor women ventured. Nor had we had any need to do so before. But now, it afforded our only chance to make a life of our own in freedom and peace. We did not know what dangers it held in its unknown depths, but we were willing to risk it, rather than endure our enforced servitude and the awful religion of the white man that was being forced upon us. We called out to the Great Lion and the Island Snake for help. And they came to our aid!" The oldest woman's voice choked with emotion, and another woman picked up the thread of the story.

"The Lion walked majestically into our secret meeting and told us that it would no longer dwell among the men in the desert, for they no longer honored us or the Lion or any other creatures. ' Their hearts have grown as hard as the dry bed of the river,' said the Lion. 'They think only of how to use and dominate those who are not like them. I will lead you into the jungle, and the Island Snake will live with you there, and teach you how to thrive in it.'

And so, on the Night of the New Moon, forty years ago, we and many other bands of women fled under cover of darkness into this jungle, taking our daughters with us. We had to leave our sons behind, for they always slept in the men's tents with their fathers. We walked all night into the jungle darkness, with only the Lion to lead us—and the fireflies, who are the Lion's helpers."

Eisha smiled as she remembered their bright flashing beauty, and how they led her into the secret entrance into the island. Now the oldest woman resumed the story.

"When morning came, we heard the distant cries of many men, who had discovered our absence and were following us. We climbed up into the trees, filled with fear that they would find us and force us to go back. But as their shouts sounded louder with their approach to the edge of the jungle, we heard the Lion's roar resound like a thousand thunderstorms upon the cliffs that surround the land. At the same time, the Island Snake slid beneath the trees in which we were hiding, reared its head up towards us, and said, 'Have no fear, my beloved ones! If any man dares enter the jungle in spite of the Lion's roar, I shall catch him in my coils and whisper much needed wisdom into his ear until he is more than ready to return to his own territory! When enough men have been taught thusly, perhaps they will see the error of their ways, change their minds and hearts, and welcome you as their equals and partners. Until then, you have nothing to fear here in the jungle. For I know the secrets of its plants, and of all that crawls or flies here. And I will teach you how to live in harmony with them all, that you might flourish.'

From that day to this, we have lived in peace in this jungle, and no man has yet penetrated its depths to find us or force us. Through the years, more women and girls have kept finding a way to escape and join us here in the jungle. There must be very few left in the desert by now."

Eisha was silent, trying to understand the story she had heard, and what it might mean for her new friends and for herself. After awhile, she spoke.

"My sisters, what will you do if you all become too old to bear children before the men repent and return you to your rightful place as their partners?"

"We have thought of that," replied the oldest woman. "If that happens, it will mean the end of our race on this island. For we will not go back to servitude; only a change of heart in the men can save us all from extinction. We will not bear and raise children in the midst of the injustice and violence we endured!" Her eyes flashed with anger.

Eisha looked at the beautiful women around her, with their gleaming, dark brown skins and their curly blue-black hair entwined with flowers. She thought of the skill and joy that would die out with them, and all the human potential that would never flower. Her heart ached and protested.

"How many men, do you think, have been taught by the Island Snake and have changed their minds and hearts?" asked Eisha.

"We have no way of knowing," replied one of the women. There was a long, heavy silence. Then, as if sparked by the still-swirling Star overhead, an idea flashed in Eisha's mind.

"I am white, like the strange man who came here," she said. The women nodded.

"You look very much like him," said the oldest woman.

"Then why can't I go to the desert, and challenge this man's teachings as one who is like him, but knows better?" cried Eisha. "Perhaps many of the men are weary of living without you, and are aware of the danger of your race's extinction. Wouldn't that make them ready to listen to someone else? And even if not, surely I could find some men who have repented in the coils of the Island Snake, and arrange a meeting between them and you. Who knows? Perhaps there is a chance of reconciliation and fruitful reunion. Then you could thrive as a people for many more generations, combining the wisdom of men and women."

The circle of women was silent. Then the oldest woman said slowly, "Eisha, there may be a chance—the only one that has come our way. But this is a difficult and dangerous undertaking for you. To do it, you will first need to spend much time with us and the other bands of women in the jungle, so that you know us well, and are shaped deeply enough by the women's ways we have developed to represent us truly and strongly. Then, you will need to cross the desert, where there are many mirages to delay and deceive you, before you come to the villages where the men dwell. And though you are white, like the man who leads them, because you are a woman, your voice will not be accorded the authority his is given. That puts you at a great disadvantage. Even the men who have grown wise through the Island Snake's intervention will hesitate to leave their fellow men to follow a woman into the jungle, which they fear greatly."

"That may all be true," answered Eisha. "But could it not be that I was led here for just such a purpose, before it is too late? Who guided the ship here? Who lit the fire that drew me to land?

Who sent the fireflies that lured me and guided me into the passage behind the cave?"

"The Lion and the Island Snake!" replied one woman after another.

"I think so too," said Eisha, and she felt a collective shiver running through the circle of women and up her spine. "There is only one way I know to test my idea," she added. And she reached for her Heart- Stone and opened her hand near the fire where all could see it. The women, having heard of the Stone in Eisha's story, watched it intently with her. It began to glow gold and then silver. The white star crystal in its heart shone brighter and brighter, until it looked like the great Star swirling and shining above. Eisha could hardly hold her hand up, so great was the weight of the Stone.

"So be it," said the oldest woman.

"So be it," chorused the others.

"So be it," responded Eisha.

"At the same time, the Island Snake slid beneath the trees in which we were hiding, reared its head towards us and said, 'Have no fear, my beloved ones!'"

CHAPTER SEVENTEEN:

THE PREPARATION

From that New Moon night, and for many more moons, Eisha lived among the women in the jungle. She shed her own clothes, which were far too hot to be comfortable in the jungle's tropical climate. She learned to make and loved to wear the feather shifts the other women and girls wore. She found out what fruits and nuts and plants were edible. She learned to recognize healing herbs and memorized their uses. She learned to weave baskets of all kinds, and mats for making the walls and roofs of houses. Best of all, she found out how to make clay pots, and decorate them with beautiful designs of her own creation. She had a special gift with clay, and soon all her newfound friends wanted her to make them a pot or two.

As she learned these skills, Eisha's creative powers grew and blossomed, and she was happier than she had ever been in her life. She formed strong and special friendships with many of the women. And, to her great delight, she was befriended by one of the littlest girls, who had come as an infant with her mother into the jungle four years earlier. The little girl's name was Lila, and she followed Eisha everywhere. Something about being with Lila made Eisha feel what she had felt when she was caring for the light-cradled Child in the cave. Eisha's joy in being in the close company of the jungle-women, learning their ways, and playing for hours at a time in the jungle with Lila was marred only by the thought that all of this would have to come to an end if she was to be true to her purpose and their need.

One day, as she and Lila were absorbed in making flower chains to give to some of their friends, she looked up to see the Island Snake watching them both from behind a tree not far away. Lila had never seen it, and its huge coils, along with the towering height of its head poised above them, sent her screaming with fright into Eisha's arms. Eisha was a bit scared herself, but she swallowed hard, sat very still, looked into the Island Snake's golden eyes, and waited. When Lila's screams subsided, the Island Snake spoke.

"You have done well, Eisha. You are now ready to go into the desert. Tomorrow night there will be a new moon. You must meet with the women in the Golden Grove when the moon is straight above you in the sky. I will come when you are seated around the Stone Circle and have lit the fire with your torches."

Then the Island Snake was gone as suddenly as it had appeared. Eisha hugged Lila to her breast, and tears of grief rolled down her face at the prospect of parting from the friends who had become so much a part of her. How she hated to leave the safe shelter of the generous jungle for the dangerous desert of mirages and men! Nevertheless, that was her call, and she did not want to escape it, hard though it would be to face what lay ahead. Slowly and resolutely, Eisha walked with Lila back to the place where her friends lived.

As she approached their jungle houses, one of them saw her coming, and called out a happy welcome. But as Eisha drew nearer, she exclaimed, "You've been crying!" When they heard these words, many of the other women came quickly to Eisha's side.

"Yes, I have been crying," replied Eisha simply. And then she told them what the Island Snake had said. The women, one by one, threw their arms around her, and mingled their tears with hers, for they loved her dearly, and dreaded her departure.

The next night, as the new moon rose over the treetops, it was a sad and slow procession that wound its way to the Stone Circle. No one spoke and no one sang. Silently, they all sat down, lit the fire at the center with their torches, and waited for the Island Snake to appear. Lila was allowed to be among them for the first time. Most girls had to wait until the special month when they began the bleeding that marked the start of their marvelous ability to conceive and bear children. But the women knew the special bond between Eisha and Lila, and they were glad to support it. Along with Eisha, they gazed into the fire or up at the sky, watching the new moon's ascent to its zenith. As Lila sat squirming in her lap, Eisha whispered in Lila's ear, "Watch, Lila! Watch for the Island Snake. It won't hurt you or me or anyone here. It is on our side, you know." Lila nodded and snuggled closer to Eisha, her dark, wide eyes gazing past the women into the shadows that surrounded the circle. Suddenly she let out a soft cry.

"There it is!" And she pointed to a shadowy place between two women opposite the stone where she and Eisha sat together. The Island Snake's great head rose slowly from the shadows and towered above the women. Its eyes and the new moon high above glowed with the same golden light.

"My beloved ones," said the Island Snake. "Eisha must leave you tomorrow. There is no time to waste. Tonight you must all accompany her to the edge of the jungle, and there bid her goodbye. If all goes well, you will see her again, and a new Day will dawn for you that will be full of harmony between women and men. Once again, your beautiful race will flourish. But great perils lie in the way to that Day. The first is the peril of the desert itself. It has grown a great deal bigger in the forty years since the first of you entered the jungle. The land continues to turn as dry as the hearts of the men who wish to posses and control you, for the soil of human hearts and the soil of the earth are of a piece. Eisha cannot cross the desert alone on foot, or she will lose her way and die of thirst before she reaches her destination. Therefore, I have provided a ship of the desert for her that will carry her through the miles and miles of burning sand to the place where men dwell. She will find it at the edge of the jungle, and it will take her where she needs to go."

The Island Snake paused, and there was a murmur of whispers around the circle. When it subsided, the Island Snake spoke again.

"Desert mirages are the second great peril. They seem very real. Eisha could easily be deceived, and her ability to help you in the right way destroyed. Even the Stone she carries is not sufficient to save her from the illusions she will encounter." At this point, the Island Snake looked deep into Eisha's eyes, and she felt as if its look penetrated to the darkest recesses of her soul, and saw all its Shadows. The Island Snake continued. "Only the eyes of a little child, who has not yet learned to deceive itself or others, can save Eisha from this peril." The Island Snake stopped and looked at Lila, and then at her mother, who sat at Eisha's right hand. The mother immediately caught the meaning of the Island Snake's words and look. She bit her lip and lowered her eyes. Eisha also understood, and turned whiter than she already was. Lila sensed the consternation of her mother and her pale friend. She whimpered, and put her arms around Eisha's neck. Her mother struggled with her feelings as she weighed the sacrifice being asked of her. She knew her daughter, as well as Eisha, might never return. And she knew she had to give her permission freely. Eisha was about to protest, but Lila's mother spoke first.

"Our whole future, it seems, hangs on Eisha and Lila," she said sorrowfully. "They are both gifts to me, and to us all. We love them, but we do not possess them. Therefore, it is not for us to grasp them when so much depends on letting them go."

A great sigh went like a wave around the circle of women. Lila's mother looked the Island Snake in the eye and said in a voice choked with tears, "I commend my friend Eisha and my daughter Lila into your keeping, O Guardian and Guide."

The Island Snake's head bent tenderly over the mother's tear-streaked face. Its tongue flickered ever so lightly, touching her cheek in a soft, loving caress. "You have freely given the greatest gift a woman and mother can give," said the Island Snake. "Greater love has no one than this. Surely, such love will someday bear the fruit of your heart's deepest desire—loving reunion as beloved and equal partners with the sons and husbands, fathers and brothers, lovers and friends you have lost to the desert and hardness of heart."

At these words, Eisha put Lila in her mother's arms and sat with her hands covering her face, overcome by the enormity of what was happening. But the Island Snake was not yet finished.

"Should you safely reach the abode of men, Eisha," it said, "you will face the great peril of being a woman challenging men's entrenched power, and a system of belief that has grown stronger each year. To help you find out whom the men are who might hear and follow you, I give you this silver serpentine belt. Wear it around your waist, with the head against your navel. Whenever you meet a man who has let my wisdom concerning women lodge in his heart, you will feel a pleasing warmth in your belly. Whenever you meet men who are dangerous, you will feel a cold sting in your belly. Pay close attention to these feelings, for your sake, and the sake of your friends!"

Eisha nodded. The Island Snake bent its head, and from somewhere in its scales picked up a coiled silver belt that looked like a miniature replica of itself in silver, and gave it to the nearest woman. The serpentine belt shone bright in the moonlight, and the women passed it from hand to hand around the circle, exclaiming over the exquisite artistry of its flexible silver scales and the finely shaped head with its amber eyes. When the belt reached Eisha, she put it around her waist, looping the tail around the head to hold the belt snugly in place.

"You must also disguise yourself," continued the Island Snake. It picked up a package and tossed it across the circle to Eisha with a swift, deft movement of its head. The package landed with a soft "plop" in her lap. She opened it, to find a loose robe and scarf-like headdress with a cord to hold it in place around her head. They were the pale beige color of desert sand, with patterned stitching at the neck and sleeves.

"These are the clothes of the men of the desert!" exclaimed the woman on Eisha's left.

"Yes," acknowledged the Island Snake. "Eisha, you must seem to be a man. One of the women can cut your hair tonight in the style customary to the men. And you must daily eat a handful of the dried herbs in the pouch that is with the robe I gave you. They will make you look and sound like a young man, as long as you do not forget to take them without fail every night. Were you to appear or speak as a woman, even the wisest and fairest men would not give the same weight to what you say as they would to a man's message. And the other men would not hear you at all. Though I know you will find doing this distasteful to you, it is necessary for our plan to succeed."

With these words, the Island Snake raised its head high above them. The crescent moon had set behind the trees. And once again, the Morning Star swirled in the sky above.

"Watch that Star!" whispered the Island Snake, and then it was gone.

"The little girl's name was Lila, and she followed Eisha everywhere."

CHAPTER EIGHTEEN:

THE SHIP OF THE DESERT

Eisha, Lila, and the women stared at the Star, and as they did, it began to move slowly towards the east and the desert. Eisha picked up her bundle of herbs and clothes. The women rose and lit their torches from the fire. Then, with Lila and her mother at her side, and the other women before and behind her, Eisha followed the Star's direction.

They all walked through the remaining hours of the night along the dark but familiar trails to the jungle's edge. Everyone was comforted, and Lila crowed with delight, when a swarm of fireflies suddenly appeared before them and led the way. It seemed like a good omen, and Lila's laughter lightened their heavy hearts.

Just as the sky was starting to turn pale gray with the coming of dawn, they came to the end of the trail. Ahead of them stretched rocky soil with a layer of ground cover and small trees that dwindled away into scrub at the sandy horizon. It was not a welcome sight!

"Look," cried Lila, pointing to their right. "What's that?" The dark and humpy silhouette of some sort of animal loomed against the dawn sky. As the sky grew pink with the light of the coming sun, the unmistakable shape of a large camel emerged.

A camel! Of course!" Eisha cried. "The ship of the desert the Island Snake promised to provide!" She stopped and faced her friends. "After one of you has cut my hair," she said, "will the rest of you give me your blessing? I know it will sustain me through whatever lies ahead."

Then she sat down on the ground beneath the outermost trees of the jungle, and the oldest woman stepped forward. With a sharp instrument, she carefully cut her hair in the style of the men of the desert.

"I will keep your hair until your return. It will help us feel closer to you," she said, gently coiling Eisha's long brown locks in her hands. There were tears in her eyes, and Eisha could not bear to look at her for more than a moment. She stood up, slipped on the robe and headdress, and knelt down on the jungle floor. All the women gathered around her in a circle, laid their hands on her head, and sang a sweet and strong song of blessing. Then they tearfully embraced her in a final farewell. Last of all, Lila's mother gave her into Eisha's arms with a passionate good-bye hug, and turned away weeping.

As for Lila, she was so sleepy she hardly noticed what was happening, and laid her little head on Eisha's shoulder as Eisha walked slowly and sadly away from the jungle and her friends towards the ship of the desert that would carry her away. As she walked, she glanced up at the sky above. The Morning Star had faded from view in the light of the rising sun. Ahead of her stood a camel of creamy white, with a ring of small turquoise bells around its neck. "Look, Lila—the camel is expecting us," said Eisha.

And indeed it was, for as they approached, it knelt in the sand. Between the two large humps on its back was a scarlet leather saddle that looked more than ample for Eisha and Lila. There was even a red silk canopy above the saddle to shield them from the sun, and in two large attached saddlebags, Eisha found water bottles and quantities of dried fruit, nuts, and seeds.

"Looks like we're all ready to go!" she said as cheerfully as she could, and hoisted Lila into the saddle. Then she climbed up behind the little girl. The camel straightened its back legs, and they almost pitched forward over its neck and nose onto the ground. Then the camel straightened its front legs, and they were up and off. The sway of the camel as it loped along was so much like the sway of the ship on which Eisha had come to this land that she thought, "No wonder they call a camel the ship of the desert!" She watched Lila anxiously as they rode, hoping she was not a child prone to motion sickness. But the little girl loved the feel of the fast-moving camel, and clapped her hands in glee.

The sun rose higher and shone hotter by the hour. Under the shade of the canopy, Eisha and Lila sat and watched the desert dunes go by, carved by the wind into fantastic formations that kept them interested for a long time. They encountered no living creature, and all about them was a deeper silence than Eisha had ever known. After awhile, Lila became very quiet, and Eisha began to think about the great importance of her mission, and how much depended on her ability to challenge, to persuade, and to lead. Why, the whole future of this land and its people was in her hands! That was a pretty impressive thing! Eisha had never experienced being in such a crucial position, and there was something intoxicating about it. She began to think more and more of her importance as they rode along...

When the sun was just beginning its westward slant, and the mid-day heat rose in shimmering waves from the sand all around them, the camel suddenly stopped. Ahead loomed the dazzling whitewashed walls of a large town. Four tall, slim towers marked the four corners. A massive wooden door in the city wall nearest them opened, and through the gate came a procession of tall, dark-skinned men, wearing robes and head-dresses of varying pastel shades in the same style as Eisha's clothes. The camel stood absolutely still as they approached. When they were only a few yards away, they stopped.

"Welcome, O famed white traveler from beyond the sea," said the leader in a loud voice. "Our prophets have told of a young white man riding a white camel who would deliver our race from extinction. We come to honor you and escort you into the city."

Eisha was both startled and gratified. This was much easier than she had expected! She didn't even have to prove her importance or establish her authority! But, out of long habit, she reached into her pocket to consult Her Stone. It felt heavy, but a glance revealed that it was a dull gray. No help there. Then Eisha's face grew stern and proud as she looked at the entourage waiting to escort her with honor into their city.

"You do well to welcome me!" she called out. "I have much to teach you, for you have fallen into great error. My wisdom will be your salvation!" With these words she urged the camel forward, but it would not budge.

"Eisha?" said Lila, "Who are you talking to?"

"Why, those men who came out to meet me," answered Eisha, pointing at the entourage a few yards ahead.

"You're telling a story, aren't you?" laughed Lila.

"No, I'm not," retorted Eisha sharply. "Can't you see who I'm talking about?"

"No, Eisha." Lila shook her curly black-haired head emphatically. "All I can see where you are pointing are some rocks."

Eisha looked down at her little friend in amazement. She rubbed her eyes. Was she seeing things? What was going on? Then the truth hit her like a bucket of cold water. A mirage! She had been taken in by an illusion! No wonder Lila had asked whom she was talking to. No wonder the camel wouldn't budge. And what an inflated fool she had been! Eisha's cheeks turned red with remorse as she recalled her high and mighty thoughts and words. "Serves me right," Eisha said to herself. Then she hugged Lila. "Thank you for being so truthful," she said. "You saved me from a mirage of illusions of grandeur!"

Lila didn't completely understand, but she liked the hug and smile Eisha gave her, and returned them both. "Eisha," she said, "do you think the camel is hungry and thirsty? Can I give it something?"

"Of course!" replied Eisha. "Let's give it something together. Feeding a camel is probably a good way to stop seeing mirages!" And she chuckled as she dismounted and lifted Lila down. Together, they gave the creamy white camel a drink of water and a few pieces of their dried fruit.

"Camels can go a long way without food or water," Eisha told Lila. "They store extra in their humps. But we don't know when it last ate and drank, so we'll look for an oasis where we can give it a lot more to eat and drink than we have in our saddle bags." So saying, she lifted Lila back up onto the kneeling camel and got on behind her. This time, they both balanced themselves better as the camel raised its hind legs, and then its front legs. Eisha tugged gently on the reigns, and they were off again, with the camel loping rapidly eastward. The sun sank slowly in the sky behind them, and cast long indigo shadows around and before them. When it finally dipped in fiery splendor behind a sand dune, Eisha saw a cluster of palm trees up ahead.

"I hope this isn't a mirage! "she muttered softly to herself. She let the camel's reigns hang loose, deciding that if the oasis was real, the camel would know it and take them right into it.

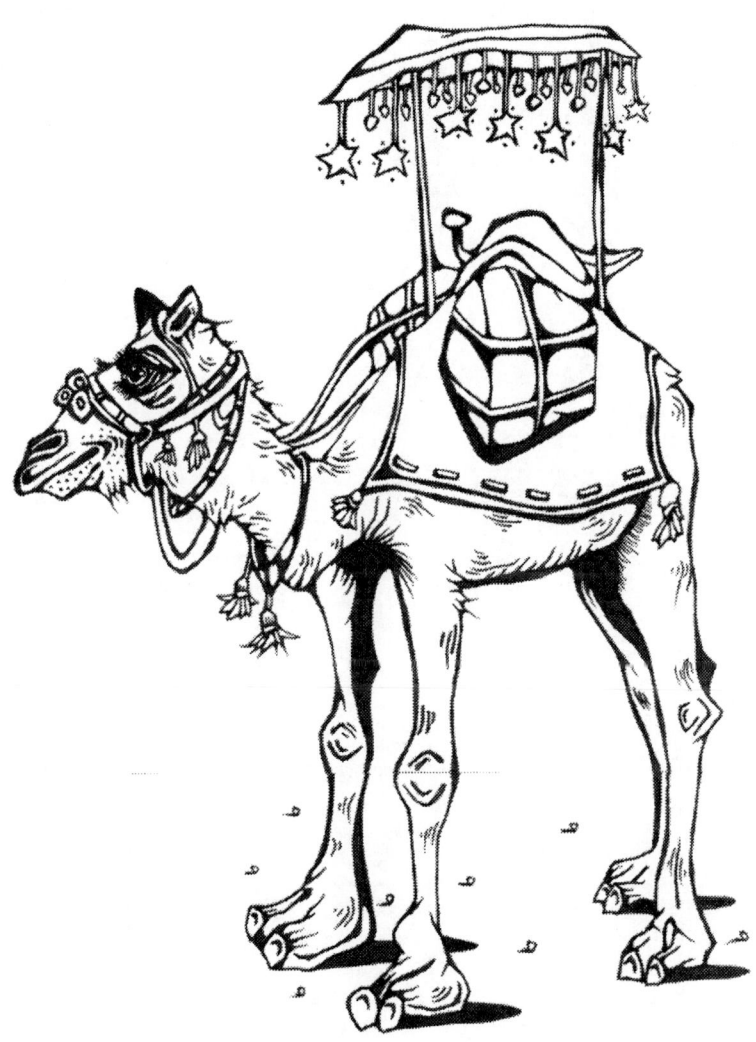

"Between the two large humps on its back was a scarlet leather saddle which looked more than ample for Eisha and Lila."

CHAPTER NINETEEN:

THE OASIS

The oasis was real, and the camel bore them to a well under the shade of the palm trees as the orange sunset turned into pale purple twilight. A group of dark-skinned women with long robes and veils over their heads and shoulders were drawing water from the well in beautifully designed and decorated water jars of clay. Eisha noticed that they looked very much like the ones her friends in the jungle had taught her to make.

When the women saw Eisha and the camel coming towards them, their faces filled with fright, and they fled and hid behind the palms. Eisha could see them watching as she watered the camel and lifted Lila down from her perch on the scarlet saddle. "My sisters," Eisha called out to them, "please come out of hiding and talk to me. I need your help."

Slowly and timidly, three of the women emerged from the palm shadows and stood a little way off, staring with surprised expressions at the strange white man with the deep voice, the creamy-colored camel with the scarlet saddle and canopy, and the little dark-skinned girl with wilted flowers woven into her halo of curly blue-black hair, and her garment of bright-colored feathers. They had never seen anything like it! The men they knew were dark-skinned and would certainly not be speaking to them in public. The camels they knew were a dirty brown, and much scrawnier. Their own little girls looked a lot like this one, but wore long white robes and veils that tripped them up whenever they tried to run and play.

"Why are you afraid?" asked Eisha gently. All three women hung their heads. Then one said softly, "Because you are a man, and we are forbidden to speak with men in public places."

"But you don't speak roughly to us, or scowl at us, and you speak tenderly to your little girl," said another. "What makes you so different from our men?" She looked Eisha in the face as she spoke. Eisha felt anger rising within her as she came face to face with what these women suffered in the desert. She wanted to find out more about the lives of those who had failed to escape into the jungle.

"It isn't my white skin that makes me different," she replied. "I have heard that a white man rules your land and that he taught your men-folk to treat you as if you were inferior and born to be their servants."

The women stared at Eisha. How did this stranger know so much? Eisha continued. "Will you tell me where I can find food for the camel and shelter for the night?"

This time the third woman spoke up. "I will bring food," she said. "And I have some cloth and rope with which we can make a tent for you near the well. As a strange man, you would not be welcome in our homes by our husbands!"

"Thank you very much," said Eisha gratefully. "One more thing. Will you bring me some women's clothes so that I can mingle with you at the well, and ask you some questions without arousing suspicion?"

The women's eyebrows shot up with shock. "No man we know would think of wearing women's clothes! It would be far beneath their dignity," said one of the women, and Eisha could tell they thought her strange indeed. Still, they seemed to instinctively trust her, for they went off to get the things she requested.

While they were gone, Eisha thought carefully about the questions she would ask. There would not be much time, for she guessed that the women would have to leave the well within the hour to prepare the evening meal for their families. She sat on the edge of the well, staring into its dark depths, with a thoughtful frown on her face...

By the time the three women returned, Eisha was ready with her approach. "Will you make a ring around me for a moment?" she asked. The three women, along with others who by now had overcome their fright and joined them, did as Eisha requested. "Now, face outward, keeping your backs to me so you can see if anyone is coming," said Eisha. Again, the women complied. A few minutes later, Eisha was wearing the women's clothes. Then the women disbanded and quickly erected a makeshift tent. Lila was so sleepy by now that she crawled into its shelter and was off to dreamland as soon as Eisha had kissed her goodnight. With great caution, Eisha re-joined the women at the well to draw water and talk.

"How many of you are there in this oasis?" whispered Eisha.

"Just twelve of us," replied one of the women. "In some towns and oases there are even fewer."

"What happened to the others?" asked Eisha.

"Many of them fled years ago in a mass exodus to the jungle. Since then, others have kept slipping away in the night. They said they would not live any longer among men who treated them like servants and possessions, and looked at them as objects made for their own satisfaction," said another woman.

"Why didn't you who are left go with them?" asked Eisha.

"Because we were afraid, and could not bear to tear ourselves away from the men. There are days when we wished we had escaped, but we cannot do it now without special help," said still another. "For a time, those who wished to escape were aided by the Island Snake and the Lion. But after awhile, they no longer appeared among us, and we became convinced that it was too late for us. So we stopped trying, or even hoping for anything better. We made our peace with our lot, and here we are, just as you see us."

"Where are your children?" prodded Eisha.

"There are very few," replied the woman nearest Eisha, and she spoke so softly, Eisha could hardly hear her. "Those of us who remain have found ways to keep from conceiving. The men know nothing about this. It is a secret our grandmothers passed on to us. The men scorn us and call us barren. But for us, it is our way of resisting their domination and religion. They have forced us against our will in many things, but at least there will not be another generation of girls and women who live in slavery as we do!" Her eyes flashed as she spoke, and Eisha's flashed in reply as she proceeded to reveal her purpose.

"I come from your sisters in the jungle," she said. "I seek the place where the white man lives who introduced these terrible changes into your way of life. I intend to challenge him and his teachings, and urge as many men as I can to throw off the oppressive ways they have accepted, and be reconciled to the women they have lost, for the sake of the future of your race and your land."

The women's astonished faces lit up with hope at these words.

"There are men who will listen," said one of the women eagerly. "Their hearts are sore and lonely. Deep down, they know they have wronged women, and they long for reconciliation and the old ways of harmony and equality. They and we will follow you if you are able to lead us to the jungle where our sisters dwell."

"I will try to find a way to do that," promised Eisha.

"If you go straight south from this oasis," said one of the women, "you will find the city where the white chief rules."

At that moment, a tall bearded figure approached the well. "You worthless women have taken long enough to chatter at the well," he yelled. "Get back here to your cooking duties."

The women gave Eisha a farewell look, and went off with their beautifully designed water jugs on their heads, walking tall and with great dignity in spite of the man's demeaning words.

"Their spirit isn't broken yet!" exclaimed Eisha as she slipped inside the tent, hoping to escape notice.

Her hope was rewarded. No one approached her tent, although she could hear the sound of people's conversation, the clanking of pots and pans, and the barking of dogs in the distance. The smell of cooking fires and spicy curry drifted through the desert air into her tent, awakening a strong hunger in her. She took off her women's robe and veil, and swallowed her usual nighttime dose of voice-deepening herbs. She ate a few hand-fulls of dried fruit and nuts, wishing she had some of the delicious-smelling curry as well. But she didn't want the company of the men that might have gone with it, so she contented herself with the simple food at hand. Then she checked Lila, who was sleeping soundly, curled up next to her little friend on a soft layer of cloth, and fell fast asleep.

"'You worthless women have taken long enough to chatter at the well,' he yelled. 'Get back here to your cooking duties.'"

CHAPTER TWENTY:

DESERT DANGER

As dawn broke, Eisha awoke. Lila was sitting up, staring solemnly at her, waiting quietly for her friend to open her eyes. Eisha and she smiled at each other, drank some water, ate some fruit for breakfast, and boarded the camel once more. It had knelt patiently all night beside the tent, as if guarding it, and seemed glad to be on its way.

After her meeting with the women at the well, Eisha was ready once more to act a man's part and do whatever she had to do to help her new friends. Once again, the camel swayed steadily through the trackless desert, heading southward toward the city of which the women had spoken. On and on they went as the sun climbed from the eastern horizon to the very top of the sky. Its heat rose in waves all around them. Lila became tired and fussy, and Eisha tried to amuse her with stories and songs, but her heart was not in it. She was distracted by her anger as she imagined the lives of the women she had met, and the things that had driven her sisters into the jungle...

Then, up ahead, she saw a band of men on foot coming towards her. As they drew nearer, she could see that they were ragged and exhausted. One of them ran towards the camel and knelt near its feet, looking up at her. "Help us," he cried. "We are lost in the desert and have no more food or water. We are afraid we will die here in this wasteland!"

Eisha looked at him coldly. "Why should I care if you live or die?" she said with icy fury. "You desert men have done so much damage you don't deserve to survive!"

The man looked up in surprise. "How can you say such things?" he demanded. "You are a man like us! What makes you so pitiless and critical towards your brothers?"

"I am NOT a man like you!" shouted Eisha. "And you are NOT my brothers! Your kind deserves no pity, and I will not offer it! Go find someone else to help you."

"Eisha," said Lila. "Why are you screaming?"

Eisha stopped screaming and looked down at her little friend. "Because I'm angry at these men for what they have done!" she explained impatiently.

"I don't see any men," said Lila, looking around with wide eyes.

That stopped Eisha dead in her tracks. Another mirage! She shook her head and hid her face in her hands. Her anger had led her into another illusion!

"Lila," said Eisha. "You saved me again! I was seeing things. Will you please hold the camel's reigns while I get down and find us something to eat and drink?" Lila was happy to have such an important task, and clutched the reigns tightly in her little hands. As Eisha dismounted, the band of men disappeared into thin air. She slowly opened the saddlebags, and got out the food and water they needed. "How could I have let myself get so angry and cruel?" she wondered.

When she got back on the camel, Lila would not let go of the reigns, for she loved holding them. Eisha humored her, and fed her fruits and nuts and sips of water. Then she fed herself, and soon they were ready to go on. Holding the camel's reigns together, Eisha and Lila guided it through miles and miles of desert towards their destination.

Afternoon wore on towards evening. As the desert began to fill with dark, weirdly shaped shadows, Eisha saw a city ahead. A huge herd of camels emerged from its walls and came thundering towards them. They were ridden by black-bearded, turbaned riders wielding curved silver scimitars that looked as if they could take off a head with one swipe. Eisha's heart filled with fear. She had no weapons. She was a stranger. She had a little girl to protect. Whatever had made her think she could challenge the power of these fierce desert men? How foolish! If they caught her and didn't kill her right away, they might strip and search her, and discover that she was a woman! Eisha shuddered as she imagined what might happen then.

"Maybe I can turn the camel around and outrun them," she thought. In frightened desperation, she seized the reigns from Lila's hands and tried to turn the camel around. But the camel would not turn. It stopped and stood stock still instead. The charging men bore down on them. Eisha screamed and covered Lila with her body, putting her head and shoulders as far down as they would go.

"Eisha! Let me go!" cried Lila, struggling to get out of Eisha's smothering embrace.

"Hush!" whispered Eisha sternly. "We are in great danger!"

"Why?" asked Lila. And she squirmed so hard she slipped sideways and fell off the saddle onto the desert sand with a loud thump. "O-w-w-w!" she wailed loudly. Eisha scrambled down the camel's side and dropped onto the sand next to Lila.

"Are you hurt?" Eisha asked anxiously, gathering the little girl into her arms. Lila cried and cried, but Eisha could not find any sign of injury except a little goose-egg on her head and a scrape on the side of her leg. When her sobs finally faded away, Eisha became aware of the deep desert silence. Suddenly she remembered. Where were the marauding men on camels who had been bearing down on them only a little while ago?

"Lila, did you see the men charging at us with their sharp, curved swords?" asked Eisha.

"No," answered Lila, wiping away her tears.

"Another mirage!" exclaimed Eisha ruefully. "Well, it showed me the fear I carry inside!" She stopped, as the meaning of her words struck her. "All the mirages have shown the feelings and thoughts inside me," she exclaimed, "—just like dreams do!"

Then, tenderly picking Lila up in her arms, Eisha wiped her face, and said, "Lila, from now on, you are going to be my leader. I want you to keep watch as we ride, and tell me just what you see. If you don't see it, I won't let what I think I see disturb us. I hope I've learned what I needed to from the mirages. I know my hidden feelings better now. I didn't want to admit my pride, or anger, or fear. Now I have to accept the fact that they exist, and can get in my way." She stopped, realizing that Lila was probably not understanding her words. Giving her a big hug, Eisha said, "I'm so glad you love me just as I am! I love you just as you are too, and I hope that will get us through!"

When they got back on the camel together and resumed their southward direction, Eisha would say every few minutes, "Lila, what do you see now?" And Lila would tell her that she saw sand and sky and sunshine and shadows, and now and then a rock or a patch of scrubby bushes. Each time Eisha thought she saw something different, she would close her eyes, put her arms tightly around Lila and say, "Lila, hold the reigns and keep the camel going straight south," and she would point in that direction. Lila would soberly comply, sensing that Eisha was going through a struggle of some kind. Thus, they proceeded toward the city that was their destination.

They were still a good ways from the city when the shadows cast by the sun setting behind the desert dunes deepened into nightfall. Slowly, the stars emerged in all their brilliance. Every few minutes, a falling star would flash through the blue-black sky, leaving a fiery trail that disappeared in an instant. There was something magical about riding the cream-colored camel through the softly glowing sands in the cool night air, with myriads of stars twinkling around them, and the camel's bells tinkling musically in the deep desert silence.

"Look, Eisha, look!" cried Lila suddenly. "The Morning Star! It is guiding us to the buildings over there!"

Eisha's heart leaped with joy as she saw the Morning Star rising over the city. It was a sign of the care of the Lion and the love of the Lady for whom she was seeking. "Could she be in this city?" wondered Eisha, and hope surged in her veins. The camel seemed to sense her eagerness, and quickened its pace. Soon the black walls of the city loomed before them in the night. The camel stopped and it was clear that it would go no further.

"I guess this is where we get off," said Eisha. As if assenting, the camel knelt, and Eisha and Lila dismounted, feeling stiff and sore from the long hours of riding through the desert. "Stay near here," whispered Eisha into the camel's ear. "We will need you for the return trip!" After removing some provisions from the saddlebags, she took Lila's hand, muttering, "I hope the camel understands!"

As the two of them walked away from the camel toward the shadows of the city wall, they heard a rough voice calling out in the darkness. "Ho! Who goes there?" Eisha looked up and saw the black figure of a night watchman silhouetted against the sky, his feet planted on the top of the broad walls that surrounded the city.

"A youth and a child seeking shelter," replied Eisha.

"You will just have to sleep next to the wall," growled the watchman. "The gates are shut for the night, and no one is allowed in until daybreak."

With a sigh of disappointment, Eisha sat down with Lila in her lap, leaned against the wall wearily, and fell asleep as quickly as her little friend.

"Eisha's heart leapt with joy as she saw the Morning Star rising over the city."

CHAPTER TWENTY-ONE:

THE BEGGAR

They were awakened by the cry of the watchman above. "The dawn comes!" he shouted. "All is well in the city!"

"I'm not so sure," muttered Eisha to herself as she rubbed the sleep out of her eyes. "But I hope all will be well soon, with the help of the Island Snake and the blessing of the Lion!" So saying, she awoke Lila, and shared some fruit, nuts, and water with her. Then they walked together through the city gate, which was already open.

The street on which they found themselves was filled on both sides with small stalls in which wares of every sort were being sold. There were oranges and sweet fried cakes, bright brass bracelets and red leather shoes, embroidered silks and carved wooden toys—and so much more that Eisha and Lila could scarcely take it all in. The sights and sounds and smells surrounded them, and the crowds of people swept them along as if they were being carried by the current of a swift river. After the days of desert silence and simplicity, it was overwhelming. Lila clung to Eisha's hands, while Eisha tried to steer them through the crowds towards a high, dazzling white pyramid of steps that rose at the far end of the street. A many-columned large-domed building sprawled at the top of the steps, and Eisha guessed that it was the palace of the white chief.

As they walked along, jostled and pushed on every side by the throngs of people around them, Eisha noticed that while some of them were fat, and dressed in gorgeous, expensive silk robes, many others were in rags, and far too thin. A few were reduced to begging. They were the ones who were blind or crippled. Eisha also noticed that there were very few women and children, and the few she saw had harried, tense looks on their faces, as if they expected something bad to happen at any moment.

Eisha grew indignant as she saw how many miserable and poor people there seemed to be alongside the rich minority. "How unfair!" she thought to herself. "I wonder if the white chief is responsible for this state of affairs." She stopped next to a young man who had two stumps for legs, and was resting after laboriously hauling himself along on the ground with his two hands. When he noticed Eisha looking at him, he held out his hand, begging for a gift. Eisha sat down on the ground next to him with Lila in her lap. She reached into her pouch for some food to give him. He looked at them in amazement. "No one has ever sat down next to me to offer a gift!" he said, and his eyes filled with tears. "And never have I seen such a beautiful child," he added, looking tenderly at Lila. Eisha said nothing, but smiled, and put one handful after another of fruit and nuts into his empty hand. He ate quickly and hungrily. Eisha wondered how long it had been since his last meal. When he was done, she said, "My friend, I am sorry I have no more than this to give you."

"You have been more generous than most," he replied.

"Would you mind telling me what happened to you?" asked Eisha.

"I will tell you," he said, "if you first tell me what a white man like you is doing here. I thought there was only one in our land, and that he lived in yonder palace." He nodded in the direction of the pyramid. "Are you related to him?" The beggar looked at

Eisha sharply, and there was a note of suspicion as well as bitterness in his voice.

Eisha became aware at that moment of the silver serpentine belt around her waist. She was silent, waiting to sense its message. She felt a pleasant warmth in her belly, and breathing a sigh of relief, answered him.

"No, I am NOT related to your white chief," replied Eisha, "I have never even seen him. But I know something about him, and I have come from the jungle to challenge him and find men who are wise and wish to live in the old ways of harmony and equal partnership with women."

The beggar looked at Eisha in wide-eyed surprise. "The jungle!" he exclaimed. "That's where most of our women and girls have fled! Were you with them in the jungle?"

Eisha nodded. The beggar put his mouth near Eisha's ear so that no one passing by could possibly hear what he was about to say. "I was one of the few men who sided with the women in my heart," he whispered. "I helped many of them escape when I understood that there was little else I could do for them while the white chief's views and rules prevailed. But one night, I was caught. The punishment for my 'crime' was having my legs cut off. That is why I am here on the street, begging. It is the only way I can stay alive."

Eisha was horrified. Lila, who was able to hear his words with her sharp little girl's ears, began to cry. She got up and put her arms around the beggar's neck, and her tears loosened both his tears and Eisha's. All three sat there on the ground, crying together.

When they were all cried out, and had sat together in silence for a while, Eisha said softly, "I am sorry and angry about the cruelty you have suffered. How long has such cruelty been inflicted on the people? How long have there been beggars and poor people among you?"

"My grandfather told me that before the white man came, women and men shared their lives and work, and lived together in peace. Everyone had enough—a simple house and garden, food in abundance, several changes of clothes—in short, everything necessary to live a decent human life. People spent their spare time making music and beautiful things, telling stories, playing games, and learning the traditions and knowledge of our ancestors."

"So!" said Eisha. "It is since the chief's ways have prevailed that people have become poor, and suffered terrible injustice."

"Yes," said the beggar sadly. "And now the rich think of nothing but how to become richer, and the poor think only of how to survive, and those who want to create music and beauty are stifled." He sighed deeply.

"How wonderful it would be," said Eisha quietly, "if you and other men could be reconciled with the women in the jungle, and return to the former way of life your grandfather told you of!"

The beggar's eyes shone with a glimmer of hope. "Is there a way?" he asked. "You were with the women. Would they come back to us?"

"I don't think they would come to the desert," replied Eisha. "But they would gladly welcome any men who wished to live with them in the jungle as friends and equal partners. They have made a beautiful and peaceful way of life for themselves there, and would share the treasures of it with men who truly love them."

The beggar looked thoughtful. "That makes good sense," he said. "I would gladly go to them, and I know many men, though most of them are poor, who would do the same. But I have heard stories of a great Island Snake and a mighty Lion who guard the jungle. No man I know has ever succeeded in entering it and finding the women, though some were stopped at the edge of the jungle by the Island Snake, and came back better for the experience!" He grinned slightly, as if remembering, and went on. "Could you lead us into the jungle to the women and girls who live there?"

"I am looking for a way to do just that," replied Eisha. "But first I must confront the white chief in his palace, and challenge his cruelty and injustice. If I survive doing that, I must find the wise men who, like you, long to return to the ways of your ancestors."

"You will be in great danger if you publicly confront the white chief and the rich and powerful men who back him," warned the beggar. "However, if anyone can, you can, for you are white and a stranger and have an air of authority about you. Besides, I can see that you are convinced that this is what you must do. I wish I could help…" He paused, and then continued with excitement in his voice. "Wait! I think I can! First, I will follow you in a way that no one will notice, and will linger near the palace. I have a few friends among the servants there, and I will stay close by and listen for news of you. You can send messages to me as necessary through one of my friends in the palace who can be trusted. His name is Sadik, and he carries water to the palace each day from the royal wells in a nearby oasis. I will also speak with the men I know who wish to return to the old ways of justice and peace. I will tell them of your purpose, and should you find a way to lead us back to the jungle, I will notify them, and they will be ready when you are."

Eisha was delighted with his offer, and nodded her assent. They shook hands warmly. Taking Lila from his arms, Eisha stood up and walked toward the palace again. Now and then, she glanced back over her shoulder, and could see the beggar pulling himself along the ground through the spaces among the people, his eyes on her, and a hopeful smile on his face.

"Eisha noticed that while some of them were fat, and dressed in gorgeous, expensive silk robes, many others were in rags, and far too thin."

CHAPTER TWENTY-TWO:

THE CHALLENGE

As Eisha approached the long flight of stairs leading to the palace on top of the pyramid, she sensed that many eyes were watching her and Lila. Her heart was beating fast with fear, but she held her head high, and began climbing the steps with as much determination and dignity as she could muster. Eisha knew that if she acted sure of what she was doing, people would probably let her proceed. And they did. Without opposition, she and Lila were able to walk all the way up the white marble steps, past the vast columns of the outer court, and through the great double doors of black ebony that opened into the throne room. But as they crossed the threshold, two guards robed in black stopped them. "What is your business?" they barked, crossing gleaming curved swords in front of her.

"I have come from across the sea, and I have an important message for your chief!" said Eisha boldly. "As you can see, I too am white-skinned, and that gives us a special kinship."

The guards uncrossed their swords and looked dubiously at her and Lila, but let them pass. They entered into the huge, domed throne room with every eye upon them. Dancing girls, musicians, jugglers, waiters bearing trays loaded with food, and magnificently robed and turbaned men with dark beards and faces drew back to create a path for them to approach the throne. It was high up on a dais that was covered by a ruby-colored carpet with a peacock design woven into it. The throne itself was a single piece of black mahogany, hand-hewn from the trunk of an ancient tree that had been cut down to make the throne. It was carved into the shape of a huge hawk whose head and fierce beak rose and curved over the chief's head. Its body formed the back of the throne, and its wings the sides of it. The effect of this majestic, ebony-black shape framing the white-skinned, red-robed chief was impressive indeed. His beard was brown and full, his eyes a steely blue beneath thick, bushy eyebrows, and he wore a turban of gold set with rubies, topped by a large peacock feather.

Eisha advanced to the steps of the dais, and stood as tall and straight as she was able. She looked up into the chief's eyes, and from her hidden belt she felt a cold tightness in her belly. Lila buried her face in Eisha's robe. She did not like the looks of the white chief. Eisha took a deep breath, and made a slight bow of courtesy in his direction.

"I come to you today as a kinsman of your own race," she began. "I came here, like you, in a ship from a land far across the sea. I was guided here by a great Lion, and the Morning Star."

A low murmur of anxious surprise ran through the crowd in the courtroom. No one was supposed to ever mention the Lion's Name among them, for the chief had declared that the Lion was nothing but an ancient superstition, and that only the thunder god, whose prophet he was, could be named at court. Moreover, some of the court astrologers had noticed the new star moving into the sky from the west, and had been troubled about what it might mean.

Eisha ignored the murmur and went on. "I found my way into the jungle in the western part of this land. There, a huge Island Snake met me, and allowed me to spend some time with the many women who live in the jungle." She looked around at this point, and saw by the alarmed expressions on many faces that the Island Snake was no stranger to them!

The chief scowled, and Eisha could tell he did not like this mention of the Lion and the Island Snake, who still had power in the hearts and minds of the people. She paid no attention to his scowl, and kept on talking. "I have observed that there are few women or children left in this desert land," continued Eisha, "and I know many of the reasons. I have seen great injustice and cruelty here. The evil spirit of domination which you, my white kinsman, brought here and taught, and still impose on these people, is reaping a bitter harvest. When men begin to unjustly treat women as inferiors, instead of with love and respect as equal partners, the door opens to injustice everywhere, and the poverty and misery which attends it."

Eisha stared boldly into the chief's eyes as she spoke, her own flashing with anger. The chief was stunned into speechlessness. So were the others in the court. No one had ever spoken in such a way to the chief!

"Tell me," exclaimed Eisha, turning to face the crowd around her. "Do you all really want this unjust way of life? Do you think it is better than the ways of your ancestors? Is it good that most of the women have fled, that there are beggars in the streets, and that your towns are full of miserable hovels where the poor live in constant hunger? Do you think there is any future for you or your people with so few children among you? Surely, you have been tragically misled by a false teacher. His white skin and foreign origin gives him no more authority than mine does! Why do you let him lord it over you when he clearly cares far more for himself and his cronies than the welfare of the land or the people?

Would you not rather rule yourselves in the old ways as your grandmothers and grandfathers did? Would you not rather be reconciled to your mothers, your sisters, your wives, your daughters, and all the women who dwell in the jungle, than live divided from them because of the hardness of your heart and the oppressiveness of your ways? I have been with them in the jungle and heard their stories. I heard the love and longing in their voices as they told me how they wanted you to come to them with changed hearts, willing to live with them again in love and peace. If you did—all the trees of the jungle would clap their hands for joy, and the cliffs and mountains would break forth into singing! Then the desert would once again blossom, and—"

Eisha could tell her words were hitting home in many hearts, but they were suddenly cut off as two men in gray robes seized her. One clamped his hand over her mouth while the other said, "With your permission, O Mighty Chief, we will remove this dangerous upstart from your presence and throw him into the deepest dungeon to await his just punishment!"

The chief, taken completely off guard, knew only that he wanted to be rid of this white man and the challenge to his authority. He nodded his permission while he scowled as fiercely as he could to hide his fear. The two men bore Eisha swiftly out of the throne room and into a long hallway ending in a flight of stairs that descended below the palace. As they carried her forcefully down one flight of steps after another, Eisha struggled desperately in their grasp. "Lila!" she cried. "What will happen to Lila? Let me go! Let me go!"

But the men ignored her cries, and carried her into the dark depths where the palace dungeons awaited those who were unfortunate enough to offend the chief. They were apparently familiar with the way down, for they went confidently and quickly without the aid of any sort of light. As for Eisha, she could see nothing. Gradually, as she stopped struggling, her other senses became acute. She smelled the mustiness of the underground air, and the sweaty odor of the men who were holding her captive. She heard the faint sound of footsteps, and the swish of robes moving in the darkness. The men's grip on her body was strong, but not painful. Then she became aware, with great surprise, that she was feeling a sense of pleasant warmth in her belly. Could it be that these men who had seized her and were even now taking her to a dungeon were trustworthy? She decided to keep silent, and wait and see, but she did relax a little, and began breathing deeply and slowly. This brought to mind the simple chant she had learned under the Sacred Tree from the red-haired woman. Eisha began to chant the words and their melody silently in her mind. "Ruach, Shaddai, Eemah, Ruach, Shaddai, Eemah, Ruach, Shaddai, Eemah." A deep peace began to well up within her, along with beautiful, refreshing memories of her night in the lotus pool, her rest in the ship's rainbow hammock, and the dance in the jungle with the women in the light of the Morning Star.

So deeply engrossed was Eisha in her memories, that she scarcely noticed when the two men put her down. But she did notice the creak of a large door opening, and the clanging sound it made as it shut. She stood there, wondering where she was, and if she had been left alone. A flame flared in the darkness. By its dim, flickering light, she saw that it was attached to a candle, and that the two men who had carried her down the stairs were now standing facing her. Eisha rubbed her eyes. Could she be seeing double? They looked exactly alike! Both had short, curly black beards, large dark almond-shaped eyes, and chocolate-brown skin. They wore gray robes and headdresses very much like her own. Both were looking solemnly at her.

Finally one of them broke the silence. "You are a brave but foolhardy young man," he said, "to speak as you spoke. Your words have made the white chief very angry, and your whiteness will not save your skin, I'm afraid!"

"But the truth you so fearlessly proclaimed might save this sad land and people," said the other, "—if enough of them open their hearts to it. As for us, our hearts vibrated as your words rang the great Bell of Truth."

Eisha could not help herself. "Then why did you cut off my words and seize me and carry me down to this dungeon?" she cried.

"It was the only way to save you from immanent torture and death," answered the two men at the same time. One of them laughed and said, "We are identical twins. This happens all the time."

"Oh!" said Eisha, and she stood there, speechless, staring at them.

"My name is Hesed, and my brother's name is Rehem," said Hesed. "We know of the Island Snake of which you spoke. When we tried to enter the jungle some years ago to find our mother and sisters, it caught us in its coils and taught us much wisdom." He grimaced and fell silent.

"When you were speaking," continued Rehem, "we looked into each other's eyes and knew our thoughts matched. You were in grave danger for speaking truth to power. We had to intervene right away, for we could tell that the chief was about to explode in rage. Since we are both in charge of the palace prisons, it would seem perfectly natural for us to do what we did."

Eisha nodded and marveled at how accurate her warm gut feeling about them had been.

"Can anyone see or hear us in here?" she asked.

"No," replied Hesed. "In this deepest of all the prison dungeons, the walls are two feet thick. When the door is closed, as it now is, no sight or sound can escape beyond this enclosure."

Eisha looked around. She was in a small, square room with stone walls, floor, and ceiling. There were no windows or openings other than the door. Several thick chains with manacles on them for holding ankles and wrists were attached to one of the walls. A hole in one corner could be used as a toilet. A stone jug in another looked like it might hold water. That was all she could see.

"How can it help me to be here?" she asked with an edge in her voice. "The chief could command me to be brought out at anytime for any sort of punishment." She shuddered as she imagined the possibilities.

"True," replied Rehem. "But there are ways to distract the chief with other matters, and we have some skills along these lines." The two brothers smiled at each other and then at her.

"We will do all in our power to make sure he is distracted and preoccupied over the fate of other prisoners in the palace dungeons," added Hesed.

"And if he does think of you—as well he might, considering the impression you made today," said Rehem, "we will assure him of your desperate condition in this dungeon. Meanwhile, as chief keepers of the prisons, we will make sure that you are safe and will personally do all we can for your comfort. Very few others besides us know where this dungeon is, or how to get to it. It is below all the others, and quite a ways from them."

"My life is in your hands, Hesed and Rehem," said Eisha gratefully. "I sense I can trust you, and I thank you for intervening in my behalf. I don't know where all this will lead, but I am glad you heard truth in my words." She paused. "Will you do one more thing for me?" The men nodded, and Eisha continued. "Remember the little girl I carried in my arms? Her name is Lila, and she is dearer to me than my own life. Please try to find her, and let me know how she is as soon as you can." Her eyes filled with tears as she thought of her little friend, alone and lost in a strange and dangerous place.

The two brothers assured her of their help, and then turned to leave. "We don't want to arouse suspicion by being gone too long from the court," said one of them. "We will return as soon as we can with food and a better light." He put his candle on the floor, and as he left with his brother, the door clanged shut behind them, leaving Eisha alone.

"Eisha rubbed her eyes. Could she be seeing double? They looked exactly alike!"

CHAPTER TWENTY-THREE:

THE DUNGEON

Eisha put the candle in the center of her cell. It was high and thick enough to burn for many hours. She walked slowly around the dungeon, feeling the walls with her hands, and the floor with her bare feet. The stone was rough and cool. It would not be comfortable to lie or sit on. Still, the room seemed clean enough, even if it was small. But there were no windows! Eisha could hardly bear the thought of going more than a few hours without seeing the sky or feeling the breeze on her skin. What was she to do now? Lila was lost. She was imprisoned deep in the bowels of the earth. How could she carry out her mission here? Was it all a terrible mistake? Should she have confronted the chief and the court with the words that had poured out from somewhere deep within her? What good would it all do now?

Eisha buried her head in her hands and felt dark waves of despair roll over her. It was a heavy, dark despair—the worst she had ever felt. And once again, pushed to her limits, she cried out, "Help! Help! Help!" But the cries bounced off the stone walls and fell to the floor in pieces of silence. Eisha threw herself down on the dungeon floor and began to cry and cry and cry.

When she had had finally cried herself out, she became aware of hunger-growls in her stomach. Luckily, she still had a few nuts in her pouch, and she ate them slowly, one by one, as if they were the berries of the Sacred Tree. "These are the best nuts I've ever tasted!" she exclaimed to herself. They did make her thirsty, however, and she peered into the stone jug that sat in a nearby corner. The candle-light revealed a shimmer of water. Eisha scooped some out in her hands, and lapped it up, relishing it as if it were the finest wine. As she drank, a picture of Lila came into her mind, perched on the camel, and riding swiftly and surely toward the jungle. This image comforted Eisha, and she wiped away the tears from her cheeks. "I think I'll take a little nap," she said to herself. Wearily, she lay down on the hard, stony floor. But she could not get comfortable. Something small and hard was cutting into the side she was lying on.

Suddenly, Eisha realized that it was her Heart-Stone! She took it out of her pocket with trembling eagerness, and held it between her fingers close to the candlelight. It began to flash fiery crimson and purple, and grew too heavy to hold between her fingers. She cradled it in her palm, and gazed into its glowing color. So! She was where she was meant to be! It was not a mistake that she was in this dungeon. Eisha began to feel very much better. "After all," she thought, "the twin brothers are on my side and watching out for me. I am out of harm's way. And anything could still happen..."

Eisha began imagining the possibilities. As she mulled them over in her mind, with the Lion and the Island Snake always somewhere in the mental pictures she was creating, an inspiration came. She would confide in Rehem and Hesed and reveal who she really was. She would tell them all about the women in the jungle and what she had learned from them. She would describe their visions, and hers, of what could be. She would tell them about the Lion and the Island Snake and her experience of them. Perhaps Rehem and Hesed could contact the beggar and his friend Sadik, the water carrier, and whatever other openhearted men they knew. Somehow, she was sure, a way would open up for their return when enough of them were ready.

Eisha was still occupied with these thoughts when she heard the creak of the door opening, and saw her friends entering the cell.

"Rehem! Hesed!" she said with relief. "I'm so glad to see you! I want to tell you what I've been thinking!"

Rehem held up his hand. "Wait! First things first, friend! We know you've been waiting a long time, and we are sorry we were delayed, but we found a way to bring some things we hope you will consider worth waiting for!" His eyes sparkled with excitement as he produced an elegant brass filigree lamp and lit it. The flame shone through the open designs in the lamp onto the walls, ceiling, and floor, covering them with beautiful patterns of light that moved and swayed with the flame. "The lamp will bring light and beauty to this dreary dungeon," he said proudly. Then he laid down a carpet he had been carrying. It was ruby red, and patterned with flowers and birds. It covered almost the whole floor. "There!" he said with a satisfied sigh. "Now we can sit down and talk in comfort."

"Wait," interrupted Hesed. "These cushions will make sitting even better." And from under his arms he produced three large cushions covered with blue and yellow silk. Eisha's eyes widened with surprise and delight. This was much more than she had expected!

"There's more!" exclaimed Hesed, and he grinned and took a quantity of soft material from a sack slung over his shoulder. "This will make a nice sleeping nest for you," he said. He arranged the material in a corner. The two brothers sat down on two of the cushions, and motioned Eisha to sit down on a third beside them.

"We have a nice supper in this box," they said invitingly, holding up a large, beautifully carved wooden box. Eisha sat down opposite them with the box and lamp between them, and they opened the box with a smile and a flourish. Inside it was a blue and yellow glazed pot. Hesed lifted the cover, and the spicy smell of curried chicken and vegetables filled the room. As her two new friends put out bowls and spoons and cups, dished out the food, and poured out sweet papaya juice, Eisha realized how very long it had been since she had eaten a good, hot cooked meal.

"This is wonderful!" she exclaimed. "How did you do it?"

Rehem smiled and said, "There are many forgotten storerooms in the palace underground, and there is always a great deal of leftover food from the daily palace banquets."

"I am very grateful to you," replied Eisha as she helped herself to the curry. "It smells so good, I can hardly wait to taste it." The twins gave satisfied smiles, and the three of them ate and drank together, enjoying the delicious food and drink without words, until their hunger was satisfied. Finally, Hesed spoke.

"My friend—we do not even know your name yet! We know very little about you. Nor do we know the thoughts you were so eager to tell us."

"Ah—yes," answered Eisha with a smile. "I think that now is the time." So saying, she rose to her feet, quickly took off her man's robe and headdress, and stood there before them in her sleeveless, bright-colored feather shift and short, tousled brown hair. "My name is Eisha," she said.

The brothers sat open-mouthed with surprise. "You—you look like a woman, but your voice is that of a man!" stammered Rehem.

"Yes. But only as long as I take these herbs." She pulled out the pouch of herbs the Island Snake had given her. "Now that you know I'm a woman, I can stop taking them and let my womanly voice and appearance return, since I will probably not be seeing anyone but you for awhile."

The men nodded, still speechless with amazement. Their silence gave Eisha the chance to tell them about herself, her journey, her time in the jungle, and the hopes she and the women held for the future. They listened with rapt attention as she spoke, and were especially eager to hear about the women and their way of life, and of the vision they and Eisha had for reconciliation and reunion.

"It sounds as if the Island Snake and Lion support your vision," remarked Rehem when Eisha had finished speaking. Eisha nodded.

"Perhaps it is they who even planted the vision in our hearts," she said.

"We must tell others what you have told us!" exclaimed Hesed.

"Indeed!" agreed Rehem. "More and more of the men we know are longing for the old ways, and are sick at heart over what has happened since the white man came and established his rule over us. I wonder if any but the few whom he has made rich and powerful really want his reign to continue."

"I was going to ask you to help me find men who would want to change and be reconciled to women," said Eisha. "I know of only the legless beggar I met on the way to the palace, and his friend Sadik, the water-carrier."

"We know them both!" exclaimed the twins together. Then they all laughed, and Eisha told them how she had met and spoken with the beggar in the city's bazaar. But as she recounted her experience, she remembered Lila, and cried, "Where is Lila? Do you know? Did you find out for me?"

Rehem and Hesed shook their heads sadly.

"We asked as many questions about her as we dared," they said. "But the only thing we heard was that she was seen in the bazaar in the company of our friend the beggar a short time after we took you out of the throne room."

Eisha was silent for a long time then, wondering whether Lila had somehow escaped with the beggar's help, found the camel, and been carried safely back to the jungle. She did not know whether the strong image she carried in her mind from the night before was wishful thinking or a glimpse of what had really happened. Her heart ached for Lila, and she realized how much she missed her little friend's lively company and innocent wisdom. Tears began to trickle down her face as Rehem and Hesed sat silently by, respectful of her feelings, and knowing that any words they might speak would be inadequate.

Finally, Eisha recovered herself, dried her tears, and remembered her mission and her solemn promises to her women friends, and said, "Could you speak to the beggar and Sadik tonight? I have a feeling we need to join forces with them now."

The brothers readily agreed, and began to make their plans. Gradually, their enthusiasm drew Eisha out of her grief, and the three of them continued talking far into the night, hearing each other's experiences, and sharing their stories and hopes and dreams. When Rehem and Hesed finally left, Eisha realized with gratitude that they were fine and loyal friends, and that with their help, there was great opportunity in her imprisonment after all. "Moreover," she remarked to herself as she blew out the lamp and snuggled into the soft cloths in the corner, "life in this dungeon cell is not as hard as I had feared!" And she fell asleep with a smile on her face.

"'We have a nice supper in this box here,' they said invitingly, holding up a large, beautifully carved wooden box."

CHAPTER TWENTY-FOUR:

THE HIDDEN PASSAGE

When Eisha awoke, she was in complete darkness. She did not remember right away where she was. But as she rolled over and felt the soft cloths around her, the memory of the day before came back with a rush. She groped for the lamp, and then remembered that she had nothing to light it with. This was not a pleasant turn of affairs! She was alone in the dark, and though she was comfortable enough, she could see nothing. She had no idea how long she had slept or what time of day or night it was. It was most disconcerting! Only the memory of her conversation with Hesed and Rehem, and the Heart-Stone's glowing color and weight kept her from sinking into gloom again. How she longed to see the sky, and breathe the air of freedom! All she could do in the deep darkness of her dungeon was feel.

And feel she did, for she grew tired of sitting and waiting. Instead, she started to crawl around the dungeon on her hands and knees, feeling up and down the walls and along the bottom edges where they met the floor. "I don't know why I'm bothering to do this!" she muttered to herself as she went along inch by inch. Suddenly, she stopped. Her hand had been pushing against rock, and now it was feeling only thin air! She put her other hand out next to it, and again felt air. She moved her hands and arms about and felt the sides of an opening just a little smaller than the secret one through which she had emerged into this land where she was now a prisoner. "I wonder what this opening leads to," Eisha thought as she pushed her head and shoulders into it. There, only a little ways away, was the familiar, twinkling light of a firefly!

Feeling sure the firefly was a sign, Eisha squeezed her body through the opening, and found herself standing on damp earth! The firefly flew toward her and then ahead, inviting her to follow, just like the fireflies that had guided her through the entrance into the land. Though its tiny light was dim indeed, Eisha's eyes had by now gotten so used to the dark that she could see where she was going if she kept close behind the firefly. "Maybe the Lion sent this little light to lead me," she thought as she walked along. Beneath her feet, she could feel the passageway sloping gently downwards. Then she became aware of the sound of water clear and near. "I wonder where the water is?" she said as she walked along.

By now the passage had leveled out, but it was making many twists and turns, and Eisha felt as if she had been walking for hours and hours. All at once, the firefly stopped and flew low over the ground to her right. She cautiously stepped after it, feeling ahead with her right foot. "Plunk!" went the foot, and was instantly soaked. She had stepped into running water! "I must have been walking alongside an underground river for quite some time," surmised Eisha. Gratefully, she sank to the ground to rest and bathe both her aching feet in the water. She had not been wearing shoes when she entered the passage, and of course, she had no food or water with her either. She scooped some of the water into her hands by feel, and lapped it up. "I'm becoming a lot better at sensing my way when I can't see it," she thought to herself with some satisfaction. "But I hope this passage will eventually lead back up into the light. I'd hate to be down here for too long." She shuddered a little in the cool underground air, and then stood up and continued walking, for the firefly was blinking far ahead of her.

As she walked more swiftly to catch up with it, Eisha felt the ground beneath her feet starting to slope upward. The ascent went on and on for what seemed like endless hours. But she persevered, fearing to lose sight of the firefly, which was the only light in the darkness. Then, up ahead, she saw a glimmer of daylight! Eisha ran eagerly towards it. At the end, she had to scramble up a steep, rocky slope on her hands and knees, which she scraped up rather badly. But finally, she made it to the opening. Thrusting her head through it, she looked around and saw that she was in back in the jungle, and all around her were the familiar trees of the Golden Grove! Above her loomed the huge head of the Island Snake!

"Hello, Eisha," it said calmly. "I was wondering how long it would take you to find your way back here from the dungeon."

Eisha looked into the Island Snake's golden eyes with surprise. "How did you know I was coming and where I was?" she blurted out.

"Oh, my friends the fireflies find their way everywhere," replied the Island Snake.

"I thought the Lion sent the firefly to guide me," said Eisha.

"We work together, you know," answered the Island Snake in a reproving tone of voice.

"I should have guessed," responded Eisha as she pulled herself out of the hole in the ground and stood up on the jungle floor. She looked around. There, not more than a stone's throw away, was the stone circle! She broke into a broad smile and walked over to it.

"I'm tired!" she said as she sank down on one of the stones. "I think I'll just sit and rest here awhile before I go back to the place where my friends live. Oh! It is so wonderful to be out of the dungeon and the dark and the desert land with all its dangers! I never want to go back there."

"Eisha, have you forgotten your Stone?" said the Island Snake gently. "Doesn't it help you decide what to do?"

Eisha nodded reluctantly, and pulled out her Heart-Stone. It lay lightly in her hand, and was a dull brown color. "I don't care!" said Eisha. "I am not going back! How can it possibly do me any harm to stay here for awhile with my friends?"

"Eisha!" The Island Snake's voice was stern. "You were not led here to simply escape and rejoin your friends! Remember?"

Eisha blushed, remembering her brave plan, and the things she had told Hesed and Rehem. But here and now, in the Golden Grove, they seemed like characters in a fading dream, and her plan nothing but wishful thinking.

"Why was I led here if I am not supposed to stay here?" she said crossly. "What am I supposed to do? Just turn around and go back to that dark dungeon? What good will that do?"

The Island Snake was silent. Eisha realized it was her job to figure out the answers to these questions for herself. She also saw that the Island Snake intended to keep close watch until she was clear about her next move. She began to think, putting together everything she had heard and learned into different combinations. Suddenly she cried, "Aha! I think I have it!"

The Island Snake, who had remained coiled nearby, lifted its head higher, and looked at her with anticipation.

"Well," began Eisha, "I think that the earthquake that happened shortly after the white man arrived caused the river to go underground. It created a passage that linked the jungle and what became desert when the river no longer watered it. Somehow, with your help and the Lion's, I found the passage. Since one branch of it links up with the deepest dungeon in the palace, anyone who knew of the connection could escape through the passage into the jungle. If you were here guarding the opening, as you were when I came out of it, you could make sure that only men who were truly willing to change and live with women as equal partners could find the women and remain in the jungle with them."

The Island Snake's eyes gleamed approval. "Well, I guess I should go back and tell Rehem and Hesed about this passage, and work with them to help as many people as possible escape," concluded Eisha.

"Ah yes, Rehem and Hesed," said the Island Snake. "Fine young men. I remember them well. I am glad you met. And you are right in all your conclusions. Of course, you couldn't know that I have used this passage for a long time, and extended it myself so that it came out in that lowest dungeon in which you found yourself!"

"That's an amazing coincidence!" exclaimed Eisha.

"On the journey you are taking," replied the Island Snake solemnly, "there are no coincidences. Now, Eisha—will you go back down into the darkness and back to the dungeon? There is no time to waste."

Eisha paused as she rose to indicate her willingness. She looked regretfully at the beautiful Golden Grove she had to leave once again—and suddenly, she remembered. "Lila is lost!" she cried out to the Island Snake. "I forgot about her in the midst of all the excitement of finding the passage and seeing you! I was taken from her in the throne room, and I haven't seen her since. Do you know anything about what might have happened to her?"

"Lila, like all little children in need, is especially cared for by me and by the Lion," assured the Island Snake. "Perhaps you will know her story one day, but right now, you must live your story, and you must not delay. I can only tell you that she escaped the desert dwellers and is safe even as we speak."

Eisha wanted to know more, but she knew better than to object. The Island Snake's sense of urgency about her immediate return to the dungeon must have a good reason behind it. At least Lila was safe, and knowing so made it possible for Eisha to save her many questions for another time. With a deep sigh, she let herself back down the hole into the dark, damp passageway. As she dropped to the ground and took her first step back, a beautiful sight greeted her. It looked as if she had stepped right into the night sky, for hundreds of fireflies twinkled like stars all around her in the darkness!

"I know the Island Snake wanted them to encourage me for the return journey," she thought gratefully. "Thank-you!" she said aloud. And she began walking back along the hidden passage back toward the dungeon.

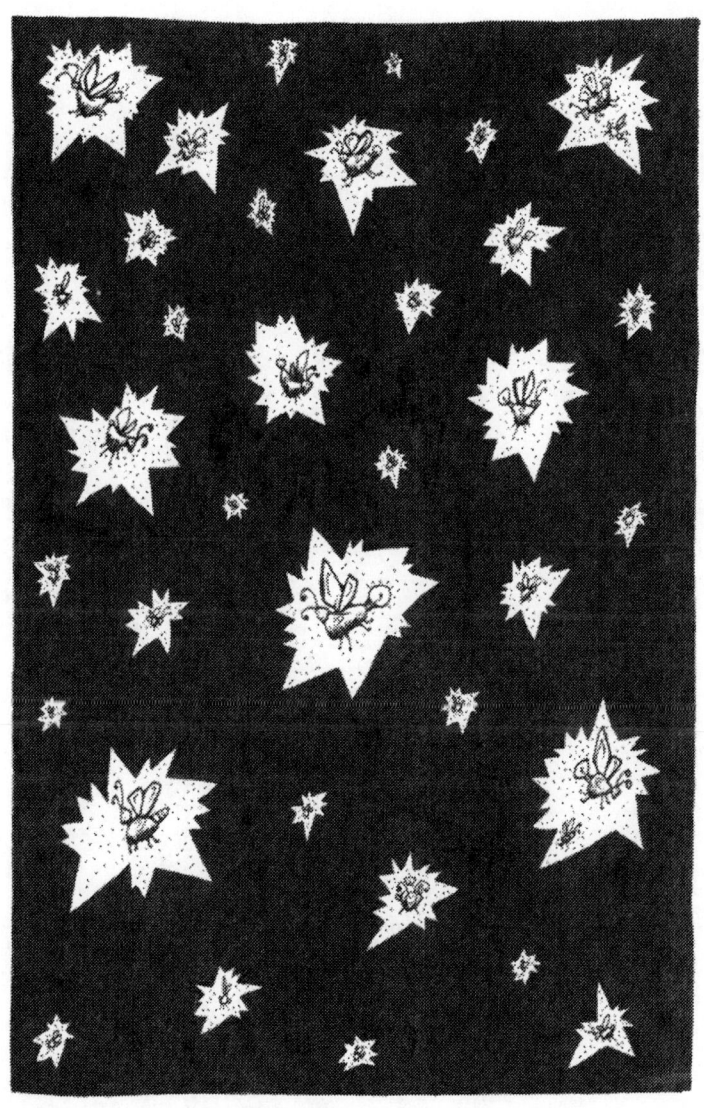

"It looked as if she had stepped right into the night sky, for hundreds of fireflies twinkled like stars all around her in the darkness!"

CHAPTER TWENTY-FIVE:

THE PLOT

In spite of the fireflies' delightful dance of light ahead of her, the way back seemed dreary and long to Eisha. She stopped often to drink from the underground river at the side of the path, and her legs and feet felt heavier and heavier. It became an enormous effort just to put one foot in front of the other. She had walked for many, many miles with very little sleep, and she was near total exhaustion. Only the company of the fireflies, the urgency in the Island Snake's words, and her own renewed commitment to her purpose kept her going. Finally, far ahead, she saw a faint glow of lamplight.

"Rehem and Hesed must be there, waiting for me!" she exclaimed, and quickened her pace. As she drew closer and closer to the lamplight, the fireflies disappeared, one by one, into the darkness, until none were left. But by then, Eisha was near enough to the opening into the dungeon to find her way by the light of the lamp that shone through it. As she hoisted herself into the dungeon, she saw the relieved and surprised faces of her friends staring at her.

"Where have you been?" they cried out together. "We've been worried!"

Sinking wearily onto the carpet, Eisha told them what she had discovered. When she had finished, Rehem said, "We've been waiting here for hours, hoping you would show up! At first, when we did not find you here, we thought the chief might have sent someone to take you away, and we were alarmed. But then we found the opening as we searched the dungeon, and guessed you might have gone through it. But we did not dare go into that unknown darkness to search for you." He shuddered.

"Anything might be down there!" added Hesed with a shudder of his own. "Alligators—bottomless holes—poisonous Island Snakes and spiders—slimy creatures of the dark—ugh! You are very brave indeed, Eisha, especially for a woman."

Eisha frowned. "Women risk their lives to give birth and protect their children. The women in the jungle risked much to get there and live there. What makes you think women are less courageous than men? Or that I am unusual for my courage?"

Hesed was silent. He felt the truth and reproof of her words, and hung his head. Eisha gazed seriously at him, as if waiting for him to speak. Rehem leaned over and whispered something in Hesed's ear. Hesed nodded. "Eisha," he said slowly, "I'm sorry for what I said. Please be patient with us. We have to learn to see women in a whole new way."

Eisha smiled. "Of course," she said.

The brothers returned her smile, and then realizing how hungry she must be, offered her a plate of bread with honey and a jug of milk. Eisha ate and drank eagerly, for she was famished. How good the simple food tasted! She could feel the strength flowing back into her body as she ate.

"It is early afternoon," said Rehem after a few moments, "and one of us should reappear in court before anyone gets suspicious. Our looking exactly alike helps one of us do double duty so that the other is free." He grinned mischievously and rose to his feet. "My brother will tell you of our conversations with Sadik the water carrier, and the legless beggar, and many others." Then, with a creak and a clang of the door, he was gone.

Hesed lost no time in telling Eisha all about their conversations. "It seems word of your challenge in the court has spread like wildfire through the whole land," he said. "The beggar told me the whole city is restless, and many men are whispering of ways to end the white chief's reign. Sadik tells me that the chief and the rich and powerful men who surround him are alarmed, for they sense a great shift among the people, and an unwelcome change coming. I am afraid they will move soon, and forcefully, to try and stop it."

Eisha took his arm with alarm. "Hesed," she said earnestly, "we must try to avoid violence. The women and I would be deeply grieved if there was killing. Can you get the word out through Sadik and the beggar to the men who desire change that if it is change they want, it must begin with them? Can you tell them that if they are ready, there is a secret way to return to the women they love and to live the ways of their ancestors in the jungle?"

Hesed nodded. "Your words have great weight, and I am sure I can spread them quickly. Sadik and the beggar seem to know the best channels by which news is carried, especially among the common people."

"Good!" exclaimed Eisha. "Now, is there a way that you and Rehem could meet with the men and women and children who want to leave—perhaps a few at a time, night by night? Could you get them down here without being noticed?"

"It would be difficult, but I think it is possible," replied Hesed.

"Once they are here in the dungeon, I can lead them through the passage to the jungle," said Eisha, "and from there on, they will be in the Island Snake's keeping."

"If this works," said Hesed excitedly, "I thing the reign of the white chief will eventually collapse. The very people who I know will leave are the ones he needs to keep things going. Without their work and their resources, he's done."

"Do you really think so?" asked Eisha hopefully.

"Well, we have this in our favor," replied Hesed. "The men in power are so preoccupied with what goes on in court, and with being entertained and served—as you yourself saw—that they pay little attention to what ordinary people are doing in the streets and towns and oases. They may very well remain unaware of the secret exodus until it is too late."

"Oh, I hope so!" cried Eisha.

Hesed rose to his feet. "I better go now," he said. "You must be exhausted after so long a time of walking with so little sleep."

Eisha nodded. "I don't think even my excitement can keep me awake for much longer," she said.

"Either Rehem or I will return late tonight," said Hesed. "I will share our plan with him. And now, good night, and sweet sleep, fair friend." And he bowed in a courtly manner and was gone. A few minutes later, Eisha was fast asleep among the soft clothes piled in the corner of her cell.

Hours later, she was wakened by the creak of the door opening. "Rehem?" she asked, sitting up and rubbing the sleep from her eyes.

"Good guess!" replied Rehem as he came into the dungeon, shutting the door carefully behind him. "Don't bother to get up, Eisha." He sat down next to her. "Hesed told me of your plan. It is a good one, but time is too short for it to work. Somehow, suspicions have been aroused about Hesed and me. We must act carefully and quickly. Fortunately, Sadik knows of a secret underground tunnel that leads from a well in an oasis a few miles north of the city to the hidden passageway you discovered. It is very small and narrow, and can only be gotten through on hands and knees, but it will serve the purpose." He shook his head. "I could not believe he knew all about the Island Snake and the underground river and the passage you told us about. He is a water bearer with many secrets and surprises!"

"That's great news!" Eisha exclaimed. "I'll bet that well is fed by the underground river. I remember that the sound of the water was very faint in the first part of the underground passageway. Then its sound became clear and strong. That must be where the river starts to flow alongside the path. It probably runs at an angle between the path I found and the oasis you described."

"Yes, I think you must be right," Hesed agreed. "And it will be easier for more people to escape without being noticed from out in the oasis. In fact, I think we could begin tonight. There are enough people ready to form a good-sized group."

"Wonderful! said Eisha. "You go and gather those who want to leave tonight, and after a little while, I will walk with the lamp down the passage to where the river joins it, and wait there to meet whoever comes, and guide them the rest of the way."

Hesed agreed gladly, and both of them followed their plan. That night, a band of men, along with a few women and children, came crawling through the tunnel that led from the oasis to the hidden passageway where Eisha waited with her lamp. As they emerged at the junction of the two hidden passageways, Eisha saw that they were led by a tall man with a grizzled gray beard, dressed in a ragged robe, and carrying a lantern and a goatskin of water on a strap over his shoulder.

"Sadik?" asked Eisha as he stepped into the circle of light shed by her lamp.

"Sadik the water bearer, at you service, Lady Eisha," he said, bowing low. Then they looked long and silently into each other's eyes, and saw the Wisdom of the Island Snake mirrored there.

"The Wisdom shines in the eyes of all who came with me tonight," said Sadik. Eisha realized he saw far more by the dim light of a lantern than most men saw in broad daylight.

"Good! They will have need of it!" replied Eisha. "Follow me, and I will show you the way."

In silence, and in the dim light of lamp and lantern, the people moved hour after hour behind Eisha and Sadik, until far ahead, the light of the opening shone, signaling their journey's goal.

"Go up through that opening," said Eisha, as she stood to one side, "and do not fear the Great Island Snake who will greet you. It will test you, but it is for good. Follow the Island Snake's direction, and all will go well."

Then she turned back down the passageway.

"Wait!" called Sadik. "Let's walk back together. I will not go through the opening into the freedom of the jungle until all those who seek to return to the women and the jungle have made their escape."

Eisha nodded gratefully, aware of how crucial his help was, and together they walked back towards the desert oasis and city dungeon, sometimes in silence, sometimes speaking of their experiences, and sometimes sharing their fears and hope for the future.

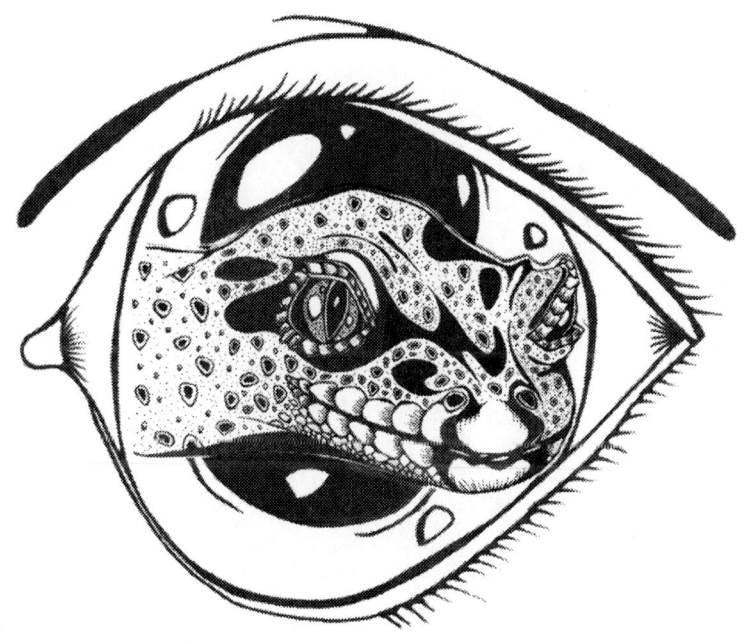

"Then they looked long and silently into each other's eyes, and saw the Wisdom of the Island Snake mirrored there."

CHAPTER TWENTY-SIX:

THE ESCAPE

Sadik and Eisha parted ways where the hidden passage and secret tunnel joined. They agreed to meet in the same place the following night, and every night thereafter, until the exodus was complete.

For the next seven nights, one band of men after another, along with a few women and children, crawled on hands and knees through the secret tunnel after Sadik, and then followed Eisha along the hidden passageway to the opening into the jungle. Wearied by her marathon walks, Eisha slept during her few free hours, after hearing from Rehem or Hesed about the wonderful change of heart going on among many men in the country, and the ways in which they were helping one another escape with as little notice as possible.

But on the eighth day, Rehem and Hesed came to her cell with troubled faces. "The chief and his men have finally noticed what is happening," they said. "In the last few days, even some of the men of the court, and a few of the dancing girls as well, have disappeared. Now the chief realizes that if this continues, there will not be enough people left to produce the food or other things upon which he and his henchmen depend. They have sent out spies to discover what is going on, and find out how and where the people are disappearing. The chief has asked about you, for he suspects you are somehow at the root of this mysterious exodus. And we too are under grave suspicion. He has commanded the three of us to appear before him as soon as possible. We must make our escape immediately, or it will be too late!"

At that very moment, the dungeon door was pushed open, and several imperial guards dressed in black robes burst into the dungeon with drawn swords, followed by the white chief himself. Unfortunately for him, something, or someone, tripped him as he strode across the threshold, and he fell flat on his face in a most undignified way. His fancy turban with the peacock feather went rolling across the floor. Eisha and her friends could hardly hide their smiles. The white chief, of course, was furious. He scrambled to his feet, put his turban back on, and glared at them. "So!" he roared, his face red with fury. "You are the ones responsible for this conspiracy! Shackle them all!" And he glared balefully at Eisha, Rehem, and Hesed while the guards pushed them roughly against the dungeon wall and put the manacles of the chains that dangled there upon their wrists and ankles. "You will have this last night of your life in which to reflect upon your mistakes," the chief continued menacingly, "while I and my advisors dine, and devise suitable ways to see to it that you die long and painful deaths tomorrow!" And he stormed out of the dungeon with the guards behind him. The door swung shut with a loud clank, leaving Eisha, Rehem, and Hesed chained in the dark.

"We'll be alright," said Eisha bravely. "Tonight, when I fail to meet Sadik at the usual place in the hidden passage, he will suspect something is wrong, and look for us here, and set us free to go with him."

"I wish you were right," replied Rehem with a deep sigh. "But I already warned him not to lead anyone into the tunnel tonight because of the chief's spies. I asked him to try to join us here without being noticed, so that we could escape together. But now it is too late. He will not be able to open the door, even if he is able to get down here without being caught. And we cannot move more than a foot from the wall with these chains on."

Eisha was silent with dismay. Their plight seemed hopeless indeed. Yet, she could not bring herself to believe that her purpose and her life would end in torture and death on the next day. Of course, it was true that many people had escaped the desert and returned to the jungle because of her efforts, along with the help of Rehem, Hesed, Sadik, and the legless beggar. Their mission was accomplished to a great extent. And if its results were what she and the women in the jungle had hoped, then the sacrifice of their lives would not be in vain. "Still," said Eisha aloud, "I can't believe the Lion and the Island Snake would let us be killed in this way. I am sure they want us to escape to the jungle with all the others." The twin brothers were silent. Apparently, they did not share her faith.

After awhile, to keep up her courage, Eisha began to softly sing her favorite chant: "Ruach, Shaddai, Eemah; Ruach, Shaddai, Eemah; Ruah, Shaddai, Eemah." Before long, the men began to chant too, for her sweet voice drew them in, and the singing somehow seemed to lighten the darkness as the last hours of their life slipped away.

Then, as they chanted together, a deep rumbling sounded in the distance, like an approaching thunderstorm.

"There has been no rain or thunder over the desert for years!" exclaimed Hesed. "Could it be—?"

The rumble became a menacing growl that grew louder by the moment until it burst into an ear-shattering, wall-shaking roar, like a thousand thunderstorms all at once! The walls of the dungeon trembled. Their chains fell off. The door flew open. There stood Sadik and the legless beggar, their eyes shining in the light of the lantern Sadik held.

"We have been waiting in the dark for many hours!" said Sadik calmly. "That is a powerful chant you three have been singing! The roaring you hear is the Lion's response to it! Come, let us take the passage to freedom!"

Eisha and the twin brothers scrambled to their feet, and followed Sadik and the beggar through the opening. Behind them, the Lion's Roar grew ever louder, and they heard the sound of walls crashing far above them. As they hurried along the passage, with the brothers carrying the legless beggar between them on their inter-twined hands, the roof suddenly caved in behind them with a crash, shutting off the opening to the dungeon.

With swiftly beating hearts, Eisha and her friends followed the downward slope of the passage. The sounds of roaring and crashing grew ever dimmer, until all was quiet as the four of them walked along in awed silence, taking turns carrying the legless beggar between them as they went. Eisha's heart was so full at the miracle of their escape that she could find no words to express her feelings. They simply rolled silently down her cheeks as tears. She saw by the light of Sadik's lantern that her friends' faces were wet with the same kind of tears. They were alive! They were free! And they were on their way out of the desert and into the jungle! Eager to get as far away from the palace as fast as they could, all four broke into a swift trot.

In spite of their speed, it took them a long time to finally reach the place where the light of the opening into the jungle could be seen. As they drew near it, Sadik blew out his lantern and heaved a huge sigh of relief. "Here we are!" he cried as he hoisted the beggar onto his shoulders and up through the opening. Then the rest of them scrambled through it.

They found themselves standing in the Golden Grove in the amber light of late afternoon, surrounded by a great crowd of women and men and children of all ages, singing and shouting and clapping glad welcome! A group of women came out from the crowd, heaped garlands of golden flowers around their necks, and kissed each of them warmly. Eisha and the men were so overwhelmed that they simply stood there with tears of joy and relief raining down their faces.

Then a little girl's voice called out, "Eisha! Eisha!" and a small, black haired child hurled herself into Eisha's arms.

"Lila! Oh Lila!" cried Eisha, hugging her to her breast. "You are here! You are safe! It is too good to be true!"

"Nothing is too good to be true, Eisha," said a golden voice, and Eisha looked up to see the Island Snake's head towering behind and above the crowd. Eisha laughed, and swung Lila around and around, singing, "Nothing's too good to be true! Nothing's too good to be true!" Soon, everyone was dancing and swinging each other around in joyous circles, singing with Eisha, "Nothing's too good to be true! Nothing's too good to be true!"

Meanwhile, the Island Snake gently picked up the legless beggar, and made a throne for him on its coils, from which he could preside over the celebration. All kinds of delicious food and drink appeared as if by magic, and the eating and drinking and dancing and singing went on for many glad hours. After awhile, Eisha joined the beggar on the Island Snake's coils, with Lila snuggled in her lap.

"How has The Return been going?" asked Eisha of the Island Snake.

"Very well indeed," replied the Island Snake. "Most of the men are learning quickly how to make the necessary changes. The women correct them kindly, but firmly, whenever they slip into superior or demeaning attitudes. And the men listen, for they have gone through a great deal to get here. They have risked much, and left much. They have submitted to Sadik's searching eyes, and followed him on hands and knees through the tunnel to where you, a woman, waited to lead them down an unknown path in the darkness. They had to trust and follow you, and then pass my test when they finally emerged into the jungle."

"What sort of test?" asked Eisha curiously.

"That is my secret!" replied the Island Snake. "The few who did not pass, or later on did not listen to the women's correction and change their ways, were escorted in blindfolds back into the desert. No doubt, this was a great encouragement to the rest of the men to learn quickly and well how to live in harmony here in the jungle!"

Eisha smiled and sighed with satisfaction. She looked out over the crowd of beautiful dark-skinned people, with their curly, blue-black hair, flowing robes, and feather dresses. They were all laughing and talking and dancing and enjoying one another with all their hearts. She spotted Hesed and Rehem with three women who looked like their mother and sisters. How happy they looked to be together again! One of the twins caught her eye, and waved happily in Eisha's direction. Eisha waved happily back. "If I ever get married," she thought to herself, "only a man like Rehem or Hesed will do!"

By now, a full moon was slowly rising over the trees. The fire at the center of the Stone Circle had been lit. The eldest woman came near Eisha, and motioned for the people to be quiet. When silence prevailed, she said, "Tonight our hearts are overflowing with joy and gratitude as we celebrate the reconciliation of women and men, and our restored hope for a future of peace and harmony together. When Eisha stood so bravely before the white chief, she said these words, which we have heard from the men who have joined us, and learned already by heart:

> "'When women and men live together again
> With justice, in love, and in peace,
> All the trees of the jungle will clap for joy;
> The mountains will break forth into singing;
> And the desert will once again blossom with life!'"

Here, and now, these prophetic words are being fulfilled, and there is much more filling full to come! We owe much to Eisha and her friends for all that they have done for us, and we wish to honor them tonight."

At these words, the crowd burst into cheers and applause. When the joyful noise had finally died away, she continued. "Now we call on Eisha and her friends to tell their stories, so that we might remember, and tell them to our children's children—now that we know we will have them to tell stories to!"

The crowd broke out in happy laughter and more cheers. Then, as the moon sailed slowly through the sky overhead, Eisha and her friends recounted their adventures while the people listened with rapt attention. By the time the story-telling ended, the moon had set behind the trees, Lila had fallen sound asleep in Eisha's arms, and the fire in the center of the Stone Circle had burned low.

As the people began to drift off to their houses to go to sleep, the Island Snake spoke softly in Eisha's ear. "Dear Eisha, you have done well indeed. But you have not found the Lady or the Child here. And you will not find them in this land, for this is not their dwelling place. Nevertheless, you are far more ready to seek and to find them than when you came. And that is what you need to do now. It is high time for you to go back to the ship, which still waits for you where you left it. I will carry you there, for that will make your return to it far swifter. Once again, there is no time to waste."

Then the Island Snake gently set the legless beggar on the ground, uncurled its coils, and let Eisha slip off. Eisha stood hugging Lila tightly, and crying. How could she leave her and the others she had grown to love so much? Yet she sensed that the Island Snake was right, and that she really did need to leave without delay.

"Goodbye, good friend," she said to the legless beggar, for she could find no other words in the face of their farewell. They embraced each other with tears in their eyes. Then she turned to her little companion.

"Goodbye Lila," she said, and hugged the little girl tight for the last time. "I will never forget you, and I will always hope that we will meet again." Lila clung to her, sobbing, and only her mother could get her to finally let Eisha go. Then, with aching heart and tear-streaked face, Eisha climbed slowly onto the Island Snake's back, and held tightly to its scales as it slid swiftly through the jungle shadows towards the cliffs that surrounded the island.

"Behind them, the Lion's Roar grew even louder, and they heard the sound of walls crashing far above them."

CHAPTER TWENTY-SEVEN:

THE RACE

Though the Island Snake moved speedily through the jungle, it was almost dawn before it reached the steep cliffs that towered between Eisha and the ship. "Hang on tight!" said the Island Snake as it began to climb straight up the cliff's rocky side. Eisha found herself almost at a right angle to the cliff, with the sky above, and the trees beneath. The rising sun on her left lit up the sheer granite rock-face, and shone hot on her body, though it was still early in the day. Eisha gripped the Island Snake's sides with her legs and arms, laid her face against its soft, dry scales and closed her eyes to keep from becoming dizzy.

As the sun reached the top of the blazing blue sky-dome, the Island Snake paused. "We're at the top," it said. "Take a last look at this land, Eisha." Eisha sat up, opened her eyes, and looked. Far below stretched the vivid green of the jungle, and to its east, the pale sand dunes of the desert. The air was so clear that she could see a city in the middle of the desert. She peered intently at it. "It looks like it's in ruins!" she remarked.

"Yes," said the Island Snake. "It is. That is where you were imprisoned. The palace and its pyramid could not withstand the Roar of the Lion. It shattered them and the white chief's rule. But he and his men are cruel and vengeful. One of his spies told him where the ship is, and the chief is determined to keep you from boarding it. He blames you for everything that has happened to him, and has vowed to take you, torture you, and kill you, or die in the attempt. Even now, they are climbing the cliffs not far from us. That is why we must continue to waste no time. Hang on now!"

Then the Island Snake started the straight-down descent. When Eisha saw the white waves crashing on jagged rocks hundreds of feet below, she closed her eyes tightly, and clung to the Island Snake's sinuous body with all her might. Waves of heat rose up from the rocks and poured down from the sun. Soon, she was drenched with sweat and could barely breathe. The crash of the waves below grew louder and louder.

All at once, she felt cool water on her feet. She sat up. The Island Snake had entered the sea and was swimming swiftly toward the ship, which lay directly ahead. When they reached it, the Island Snake slid over the side and onto the deck. "Quickly Eisha!" it said. "Go down into the secret hold of the ship. The chief and his men are approaching! Soon they will board the ship. They must not find you!" The Island Snake put its huge head next to Eisha's, and gently flicked a kiss on her cheek with its velvety tongue. "Farewell, friend. Be brave, and know that I and the Lion will never forsake you." Then, with a great splash, it was gone into the depths of the water.

When Eisha looked up from the water, she saw the figures of men wading into the waves, pointing at the ship, and shouting. With a sick feeling in her stomach at the thought of her beautiful ship being boarded by such vengeful and violent men, she quickly descended the ladder into the upper hold where the cabins were, and then went down the rope ladder that took her into the secret hold, closing the hatch securely above her head as she did so.

Once again, she was surrounded by the cool green and blue sea-light that shone through the transparent walls. The rainbow hammock hung there, as if waiting to cradle her in its soft folds. Eisha took a deep breath, walked over to the hammock, and lay down on her back, half-expecting to see the Lion curled up on the rafters above. But no Lion was visible above or below or anywhere else in the hold. Eisha remembered the Lion's promise, "Should you need to hide, here no one will find you," and she clung to it as fiercely as she had clung to the Island Snake's back.

Suddenly, she heard loud voices and the sound of footsteps above. Her heart began pounding with fear. She shrank into the hammock and pulled the folds of its finely woven sides over her body.

"I could swear I saw someone board this ship only a few minute ago," shouted a rough male voice.

"I thought I saw a huge snake slip into the water under the ship!" exclaimed another.

"I think you're both seeing things!" barked a third voice. "Search the ship, men, every inch of it, from stem to stern!"

"It's the white chief's voice!" exclaimed Eisha to herself, wincing as she heard the stomping and crashing and ripping sounds of the angry men searching the ship to find her. Every muscle in her body was tense. The search seemed to go on forever.

Finally, the noises stopped. "Well, there's no one on board, I swear to it!" said a voice. "Why don't we just take the ship for ourselves, and sell it on Market Island. We could probably get a good price for it."

"Now you're thinking!" exclaimed the voice of the chief. "I've been to Market Island many times. It's less than a day's sail to the west from here. Everyone from the islands of the Inland Sea goes there to buy and sell and trade. We can trade this ship for one that can attack and outrun other ships. With the capital in ruins, and the people scattered and no longer under our control, we might as well make an adventurous living as pirates! This ship is our chance to enjoy a life of plunder and riches!"

A chorus of voices shouted approval. When the shouting died down, someone said, "Did you notice the linens and dresses and bedding? They are all beautifully embroidered with leaves and flowers and such. Do you suppose this is a woman's ship?"

"A woman's!" exclaimed the white chief scornfully. "Women can't sail ships. And I'm surprised the white man could! Did you notice how prissy he looked at court when he made that silly speech? And he looked even more womanish in his long feather shirt when I caught Hesed and Rehem in the dungeon with him the night they escaped! The only thing masculine about him, if you ask me, was that deep voice of his. Men of his kind like to dress up in women's clothes, you know. And they often have women as friends, although they wouldn't know how to use them like real men do!" There was a loud chorus of rough laughter at these words. Eisha's face burned with anger and disgust. How she would love to take them by surprise and throw them all into the sea! But she knew she could not. It would be deadly to betray her presence in any way.

Soon, the ship began to move, and Eisha lay in the hammock watching as the gracefully waving sea-plants and schools of brilliantly colored fish slipped by. As the hammock rocked gently with the motion of the ship, a wave of homesickness swept over Eisha. She remembered how her grandmother would rock her in her arms whenever she was upset. She longed to be safe and secure again in her very own home, surrounded by people who loved her. Tears began to roll down her face, and she cried as softly as she could, so no one would hear her. Finally, in spite of her sadness and fear, she slowly relaxed, her eyes grew heavy, and in the quiet peace that pervaded the secret hold, Eisha fell fast asleep.

"Eisha gripped the Island Snake's sides with her legs and arms, laid her face against its soft, dry scales and closed her eyes to keep from becoming dizzy."

CHAPTER TWENTY-EIGHT:

THE HUNT

"Are you keeping this ship on the course I told you?" said a loud and angry voice. Eisha was startled awake, and listened closely.

"Of course!" came a cross retort. "Don't you think I know how to sail a simple ship like this one?"

"Well then, why do I see land straight ahead?" asked the chief. "I've sailed this area before, and there shouldn't be any land for several hours yet, unless we are off course."

"We've been moving due west, chief," replied the other in a conciliatory voice. "Maybe there's a current in the sea at this time of year which carried us out of the way. Shall I keep going toward the land?"

"Might as well," growled the chief. "Maybe I'll recognize it and get our bearings."

After awhile, Eisha heard a cry overhead. "Land ho! Drop anchor!" A few moments later, the ship stopped moving.

"Aha!" she heard the chief say loudly, "It looks like Buffalo Island. There's a herd of beasts here that will give us the pleasure of good hunting, and we need meat. There's nothing to eat on this ship but some thin wafers of bread!"

"But chief," objected a voice Eisha had not yet heard. "Is it wise to hunt here?"

"We're only going to kill a few buffalo," insisted the chief. "One for food, and a few for sport. What's the matter—are you afraid?"

"No," replied the protester. "But I've heard that this is the only herd of buffalo left in all the islands of the Inland Sea. Can't we just wait until we get to Market Island and get some meat there?"

"Nonsense!" roared the chief. "I'm in the mood for a hunt. And I'm not going to fail to find and kill my prey this time! Who's man enough to hunt those buffalo with me?"

A chorus of voices answered him. "I'm for it! I'm ready! Let's go get 'em!"

Eisha heard the sounds of the men leaving the ship. Soon, only silence prevailed. Cautiously, she crept out of the hammock and began ascending the ladder. "I wonder if it's safe," she thought. "I hope all the men are gone." At that moment, she remembered the Stone. It was still in the pouch she had attached to the silver serpentine belt under her feather shift. When she took her Heart-Stone out, it felt heavy, and glowed a brilliant blue and green, like the color of the sea in sunlight.

"Good!" breathed Eisha with relief, and after replacing it, she opened the hold and entered the hallway between the fore and aft cabins. What she saw made her gasp in dismay! Clothing and utensils and curved swords and leather belts were strewn everywhere. There was no beauty or order left in either of her rooms or the hallway. Sick at heart, she ascended the steps to the deck and cautiously looked around. No one was visible on board.

But not far away, with their backs to her, was a band of dark-skinned men, led by the white chief, with their hunting spears held high over their heads to keep them from getting wet. Eisha kept herself hidden behind a pile of rigging, and watched as the men waded onto shore. They seemed in quite a hurry, especially the white chief. But as he charged towards shore, he slipped in the water, and the other men, who were all crowded close together, fell in a heap on top of him, their spears flying in all directions. Eisha stifled a laugh as they shouted and splashed about, fishing for their spears and looking ridiculous indeed. Finally, they recovered their weapons and their footing, and continued toward land. High above them, on the edge of the hill, stood a magnificent black buffalo, its hump and horns and bearded head dark against the brilliant blue sky.

"After it!" cried the chief as he began charging up the hill. The buffalo did not move.

"It must not know it has anything to fear from humans," thought Eisha. "The other buffalo will be easy prey too." She felt nauseated and closed her eyes as she imagined the carnage that was about to begin. At that moment, a great roar broke the silence. Eisha's eyes flew open, and her mouth made a big "O" of surprise! A huge herd of buffalo was charging at great speed over the crest of the hill! Behind the herd of buffalo was the great figure of the Lion, roaring and chasing the herd towards the sea!

A split second later, the herd swept furiously down the slope of the hill. Too late, the hunters realized their danger. Within moments, the herd of buffalo, which they had intended to kill, trampled them down with heavy bodies and sharp hooves. Then, as suddenly as they had thundered down the slope, the buffalos stopped at the edge of the water. There was no sound at all but the rhythmic plash of the waves. There was no sign of the men's bodies visible among the milling animals. Eisha looked up, and saw the silhouette of one lone buffalo, still standing at the crest of the hill.

She shuddered and looked away, filled with mixed feelings at what she had seen. Somehow, it seemed a just and fitting end to the lives of cruel and vengeful men intent on hunting and killing both her and the buffalo. Still, it was a sobering sight, and she shuddered again as she remembered it. Then she turned her back to the island, pulled up the anchor, and worked at the sail until it caught the wind full force in its silky blue curve. Swiftly and silently, the ship moved out to sea, and Eisha was alone again, safe and sound, as the wind blew her towards her next destination.

"Eisha looked up, and saw the silhouette of one lone buffalo, still standing at the crest of the hill."

CHAPTER TWENTY-NINE:

THE MISTY ISLES

The next few days were calm ones, with very little wind. The ship moved leisurely across the water in a westerly direction, and Eisha had plenty of time to do what she could to restore beauty and order to the ship. She threw all the men's clothes and weapons overboard, for the very sight and smell of them made her queasy. Then she scrubbed and mended and folded and put away, until everything was almost as ship-shape as it had been before the white chief and his men had pirated the ship.

Once this work was done, Eisha spent many hours of many days relaxing in her rainbow hammock in the transparent hold, watching the ever-changing panorama of sea-life around her, and reflecting on her adventures on Snake Island. Now and then, when she remembered Lila and her friends, she would weep for her loss. But it felt like good grief, and she made no attempt to stifle her sadness or hold back her tears. She sensed her grief was part of a healing process she needed to go through after the daunting experiences she had just endured.

For a time, Eisha was content with the slow pace of the ship, for it gave her the opportunity she needed to recover. But one day, she began to feel restless and eager for some change. She had been alone long enough. She longed for the sight of a human face—or at least, a friendly one—as she stood at the prow of the ship, looking ahead at the water that stretched endlessly toward the sky in every direction. It was warm in the morning sun, and she was wearing the brightly colored feather shift that her friends in the jungle had taught her to make. It made her feel closer to them somehow.

All at once the light of the sun grew dim, and a chilly breeze swept across the deck. A great cloud of mist was advancing toward the ship, and the ship was sailing straight into it! Within minutes, Eisha found herself surrounded by thick fog, unable to see anything that was more than a few feet away! "Oh no!" she exclaimed. "What if the ship runs into something? I can't see far enough to tell where to steer it."

But steering was only necessary if the ship was moving, and by now, the ship was as motionless as if someone had dropped the anchor. "Now what?" thought Eisha as she stared into the mist. But there was no answer to her question. There she was, in the middle of a thick fog, in the middle of the ocean, with no star to guide her and no sense of direction in the misty whiteness that enclosed her. "Well, it's waiting time again," said Eisha ruefully. And she headed for the hold deep at the bottom of the ship. At least she could lie there and watch the fascinating sea creatures float by through the underwater forests of waving sea plants.

As she lay down in the rainbow hammock to ponder her predicament, she chanced to look up—and there was the Lion again!

"I was hoping you'd come down here, Eisha," said the Lion, leaping down from the rafters to stand beside the hammock.

"Oh, dear Lion!" cried Eisha, throwing her arms around its neck. "Thank you for saving me from those cruel men!" The Lion replied by tenderly licking her face, as if Eisha was one of its cubs, and then began the purring song that had drawn Eisha into the Cave so long ago. Eisha rested her face and head against the Lion's mane and let the song vibrate through her until the Lion finally spoke.

"Eisha, you are approaching the Misty Isles. Very few of your kind have ever seen them. Two sisters live on one of these islands. They are grand-daughters of the Lady whose Lion I am, and whom you still seek. They will help you in your search for the Lady and the Child. Though they may seem a little strange, they have much wisdom to share, and you will do well to seek it from them. You will find it important to learn the art of asking good questions. They, on the other hand, will not ask you any questions. But they will listen gladly and attentively to anything you want to tell them about yourself and your search. Not about others, mind you. Just yourself."

Eisha wondered at the Lion's words, but she had pressing questions to ask about her recent experience on Snake Island. "Will you tell me," she said, "about you and the Island Snake? Before I met it, I thought all Snakes were alike, and were like the one that lured me away from the Child. But the Island Snake was very different. It spoke to a different part of me too." Eisha paused and reflected for a moment. Then she added, "I used to fear and hate all snakes. Now I am willing to wait and see what kind they are before I judge them."

The Lion looked Eisha in the eye. "You grow wiser, Eisha. Snakes are as different from each other as humans are. The Serpent who took you from the Cave is no friend of mine. It has tempted many women to be untrue to themselves, and has lured them into false ways of being feminine. To follow its way is to end up being a stranger to one's true self, and therefore a false person. Nevertheless, though the Serpent neither knows nor intends it, its temptations can work for good, as in your case. So, in a strange sort of way, we are partners. As for the Island Snake, it is my good friend. Its great desire and work is for the wholeness and well being of all who live in these isles. We work together in all the islands of the Inland Sea."

"Was it really you who roared that night in the desert, and set us free?' asked Eisha with wide-eyed wonder.

"Yes indeed," answered the Lion. "It was part of the plan the Island Snake and I have for the wholeness and flourishing of all the islands' people and creatures. Especially the children. That is why you did not need to stay with the lost children in the hut in the forest. They are in our care. Remember? And that is why Lila returned safely to the jungle before you did. And that is also why you are safely here with me now. There is a little child who still lives in you, Eisha. Though you have often forgotten it, I never forget that child. She—you—are very, very precious to me."

Eisha felt a lump in her throat and an overwhelming urge to cry at these words. "Why am I wanting to cry?" she wondered to herself. "Am I sorrowful or joyful?"

"You are filled with sorrow and joy," said the Lion, as if reading her thoughts. "They are sisters—like the ones you are about to meet in the Misty Isles. Now—go back up on deck, for the ship is about to move again, and you will need to do some careful steering through the Guardian Rocks that protect the approach to the place where they dwell." The Lion licked Eisha's face once more with a tenderness that again brought tears to her eyes, and gently nudged her out of the rainbow hammock.

"'You are filled with sorrow and joy' said the Lion, as if reading her thoughts."

CHAPTER THIRTY:

THE MEETING

Eisha climbed eagerly up and out of the hold. She was ready for a change and a challenge, and very curious about the two sisters the Lion had described. Once on deck, she looked around to find that the mist had lifted. She was no longer in a fog. She could see perfectly well again in every direction. And it was a good thing she could, because a stiff breeze had sprung up and was bearing the ship directly towards a series of huge, dangerous-looking rocks that jutted high out of the water ahead.

Eisha sprang to the sail, and let it go slack, so that the wind would barely move the ship. Then she took the tiller in hand, and carefully and slowly steered the ship around the first rock, and then swung to the left and squeezed between a pair of rocks that towered almost as high as the mast. The swift currents and crashing waves pulled the ship one way and then another. With pounding heart and clammy hands, Eisha finally made it through the Guardian Rocks into a small, narrow harbor that lay just beyond them. As she steered the ship into its calm waters, her body went so limp with relief that she had to quickly sit down on the deck.

When Eisha had recovered her strength, she lowered the anchor and looked toward shore. There, a small distance away, stood two tall women, gazing at the ship and at her. The one on the left had skin the color of worn red brick, and thin, frizzy white hair sticking out in all directions. She looked old and sad, even from a distance. Her face was lined with wrinkles so deep they looked like black furrows plowed into fertile earth. She was dressed in a long ash-gray robe that could not conceal the thinness of her body.

Next to her stood a woman with skin the color of pink primroses in spring. Her face was painted with turquoise serpentine shapes that followed the curves of her face in a skillful design. Her hair was like spun gold, and hung in long loose braids over her ample breasts. She was dressed in a rose colored robe, and crowned with a headdress of white sea eagle feathers. Even from a distance, her face radiated joy and vitality.

Behind the two women, small, smooth hills rose in emerald-green folds against a turquoise sky. A few small trees, twisted by the sea winds into fascinating shapes, crowned the hilltops. Eisha gazed with wonder at the two strange sisters and the land behind them. Then she took a deep breath, plunged into the water, and swam the short distance to shore.

When she reached the beach where the women stood, they both held out their arms in welcome, as if they had been waiting for her. The old, red-skinned woman wore a long necklace and dangling earrings of clear crystals in the shape of teardrops. Eisha looked into her dark eyes, and they shone with a depth of sorrow beyond all telling. When Eisha shifted her gaze to the young pink-skinned woman, she saw that a majestic sea eagle was perched on each of her shoulders, with each one's beak next to one of her ears, as if they were whispering secrets into them. Her eyes were sea-blue, and sparkling with joy. A double lei of multi-colored seashells hung around her neck. Her ears were hung with tiny conch-shells. Both women were silent as they returned Eisha's gaze. There was an awkward pause as she stood before them, hesitant to welcome the embrace they offered her. Then Eisha remembered what the Lion had said. "Learn the art of asking good questions."

"I am Eisha," she said politely. "Will you tell me who you are?"

"Welcome, Eisha," said the thin old woman. "My name is Lupa. The meaning of my name is Sorrow. It is a clue to who I am."

"We are glad to see you, Eisha," said the buxom young woman. "My name is Euphra. The meaning of my name is Joy. It is a clue to who I am."

I don't know what my name means," replied Eisha. "But perhaps I will find out some day. By then, maybe I will know better who I really am."

There was a long silence as the two women looked long and hard at Eisha. She became very self-conscious about her bare, browned legs, and the strands of her short, wavy brown hair which were being blown by the sea-wind into her lively green eyes. "I wonder what they think of me," she thought to herself. But aloud she said, "Will you show me where you live and give me a place to stay tonight?"

"Of course," the two sisters said in chorus. Then they each took one of her hands, and Eisha climbed between them up and down the soft green hills until they came to a valley with a grove of weeping willow trees.

"My home is in the midst of these trees," said Lupa. "Tomorrow I will welcome you into it if you ask for entrance."

"Oh, I will, thank you," replied Eisha.

"Don't be too sure!" said Lupa, and with these mysterious words, she released Eisha's left hand and disappeared among the deep green shadows of the willows.

Euphra continued to hold Eisha's right hand and led her to the top of the next hill. On it stood a round house of large, multi-colored stones, topped with a flat roof. A garden of flowers and vegetables grew on the rooftop. A curving stone stairway led up to the roof. Euphra led Eisha up the steps and through the roof garden to a small white love seat next to a low stone parapet.

When they sat down, they could see a long way over the emerald-green hills in every direction. The two sea eagles, who had stayed perched on Euphra's two shoulders all during this time, flew up and away into the sky toward the sea. By now, the sun had sunk into the water, and clouds painted with fiery hues of orange, coral, and pink hovered around the place of its setting. The fragrance of the flowers around them filled the air with sweetness. Little wisps of dewy white vapor floated over the valleys. The rustling and chirping of birds coming home to roost for the night in a nearby orchard created an evening lullaby. Suddenly Eisha was filled with a feeling that she had been here before. But how could that be?

She turned to Euphra with a puzzled face. "I feel as if I've seen this before," she said. "Is that possible?"

Euphra looked surprised. "You have a marvelous memory!" she exclaimed. "Yes, Eisha, you have been here before. It was when you were very little. Your grandmother used to visit here every summer, and after you were born, she always took you with her." Now it was Eisha's turn to look surprised.

"That's amazing!" she said. "It's as if I've come back almost full circle, isn't it? Why here, I wonder?"

"Not quite full circle yet," answered Euphra mysteriously. "But you will soon realize why you are here."

Eisha was puzzled by her response, but she pressed on, for her active mind was full of more questions.

"Why are you and your sister so different?" she asked.

"We are not quite as different as we look," replied Euphra. "In fact, we are like two sides of the same coin."

Eisha was completely baffled by this answer. But she tried again. "Why was I blown or led here to you?" she said.

"Because you are searching," responded Euphra.

"Oh—yes!" said Eisha eagerly. "I am. I'm searching for the Lady and the Child. Do you know anything about them?"

"Indeed I do," replied Euphra. "A great deal. The Lady, as the Lion probably told you, is our Grand Mother. The Child is one of many children who come to this island."

"Do you know where they are?" asked Eisha.

"You are not ready for the answer to that question yet," responded Euphra with a smile. She rose to her feet. "I think the other questions buzzing in your head can wait until tomorrow. You need nourishment and rest." And she motioned Eisha to follow her down the stone stairs and into the house.

"She was dressed in a rose colored robe, and crowned with a head dress of white sea eagle feathers."

CHAPTER THIRTY-ONE:

THE HOUSE OF JOY

As they paused at the threshold of the arched doorway that led into Euphra's house, Eisha saw letters carved in stone on the lintel that said, "House of Joy." The evening light shone into the single round room through three long, large open windows topped with arches. The one opposite them faced north, and the other two faced east and west. In the middle of the room was a round stone table with a low curved stone bench around it. A single white candle burned at the center of the table. Beneath the east window was a low bed with a fluffy white comforter and pillows on it. "This is your bed while you are here, Eisha," said Euphra with a smile.

"Oh, thank-you," replied Eisha. "But—isn't this your bed?"

"At this time of year, I often sleep in the roof-top garden under the moon and stars," replied Euphra. Then she walked over to the hearth of a small fireplace between the west and north windows. A big black pot was suspended on a rod over a merrily burning fire, and when she lifted its cover, the delicious smell of good soup filled the room. She looked at Eisha as if waiting for something. There was a long pause. Then Eisha remembered to ask a question.

"May I have something to eat?" she asked.

"Gladly—as long as you ask!" replied Euphra, and with a smile she ladled out two big bowls of the steaming soup, and set them on the table with a loaf of fresh-baked bread and a plate of vegetables fresh from the roof-garden. She poured fruit juice into two stone wear mugs, and lifted hers up in a silent ritual of thanksgiving. Eisha did the same.

Then, as they ate and drank, Eisha told Euphra about her adventures and her search. Euphra listened carefully, and her eyes often sparkled with delight in response to parts of Eisha's story. When the sharing-supper was over, Euphra put out a basin of hot water and a fresh towel and washcloth for Eisha to use, and then went toward the door.

"Where are you going?" asked Eisha a little anxiously.

"To make the rounds of the island with my sea-eagles," replied Euphra courteously. And with that, she was gone.

Eisha washed up, and tired from the rigors of the day, she lay down under the soft feather comforter by the east window, and fell fast asleep. During the night, she had a vivid dream.

She was standing on the seashore at night. A huge golden moon glowed low on the horizon. A path of golden moonlight shimmered on the water between the moon and her feet. Two sea eagles came from behind her, flew over the moon-path and disappeared into the moon. She started walking on the shimmering golden light toward the moon. When she reached it, a round door swung open, and she stepped inside. There, facing her with arms wide open in welcome stood the Lady! She wore a silky robe of sky-blue—just like the sail on Eisha's ship. Her long white hair flowed behind her as if a wind blew it back from her face. Her eyes were dark green, like Eisha's own, and her face was filled with eager longing. The two majestic sea eagles hovered over her head. At her feet, bathed in light, sat the Child Eisha longed to hold. It was now about a year old, and had curly brown hair the same color as Eisha's. The Child was playing with a shining silver ball that reminded Eisha of the Morning Star as it swirled and spun in its hand. The Child looked up, and with a delighted laugh held up the silver ball towards Eisha. It shone brighter and brighter, and grew larger and larger, until it covered the sight of the Lady and Child.

Eisha cried out and woke up with the light of the Morning Star shining into her face through the east window by her bed. She lay awake for more than an hour, watching the Star and pondering her mysterious dream. "The Child holds the Star... the Lady's robe is like the sail of the ship...Euphra Joy...her sea eagles led me to them..." but the thoughts faded away, and she fell asleep again.

When she next awoke, the morning sun was shining in her face, and the song of birds filled the air. Eisha rose quickly, washed up, ate a piece of leftover bread, and walked out of the house into the new day. No one was in sight. The dewdrops on the grass-covered ground reflected back the sun's brilliance like a million tiny mirrors. A small path led from the door to the fruit orchard she had seen from the rooftop the evening before.

"A walk will do me good," Eisha said to herself, and she took to the path with quick, light steps. As she walked, she took deep breathfuls of the fresh, dewy dawn air, and began humming a song to herself, timing it to match the rhythm of her steps. "This is fun," Eisha said to herself.

Before long, she was near the orchard. To her surprise, the sound of children laughing and playing rose up to greet her. As she entered the orchard, she saw dozens of brightly colored little tents pitched under the fruit and nut trees that grew everywhere. Children of all ages were emerging from the tents, or climbing the trees and picking fruit and nuts, which they tossed down to their playmates below. A group of them were running and laughing among the trees as if they were playing a game of tag. A few of them nearest Eisha quickly realized her presence and ran up to her.

"Want some fruit?" asked a little boy, holding up a big red apple to her.

"Thank you!" replied Eisha, and she smiled and took a big, crunchy, juicy bite of the sweet apple. "Where did you get those beautiful little tents with all the bright-colors and drawings on them?" asked Eisha.

"Oh, we made them," replied one of the little girls in a nonchalant way.

"You did?" exclaimed Eisha. "How do you do it?"

"Oh, the lady who lives in the round stone house gives us big pieces of cloth and paints, and we make the designs. Then she hangs the cloths up on a line in the sun and the wind for this many days." The little girl held up five fingers. "And then she helps us make them into tents. We go to sleep in them every night when the sun sets. I have my very own tent, and so do all my friends." With these words, she ran off to play.

Eisha walked around the orchard for a little while longer, enjoying the sight of the playing children, and the taste of the fruits and nuts they kept offering her. Every now and then, she would stare hard at one of their faces, feeling sure she had seen it somewhere before, but unable to remember where or when. "What a wonderful thing—to be a child here and have your own tent, and a place like this to play!" she thought to herself, remembering how different her own childhood had been.

Finally, she turned back to the stone house to find Euphra, for she was fairly bursting with new questions. As she neared the house, she looked up, and there stood Euphra among the flowers on the roof, looking down at her with a smile. The two sea eagles were once again perched on her two shoulders, with their beaks next to her ears.

"What secrets are they telling you?" teased Eisha as she looked up.

"They are telling me that you had a special dream last night," replied Euphra. Eisha's eyes and mouth flew open with surprise. "Come up on the roof with me, if you want to tell me your dream," said Euphra.

Eisha bounded up the winding stone stairs and followed Euphra to the love seat where they had sat together the evening before. Then, as they looked out over the green, green hills and valleys toward the misty blue sea in the distance, and bright yellow and orange butterflies danced in circles around the flowers and over their heads, Eisha told her dream. When she had finished, Euphra said, "Ah! You are nearing the end of your search for the land that lies east of the sun and west of the moon."

Eisha gave a start of recognition. "That's where the Lion said the Lady and the Child might be found," she said.

"Yes," answered Euphra. "You have only one more voyage before you reach your destination."

Eisha sighed. "Will it be a very long way for me to sail?" she asked.

"I do not know, my dear. But that is in the future. You are here, and this is now, and the present is all we have—"

Her words were interrupted by the sound of little feet scurrying up the steps, and a moment later, three small children burst onto the rooftop and ran towards them.

"Who are these children, and all the rest of the ones I saw in the orchard?" asked Eisha. "Where do they come from? And why are they here?"

"Wait, Eisha!" said Euphra, holding up her hand. Then she knelt down beside the three children and gave them her complete and undivided attention. One of them, a little redheaded girl, wanted to show her a fuzzy green caterpillar she had found in the orchard, which was now inching its way up her arm. Another one, a little blonde boy, had a piece of fruit and a little bouquet of flowers he wanted to give her. The third child was crying quietly, her little face wet with tears as she held out a dead butterfly in her open palm.

Euphra admired the caterpillar with the little red-haired girl, enthusiastically accepted the gift of fruit and flowers from the little boy, and then turned to the sad little girl. The other two children ran down the stairs to rejoin their playmates. Euphra tenderly wiped the tears from the little girl's face, and looked sadly with her at the dead butterfly.

"Even beautiful butterflies die," she said gently. "And you are right to be sad. Would you like to sit on my lap while I talk with Eisha here?" The little girl nodded. Euphra took her in her arms and then sat down with her next to Eisha and said, "Now I will try to answer your questions, Eisha. The children on this island come to us from all over the islands of the Inland Sea. They are the ones who are neglected, abused, and lost, because no one pays attention to them or really cares for them. But when they fall asleep, they are brought here, where they are loved and played with and cared for and delighted in! They never lack for attention or a chance to blossom as the wonderful little creators and players that they are."

"How do they get here?" asked Eisha with great curiosity.

"The Lion hears their cries, and brings them here in many different ways," answered Euphra. "Lupa cries with them and I laugh with them. She sings them to sleep with sorrowfully sweet lullabies, and I waken them with merry morning songs. She bathes them with living water from the stream that waters her house, and I shelter them in tents of luscious color. She puts soothing ointment on their hurts, and I fill their stomachs with good food and drink. She teaches them to fight fair, and I teach them to make peace. In turn, they fill our hearts with love. They teach us how to play each day, and enjoy it to the fullest. They show us how to feel, how to forget, and how to remember. Without them, the hills would turn dry and brown, the garden would wither, the orchard would die, and our very souls would shrivel up."

Euphra stopped speaking. There was a long silence as Eisha thought about her words. All at once, the memory of the lost, crying children she had found in the winter forest flashed through Eisha's mind. "So this is how the Lion took care of them!" she thought. "No wonder some of them looked familiar.

I'm so glad they are here!" Then she became aware that the sad little girl in Euphra's arms had begun sobbing softly again.

"Come," said Euphra to the little girl. "Let's take you to Lupa's house. She will help you bury the butterfly and grieve its death." She took the little girl in her arms, and beckoned Eisha to follow her. Down the steps they went, and then down the hill to the valley where the weeping willow trees grew.

"Eisha saw letters carved in stone on the lintel that said 'House of Joy'."

CHAPTER THIRTY-TWO:

THE HOUSE OF SORROW

As they entered the deep shadows of the grove, Eisha turned to Euphra and asked, "May I go into Lupa's house?"

Euphra replied, "Yes, you may enter Lupa's house—after she and the child are through. But only if you ask her to help you grieve over the hurt in your own soul. You cannot enter her House of Sorrow without entering your own pain." Eisha nodded. "Wait here under the willows, and listen to their weeping," continued Euphra, and she pointed to a broad, flat stone, just right for sitting, at the side of a little brook that babbled its winding way through the grove. "When you are able to weep with them, not only over your own pain, but the pain of all the islands and those who live in them, the door of Lupa's house will open to you." With these words, she walked away from Eisha, holding the sad little girl in her arms.

Eisha sank onto the sitting stone and began to quiet herself and listen. Gradually, the trickle of the water over the stream's stony bed began to sound to her like the running tears of countless children. She imagined the pain they endured—being ignored, neglected, laughed at, stifled, put down, beaten, and violated. The imagining awakened her own long-buried memories of childhood neglect. She remembered the many times she had called for her mother as she lay sobbing on her bed; but her mother never came. She remembered how sternly her father treated her, how much he criticized her, and how seldom he played with her. She remembered the many lonely days when she longed for another child to play with. Soon, the tears began running down her face as she felt the pain of her own little child and of all little children more and more deeply.

After awhile, the pain subsided, and Eisha wondered if she was ready to go into Lupa's house. She looked at her Heart-Stone. To her surprise, it lay lightly in her hand, and was a dull gray color. "But I did what Euphra said," thought Eisha. "There must be some mistake." And she decided go to Lupa's house anyway, for she had endured quite enough grief and pain. But though she searched long and hard, she could find no sign of the house in the willow-grove. Finally she admitted to herself that perhaps the Stone was right, and she returned to the sitting-stone where she had cried as she felt the pain of children.

Then she heard the wind in the willows, and it sounded like the sighing of countless women. In her imagination, the willows, with their drooping branches, even looked like huge women bending over the brook, their long green hair trailing in the water, hiding their grieving faces. Eisha felt the pain they endured—the subtle contempt, the neglect, the stifling, the beating, and the violation. And now she began to sob and sob as if her heart was breaking, for she felt again the ways in which she had been hurt as a woman. She remembered how often she had been told as she grew up, "You can't do that. You're just a girl." She remembered the first time one of the young men in the castle had tried to force himself on her, and how angry and frightened she had been. She remembered how the men in the castle ignored and interrupted her when they sat around the table together. All these things, and many more, rushed into her mind, and Eisha wept and wept with the pain of countless other women.

Finally, her tears subsided, and Eisha looked up to see a door slowly opening in the side of a small hill on the opposite side of the stream from where she sat! She quickly waded across the stream, and approached the door. It was exactly the same emerald green as the mossy hillside in which it was set, so that it was nearly invisible when it was shut. But now it was wide open, and as she came up to it, she looked down and saw a mat in front of the door that said, "Welcome to the House of Sorrow." She looked up, and there stood Lupa, gray-robed and white-haired, with her grief-furrowed face, holding a purple candle.

"May I come in?" asked Eisha.

"I see you are ready," replied Lupa, gazing into Eisha's tear stained face. "Come, and tell me what you grieve." She led the way by the candle's light into her dim cave-house, and motioned for Eisha to sit down beside her. Once again, Eisha told her story. As she did, she noticed that whereas she had focused on the exciting and beautiful and good parts when she was telling it to Euphra, now she was focusing on the sad and painful and ugly parts. She realized that her story changed according to who was listening, and her own frame of mind. And she realized that each telling, though different, was true in its own way.

Lupa listened, and when Eisha had to stop, because her voice choked with tears, Lupa's tears flowed down her face. Eisha felt that no one had ever understood her grief and anger and hurt as Lupa did. When she was finally finished, the old woman rose slowly and started towards the door. Eisha was dismayed to see that she was leaving, and said, "Where are you going?"

Lupa turned and replied, "I'm going to find some healing herbs for you." And then she was gone.

Eisha sighed deeply, and looked around the room. It was windowless and dim, but by now her eyes had adjusted to the dark enough to see what was around her. The seat on which she and Lupa had been sitting together was a long, smooth log with a flat surface. It was set against one of the walls, which functioned as a backrest. In the center of the cave-like room was a round pit with a fire burning in it. The fragrant smoke of cedar wood ascended through an opening in the roof directly above it.

Bunches of dried herbs and flowers of many kinds hung upside down from invisible hooks in the ceiling, and added their fragrance to that of the cedar smoke. A low chest stood against the opposite wall, with shelves above it stacked with wooden bowls and plates and cups. Near the log seat was a little table covered with small, curiously shaped jars of ointments. To the left of the doorway, the nearby stream came in through a small opening in the bottom of the cave-wall, ran across the floor, and out through an opening on the other side. Eisha sat looking and imagining Lupa treating the children as Euphra had described, until Lupa herself came back into the room with a handful of fresh herbs in one hand. She busied herself with boiling water in a pot over the fire, and steeping the herbs in it. Then she held out the pot to Eisha and waited.

"What is it?" asked Eisha.

"It is a liquid that refreshes both body and soul after a bout of sorrow," said Lupa. Eisha took the small, steaming pot and sipped the hot, fragrant liquid until it was gone. It had a strong mint flavor, mixed with tastes both bitter and sweet. She gave the pot back to Lupa with a grateful look. Then the two looked long into each other's eyes until Eisha asked, "What would be best for me to do now?"

Lupa's face creased with a rare smile. "I'm glad you remembered to ask," she replied. "I suggest that you go and play with the children, Eisha. Let them teach you what they have taught us. You have not played for a very long time, and your soul will green with new life as vibrant as the hills of this island, if you learn again to play and be like a little child." Then she waved Eisha out the door, and Eisha walked with a light step and even lighter heart through the willow grove in the shadowed valley, and up the sunny emerald green hill to the House of Joy.

This time, Euphra was standing at the door with sparkling eyes. But she said nothing as Eisha stood there, facing her, until

Eisha asked, "Why am I so light-hearted and footed after being in the House of Sorrow?"

"Because you have left your burden there. You bravely entered into your pain, and the pain of other women and children; you shared it openly with another who listened; and you willingly drank nature's healing potion," replied Euphra. "The House of Sorrow and the House of Joy are near each other, because when you enter one, you need to enter the other. And that is why Lupa and I are sisters who live and work together. Were we separated, there would be no true sorrow, or joy, or healing for the children and pilgrims who come to this green haven in the Inland Sea."

Eisha nodded, although she knew she did not understand the depths of Euphra's words. But she did know that what she needed and wanted now was to play with the children. "Are the children still in the orchard?" she asked Euphra.

"No," smiled Euphra. "They are playing on the beach where you came ashore."

"May I go and play with them now?" asked Eisha.

"If you still know how," answered Euphra. Then she turned back into the House of Joy, and Eisha walked down the hills towards the beach.

"She looked up, and there stood Lupa, gray-robed and white haired, with her grief-furrowed face, holding a purple candle."

CHAPTER THIRTY-THREE:

THE PLAYFUL PLACE

The sound of laughter and splashing greeted Eisha as she came down a grass-covered slope that ended in a crescent of silvery white sand. Dozens of children of all ages were splashing in the water, or building sand castles, or collecting seashells and moss and seaweeds to decorate their buildings. Euphra's two great sea eagles perched on a high rock just offshore, as if they were keeping a close eagle eye on each child. The sun sparkled on the sand and water, caressing Eisha's bare arms and legs with welcome warmth. She walked slowly onto the sand and sat down next to a group of children who were working on a very ambitious sand castle, complete with a double moat, and numerous towers and courtyards.

After Eisha had watched them wistfully for a while, a little boy with dark, curly hair said, "Do you want to play?"

"Sure," she said. "But I'm not sure how."

"Just watch us, and do what we do, and then whatever you feel like doing," said an older girl nearby, with a curious glance at Eisha. So Eisha began by watching. She noticed how earnestly and soberly the children worked at creating the sand castle. Yet, their work was often punctuated with cries of delight as they stopped to admire their handiwork. Each one contributed something, and all worked together, though without any visible kind of organization.

They worked in happy harmony until two children began to disagree about the shape of a courtyard. The boy wanted it to be square. The girl wanted it to be round. Each one argued, trying to convince the other, but to no avail. Finally, in frustration, they began to call each other names and scowl blackly at one another. At this, a third child intervened. "Hey —that's not fighting fair like Lupa showed us," he cried. "No name calling? Remember? Just say what you think or feel or want."

"I did!" exclaimed the girl, stamping her foot. "But it didn't help one bit. He just won't listen."

"Neither will you," shouted the boy.

"Square, square, square—that's all you are!" said the girl, sticking out her tongue at him.

"You're just a big round zero!" retorted the boy, and made a face at her.

"Why don't you go shut yourself up in a nice square box!" yelled the girl angrily.

"Why don't you just scrunch yourself up into a big round ball and roll into the sea!" shouted the boy.

"Calm down, both of you," said the peacemaker. "Why don't you tell me what each of you wants, and maybe I can help you." So both quarreling children presented their arguments. But the peacemaker could not get them to compromise. Square or round it had to be. Finally, he turned to Eisha, who was watching nearby.

"What do you think? he asked.

"I think you're a good peacemaker," she said. "Lupa taught you well. And I think the castle is just grand!" The children glowed with pleasure. "How about this idea?" offered Eisha, looking at the boy and the girl who had disagreed. "Put a round courtyard inside a square one—like this." She drew a diagram in the sand with her finger. "That way, you have the advantages of both, and a unique design besides." The boy and girl grinned with delight and hugged each other.

"That's perfect!" cried one.
"It'll be fantastic!" cried the other.
"Will you help us?" they said together.
"I'd love to," replied Eisha. And so she did, searching with them for beautiful shells to outline the circle, finding plants to put in the corners of the square, and feathers as flags for the towers. She helped them dig the moat so deep and wide that small driftwood ships could sail in them. She became completely engrossed in her play with the children, and lost all track of time until she heard the sound of a flute playing a melody in the distance.

"That's our supper song!" cried the children, and they began running up the green slopes, leaving their creations behind to be washed away by the incoming tide. Eisha marveled at their ability to live in the moment, and leave go of what they had created. She climbed up the hill behind them, and then sat down on the grass near the House of Joy with them. Euphra came out with loaves of bread, jars of honey, fresh fruit and vegetables, and jugs of juice. They all sang their supper song together as Euphra played the flute.

"We harvest Your bounty. Thank You!
We feast on Your beauty. Thank You!
We are fed by Your goodness. Thank You!"

Then they ate and drank and talked and laughed together until the sun began to sink behind the hills. As Euphra took the food and dishes into the house, the children walked with Eisha to the orchard, where the birds were settling into the branches. Each of the children crawled into his or her brightly colored tent for the night. Eisha laid down on her back in the orchard grass, and gazed up at the dusky blue sky-shapes that shone through the tree branches. The birds became still, and she heard Lupa's voice, soft and deep, singing a lullaby.

"Sweet and low, sweet and low,
Wind of the western sea,
Blow, blow, breathe and blow,
Wind of the western sea.
Eisha has come to rest in her nest,
While the silver moon sails in the west.
Blow her home o'er the sea,
Where her Little One,
Where her Lovely One waits."

A great longing welled up in Eisha as she lay there listening to Lupa's lullaby. "Oh—if only they are still waiting for me," thought Eisha. "How long will it be before I see them?" She spoke aloud, and from somewhere nearby, Lupa's soft, deep voice answered.

"As long as it takes, Eisha. As long as it takes you to learn to play and be a child again, and after that, sail over the sea to the land that lies east of the sun and west of the moon." Then all was silent, and Eisha fell asleep in the orchard under the stars, still wondering how long.

The next day, and the next, and for many days thereafter, Eisha joined the children at play in the orchard, on the beach, in the sea, and up and down the hillsides. She was treated and cared for by the two sisters as if she really were one of the children. She had no responsibilities beyond theirs. She made a tent for herself covered with pictures she herself painted of the Lion and the Island Snake and Lila and the Golden Grove and the Sacred Tree and the Lotus Pool. She slept and rose with the children, laughed and cried like the children, and wondered at the beauty of each day with them. Together they made up games and songs and dances. The hurt in her heart over losing Lila began to heal. The fears and tensions of her journey faded away. Her soul was filled with love and laughter, and her whole being greened with new life.

Then one morning, one of the little girls poked her head into Eisha's tent and offered her a little acorn-cup of dawn dew to wake her up. As Eisha hugged the little girl and thanked her, she realized that she really was like one of the children. She had learned to play, and create, and live in each moment with childlike energy and openness. Perhaps she was finally ready to go.

Eisha decided to ask Euphra about it at breakfast. "I am feeling ready for the last part of my search," she said as she took a bite of the bread and honey Euphra had prepared for her. "Do you think I'm ready too? And do you have any advice for me before I leave?"

"I'm glad you asked," smiled Euphra. "Yes, I think you are ready now. And my advice is this. Remember your dream. Ponder what the Lady and the Child and the moon and star and all the other things in the dream mean to you. Meditate on them and consider how what happened in the dream is connected to what is happening in your life. Open your heart to the dream's message. For all memorable dreams have messages of great wisdom. Listen to them, and they will guide you to your unique destiny and the fulfillment of your heart's desire."

Eisha nodded. "I imagine I will have plenty of time to do that on the voyage ahead," she said. Then Euphra embraced Eisha, took the golden conch shells from her ears, and put them in Eisha's. "Here," she said, "let these always remind you of the joy that listening brings."

"O Euphra, thank you!" cried Eisha. "They are so beautiful. I'll always remember you when I wear them, and all the gifts of joy you have given me." Though she was eager to begin her last voyage, it was hard to leave Euphra, and Eisha couldn't help clinging to her for a few moments when they hugged each other good-bye. She felt a strange mixture of sadness and gladness as she walked down the hill towards the harbor.

On the way to the ship, Eisha was suddenly surrounded by her little playmates, who insisted on going along with her.

Together, they went down into the valley and through the willow grove. There, Lupa came out of her house and embraced Eisha for the last time. Both of them wept at the parting, for their shared grief had knit their souls together. "Here," said Lupa, taking the necklace of crystal teardrops from her neck and placing it on Eisha's. "Let these always remind you of how precious the gift of tears is."

"Your tears have been a great gift to me already," replied Eisha. "Thank you for them—and this necklace. I will wear it always to remind me not to stifle my tears, but let them flow with the healing power you showed me they have."

Then they kissed goodbye, and Eisha and the children continued down to the beach where they had played so many happy hours together. Of course, every one of the children wanted a farewell hug and kiss, and by the time Eisha was through, she felt she had a store of loving hugs and kisses large enough to last her for a very long time! Finally, with a farewell wave of her hand, she swam out into the water and towards the waiting ship.

"Dozens of children of all ages were splashing in the water, or building sand-castles, or collecting sea-shells and moss and sea-weeds to decorate their buildings."

CHAPTER THIRTY-FOUR:

THE LAST VOYAGE

When Eisha climbed aboard the ship, the first thing she saw was the Lion, sitting on the deck near the sail, waiting for her. It sat with its tail waving back and forth, and a playful look in its eye. Beneath its huge front paws rested a silvery ball that reminded Eisha of the one the Child played with in her dream. She was not sure what the Lion wanted. Was it inviting her to play? Somehow, Eisha had never seen the majestic Lion as playful! "Of course, that might be because there wasn't much play in me," thought Eisha ruefully.

As if to answer her, the Lion sprang to its feet and rolled the ball towards Eisha. Eisha smiled, caught the ball, and threw it up in the air as far as she could. The Lion leaped high into the air and caught it in its mouth. Then it tossed the ball towards Eisha with a deft movement of its head and a bat of its paw. Eisha laughed with delight, barely caught the ball on the fly, and returned it high in the air towards the Lion. Back and forth and up and down went the silver ball, shining in the sun as Eisha and the Lion played together. Finally, when the ball was high in the sky between them, they both leaped for it at once, and Eisha fell down on top of the soft furry body of the Lion. They rolled over and over on the deck, Eisha laughing loudly with delight, and the Lion purring like a big cat. It was very gentle with Eisha, and though its size and strength at such close range were almost overwhelming, Eisha had no fear of being hurt, and let herself go in playful abandon. Finally, panting and laughing, she and the Lion sat and rested together on the deck.

Eisha said, "That was wonderful fun!"

The Lion said, "Little Eisha-cub, you now have the heart of a child, and the courage to live it out!"

"I hope so," replied Eisha. "But how am I going to get to the land east of the sun and west of the moon with no wind to blow me there? The sea is as still as glass."

"There's a good wind out on the open sea," said the Lion. "All we have to do is get you safely past the Guardian Rocks, and you will be on your way. And look! Here comes help!"

Eisha looked up, and saw Euphra's two great sea eagles flying towards the ship. They looked much larger than when they sat on Euphra's shoulders.

"Pull up anchor! Hoist the sail! The wings of sister Joy will bear you away!" cried the Lion.

As Eisha raised the anchor and then the silky, sky-blue sail, the two sea eagles hovered near it, flapping their great wings, and creating a breeze that slowly moved the ship out of the harbor. Eisha looked back, and the last thing she saw was the crowd of children waving at her from the shore of the emerald green isle until the Guardian Rocks hid them from view.

This time, the currents were much less strong, and the sea was calm, even around the rocks. The breeze from the birds' wings was just enough to help her steer the ship around and between the rocks with very little danger, until they reached open sea. Then, with a farewell cry, the sea eagles soared in a spiral high into the sky until their forms were absorbed into the blue.

"Now, sail due east, Eisha," said the Lion. "There is nothing but open water between you and the land that lies east of the sun and west of the moon. At night, when the Morning Star rises in the east, keep on course by sailing directly towards it. When it reaches the top of the sky, stop, drop anchor, and sleep. There are many shallow reefs along your course, and you will never have trouble finding a place to anchor. When the sun rises in the east in the morning, set your course straight towards it. In the afternoon, drop anchor again and rest. Eat and drink, putter, and ponder your experiences and your dreams. Write about your search and your discoveries in the logbook in your cabin. It will be a great help to some other searcher someday. Take time to read the ancient Book and meditate on its mystical mandalas. In this way, your rest and reflection will prepare you for whatever lies ahead." Then the Lion licked Eisha's face, and turned to go down into the secret hold at the very bottom of the ship. But just before it disappeared from view, it turned and rolled the silver ball towards Eisha. "Above all," said the Lion, "don't forget to play!"

By now, the ship was out of sight of any land whatsoever. A brisk breeze sprang up out of the west, the blue sail billowed out, and the ship went flying eastward over the white-waved sea. The water was a glorious, brilliant blue, with patches of turquoise where there were reefs not far below the surface. Sun-sparkles danced on the water everywhere. And then, to Eisha's huge delight, a whole school of white dolphins surfaced and began playing around the ship. She watched them all morning long.

Every morning thereafter, they came to welcome her, as if they were escorting the ship to its destination. They leaped, somersaulted, and blew waterspouts out of the holes on the back of their heads.

One day, as she watched them playing with each other, Eisha remembered the silver ball. On an impulse, she threw it out to the dolphins. In a flash, they leaped out of the water and tossed it to each other, and then to her. It was wonderful fun, and from that day on, Eisha played silver-ball-catch with the dolphins every morning.

All this continued for many days and nights as Eisha followed the Lion's instructions. Each night she sailed by the light of the swirling Star that reminded her of the silver ball. Each day she sailed into the rising sun until noon. Often, as she rested and read and wrote in the afternoon, a brief shower would pass overhead, leaving fresh rainwater in the rain barrel on the deck for Eisha to drink, and a trail of rainbow hanging in the sky for a few magical moments. There was much to ponder in the ancient Book, and much to recall, reflect, and write about in the log. Eisha was glad for the time to uncover more of the meaning of her journey, and she began to see purpose and design in her experiences as she re-viewed them. Her only problem was being patient. Often she would remember Lupa's words. "It takes as long as it takes." And when she went to sleep at midnight, with the Star high overhead, she would sing Lupa's lullaby to herself, and it would help.

But oh, how glad Eisha was when one night, she saw a black spot on the horizon that grew larger and larger until she was sure, even in the darkness, that it was land. "Surely it is the land that lies east of the sun and west of the moon," she thought, "because the Lion said there wasn't any other land before it if I kept on course, and I'm sure I have."

That night, when she dropped anchor and went to bed, she was so excited she could hardly sleep. When she finally did, she had another vivid dream.

She was on the small rooftop courtyard of a large castle. Suddenly, the castle collapsed into ruins. She found herself flying high over the trees and away from the castle. Whenever she moved her body a certain way, she would go higher. She experimented flying high and low, and covered a great deal of territory. But after awhile, she could no longer rise higher, and she found herself flying low over the ground through a woods. All at once, she noticed a huge alligator lying in the path. She tried to rise above it, but it seized her shoulder in its powerful jaws. She began to struggle, but it was useless. Then she did the only thing she could think of. She stopped trying to escape. When she did so, the alligator released its grip and lay perfectly still. She too, sat perfectly still. Fall turned to winter, and winter to spring. Then she got up, and walked away into the lacy green woods.

 Then Eisha woke up. "What a strange dream!" she thought. "I wonder what this one means!" But when she looked out of the porthole above her bunk, all thought of her dream vanished as she saw the land by daylight that she had dimly perceived during the night.

"From that day on, Eisha played silver-ball catch with the dolphins every morning."

CHAPTER THIRTY-FIVE:

THE SWAMPEYS

Eisha dressed quickly, and raced up on deck. Straight ahead, only a few miles away, was the coast of the land that was her final destination! Here she would find the Lady and the Child, if all went well. She looked carefully at the land that lay east of the sun and west of the moon. It looked like a very large island indeed—if it was an island at all. The part nearest the ship was flat, and covered with huge live oak trees with Spanish moss draped from their branches. The shoreline looked like marshland, with thick stands of bull-rushes and marsh grasses growing up from the water. She could see flocks of waterfowl flying in low, wavy lines over the marshes in the early morning light.

"I think I'll see if there's a channel through the marsh I can take, so I can get out on dry ground," Eisha said to herself. "I don't like the idea of wading through those marshes, and stepping on who knows what sort of creatures that live there!" She pulled up anchor, and a rising dawn breeze was enough to move the ship closer to land. It took some exploring, but eventually Eisha found a channel of water fairly clear of vegetation, and followed it toward land until the water was too shallow to go any further.

"I guess I can't get as far as dry ground after all," she said to herself as she leaned over the ship's railing and looked at the marshy water in which it stood. "I'll just have to get wet. I hope the water's not too deep, and I hope I don't have to walk too far in it." So saying, she put some food and water and an extra change of clothes in a sack, and attached the rope ladder to the side of the ship. Just as she was ready to climb down it, the Lion appeared on deck.

"Goodbye, Eisha," said the Lion. "Go well."

"Goodbye?" asked Eisha in surprise. "Are you going to leave me?"

"No. It is you who are leaving me and the ship."

"But I'll be back," protested Eisha.

"No, Eisha. You have found the land where you will discover what you are searching for. There is no need to take the ship anywhere else. I must now prepare it for the next seeker. And you must be prepared to journey and search on foot until you find the Lady and the Child."

Eisha was dismayed. The ship had become a home to her. She didn't want to leave it for good. What would happen to her clothes and the ancient Book and the log she had written in for so many hours?

"Eisha, let go," said the Lion sternly, reading her face and her thoughts. "If there is anything you truly need, it will return to you because you were able to give it up. As for the rest, it will meet someone else's need. Besides, Eisha, no one needs two homes." And with these words, the Lion licked her face tenderly and said, "Until we meet again!"

Eisha climbed reluctantly down the rope ladder, feeling quite put out. "The Lion practically pushed me off my own ship!" she muttered to herself. Then she remembered that it was really not her ship at all, and that the Lion was worthy of her trust. So she swallowed her anger, and with a resolute sigh, began wading slowly through the watery marsh towards land. The black muck at the bottom sucked at her shoes, and soon filled them. The reeds got all tangled up in her legs. The water was waist-deep, and the going was slow and hard.

All at once, Eisha felt a sharp, painful pinch on her ankle. "Ouch! Help!" she cried as she slipped, swayed, and fell into the water. Her eyes were still open when she went under, and she saw a big crab scuttling away from her. "That must have been what pinched me!" exclaimed Eisha to herself as she struggled to get back on her feet. "What a pain!" Then, sputtering and complaining, she got back up and began walking again. Her sack and her clothes were dripping wet, and her shoes were like lead weights on her feet.

"This is awful!" thought Eisha as she struggled onward. "What a way to begin my adventures in the land of my dreams!" Fortunately, she was not clawed again, and made it to dry land without further incident. After resting for a while in the sun until she was almost dried out, she picked up her sack, and started walking inland through the live oak forest. It was dim and sun-dappled, and the air was warm and humid, smelling of decaying wood and stagnant water. There was no visible path, and Eisha was afraid she would get lost if she went any further in. "Ill just walk as close to the shore as I can," she said to herself. "That way, I at least know I'm not going around in circles." So she walked along with the depths of the forest on her left, and the salt marsh and sea on her right.

Presently, she heard voices. They were angry voices, and though she could not understand the words at a distance, she could tell that a quarrel was going on. A short while later, a group of short, squat human figures with green, frog-like skin and sprays of gray-green hair like Spanish moss emerged from the marsh on her right. When they saw Eisha, they stopped and stared.

"Who are you?" asked one of them, his eyes bulging with surprise.

"Eisha," she replied. "And I'm afraid I might be lost. This is the land that lies east of the sun and west of the moon, isn't it?"

"That we cannot say, stranger," he returned. "But we can say that this land is our land, and you'd better have a good reason for trespassing on it!"

"I don't mean to trespass," replied Eisha as politely as she could. "May I ask what people am I speaking to, who lay claim to this marshland?"

"We are the Swampeys, and I am Bashda, leader of our band," said another of the squat green men as he stepped forward with a belligerent air. "These others have names, but you do not need to know them. I am the one who will deal with you—and them." And he turned to glare at the Swampey who had spoken in his stead to Eisha.

"Bashda," said Eisha, "I am here on a search. I am not sure which way to go, so I am walking along the coastline—"

"Walk away," interrupted Bashda, "but beware of the Forest Folk. They live in the huge and ancient live oak trees, and they will not welcome your intrusion into their forest preserve."

"H-m-m," mused Eisha. "Sounds like you and they are not the best of friends?"

"No friends at all," grunted Bashda. "They're a queer bunch—very different from us, and much less friendly, if I say so myself. Don't you agree, Swampeys?" He turned to his comrades.

"Right you are," they chorused.

"Well, how can I keep out of trouble with them?" asked Eisha.

"Just stay as close to the marsh as you can," replied Bashda. "Get your feet wet, if you have to. But watch out for the alligators that lurk in the swamp along the edge of the forest. They'll get you every time!" And he grinned up at Eisha as if the prospect pleased him. She did not like the feel of his words or the body language of the short squat green men around her. There was a sense of submerged hostility in them that troubled her.

"How do you avoid the alligators?" asked Eisha.

"Never get near 'em!" retorted Bashda with a smirk, and he and his companions burst into croaks of laughter at Eisha's expense. Eisha turned red with irritation, but bit her lip and asked another question.

"What do you do if you see one?" she asked.

"Run into the forest," replied Bashda.

"I thought you said the Forest Folk didn't like intruders, and were very unfriendly," protested Eisha.

"Right you are," chorused the squat green men.

"But they're not as unfriendly as the alligators," added Bashda. And once again, croaks of laughter filled the air. Eisha decided to change the subject before she lost her temper.

"What were you so angry about before you saw me?" asked Eisha. The question seemed to take them aback.

"Angry? We weren't angry!" exclaimed Bashda as he glared defensively at Eisha.

"Well, you were quarreling, weren't you?" asked Eisha, pursuing her advantage.

"Oh sure," replied Bashda. "We always do. It's how we get along!" More croaks of laughter burst out. "But we aren't angry. Not at all. We just say what we mean, no holds barred. It's a lot better than those Forest Folk. They just make empty chatter and pretend to be cheerful. They fritter their time away playing among the trees and carving things out of wood and doing other useless and silly things."

"What do you do instead?" asked Eisha curiously.

"We fish and hunt—mostly alligators." The Swampeys grinned grimly.

"Hunt alligators!" exclaimed Eisha. "I thought you avoided them."

"One or the other," retorted Bashda. "We try to get them before they get us as often as we can."

Eisha was tiring of the conversation, and Bashda's attempts to be clever. "What would you advise me to do?" she asked, hoping to end the conversation on a constructive note.

"Get out of our territory as fast as you can," replied Bashda with a warning scowl. "There are other bands of Swampeys around who will not be so patient with you and your questions as we have been. They might even tie you up and throw you in the swamp, just for the fun of seeing an alligator devour someone else for a change."

"Thanks for nothing," muttered Eisha under her breath, and with a short, polite bow of her head in their direction, she moved quickly onward along the edge of the swamp.

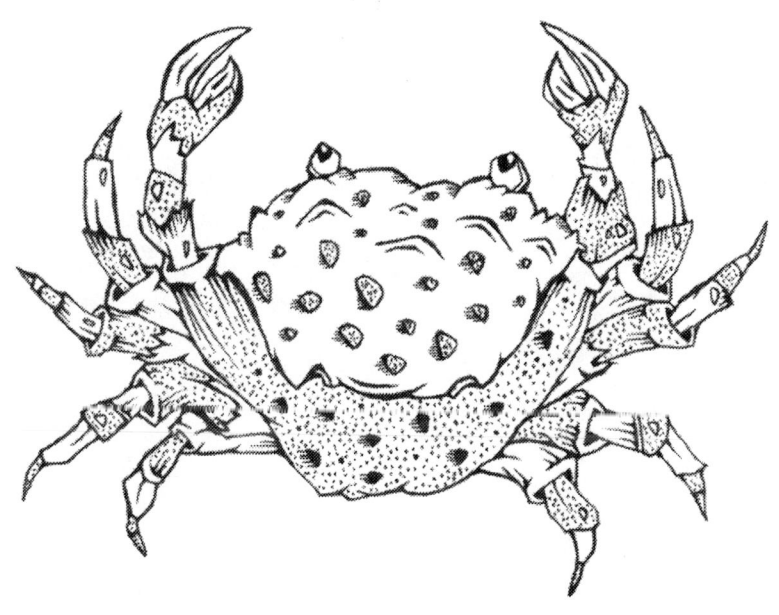

"Her eyes were still open when she went under, and she saw a big crab scuttling away from her."

CHAPTER THIRTY-SIX:

THE FOREST FOLK

The day was getting hotter by the minute, and as Eisha trudged along between the edge of the forest and the edge of the swamp, the sweat trickled down her face and into her eyes. She watched and listened carefully for any sign of other Swampeys, for she wanted nothing to do with them. Even if they were not as dangerous as Bashda had said they were, she found them decidedly unpleasant. She still felt the irritation they had aroused in her. The hot, tense walk she was enduring added to her irritation, and the anger she had felt at the Lion for making her leave the ship for good rose up inside her again. "What a horrid way to come to the end of my voyage," she said. "I don't see how the Lady and the Child could possibly dwell in such a land as this. Ugh! There must be some mistake."

At that moment, a log floating near the edge of the swamp next to her moved in a most unlog-like way. Eisha jumped away from it in fear. It was an alligator! It was hauling itself out of the water on its ugly, stumpy front legs! Eisha bolted. Into the forest she ran as fast as her legs would carry her. When she looked behind her, she saw that the alligator was moving at amazing speed behind her. In fact, it was gaining on her! Desperately, she flung the sack of extra clothes and food down behind her, hoping to distract it. Then, seeing a tree with low branches ahead of her, she ran for her life and hauled herself up into the safety of its broad limbs as quickly as she could. Below her, the alligator roared its angry disappointment, and then crouched at the base of the tree, waiting for its prey to come down.

"Now what?" Eisha thought, and looked all about her to see what else she could do to escape. She noticed, with a sigh of relief, that the branches of the great live oak in which she sat spread out close to those of another tree, which in turn spread its branches out far enough to almost touch yet another—so that it looked as if one could move through the tree branches high over the ground for a good ways. She saw that doing this would take her deeper into the forest, and would put her in danger of running into the Forest Folk. Eisha hoped Bashda had spoken truly when he said they were not as unfriendly as the alligator that even now roared in anger below her as he waited for her to come down. Then, as quietly and carefully as possible, Eisha balanced herself on the branches, now crawling, now walking, and managed to make it to the next tree, and the next. But to her dismay, the alligator noticed, and followed her from one tree to another.

"This is terrible!" said Eisha aloud. "How am I going to ever get away?"

"Not by scrambling through the trees the way you are," said a voice above her. Startled, Eisha looked up, and saw three small human-looking figures with light brown skin, furry brown hair, and long, bushy tails that curved up behind their backs. They had bright black eyes, and wore jump suits that looked as if they were made from a fine, bark-like fiber. Their bodies were lithe and limber, and they had smiles on their faces as they looked at Eisha in a friendly but curious way.

"Are—are you the Forest Folk the Swampeys told me about?" asked Eisha fearfully.

"Yes—we are the Forest Folk, but what they might have told you about us to make you so fearful is probably not true."

"They said you were unfriendly and didn't welcome intruders like me," said Eisha, still feeling nervous as she sat down on a broad branch, with the alligator below her and the strange little Forest Folk above her.

"Don't believe everything you hear," said another. "The Swampeys are the unfriendly ones, as I imagine you already know. We welcome you, and we welcome all who come into the forest—even alligators!"

"Then why did the Swampeys warn me against you?" asked Eisha.

"Because," said the third of the little Forest Folk, "they don't like us. They are angry and suspicious types, but they won't admit it. They call us unfriendly, but they are the ones who want nothing to do with us."

Eisha was puzzled by their words, and realized that she would have to try to figure out for herself who was telling the truth, and whom to trust. She knew she didn't much like the Swampeys. And she felt an immediate liking for the Forest Folk. How she wished she had her silver-Island Snake belt to help her know whom to trust, as it had in Snake Island. But it was on the ship, with most of her other possessions. Then she remembered the Stone. At least she still had that! She reached into her pocket. It wasn't there! Frantically, she searched her other pocket. It wasn't there either!

"Oh no!" cried Eisha. "It must have fallen out of my pocket when I fell into the swamp-water!" She felt utterly bereft. All during her voyage, she had relied on the Stone to guide her. Whatever would she do without it? She burst into tears.

"Can you tell us what's the matter?" asked one of the Forest Folk, coming down to sit on the branch nearest her.

"The Lion gave me a wonderful Heart-Stone," she sobbed. "It helped me over and over when I didn't know what to do. And now it's lost in the swamp!"

"That's too bad," said her companion sympathetically. "I wish we could help you."

Eisha looked at him through her tears. "I wanted to use the Stone to help me know if I could trust you," she said slowly. There was a long, awkward silence. Suddenly, Eisha realized how discourteous she was being. And she decided to trust what her heart was telling her, since now that was all she had to guide her. "I'm sorry for implying that I maybe shouldn't trust you," she said.

"Oh, we understand," replied one of the Forest Folk from a branch above her. "After all, the Swampeys gave you reason to be suspicious."

"Well, I didn't like them, and so I am not going to believe what they said about you," said Eisha. "I'll just take a chance and trust you anyhow, because that's what I feel in my heart!"

"O good!" exclaimed the three Forest Folk in unison.

"Tell me your names," said Eisha.

"We are Elim, Eshel, and Elan," said Elim, pointing to the others as he said their names. "And we live among these trees with many other Forest Folk."

"I'm Eisha, and I'm journeying through this land, looking for the Lady and the Child," replied Eisha.

"Welcome, Eisha! What can we do to help you?" asked Eshel.

"Get me safely away from this alligator!" exclaimed Eisha, looking downward with a shudder.

"I'm afraid that's not possible," replied Eshel.

"What? Why not?" exclaimed Eisha.

"Because this is your alligator to deal with. It will not go away until you do."

"But it'll devour me if I get near it!" cried Eisha.

"Will it?" asked Eshel.

"Of course! That's what alligators do!" insisted Eisha.

"Do they? Who says?" asked Elan.

"Bashda!" retorted Eisha with exasperation.

"Do you believe him?" prodded Elan.

"Not necessarily," replied Eisha. "But this alligator surprised me along the path, chased me into the forest, roared angrily at me when I climbed into the trees, and followed me here. See! It is waiting to get me right now!" And Eisha pointed below her.

"Perhaps, if you didn't run away from it in fear and disgust, it would no longer threaten you," suggested Eshel gently.

"What am I supposed to do, go down and hug it?" protested Eisha sarcastically. The three Forest Folk just looked at her, and there was a long, meaningful silence. During that silence, the memory of the dream she had on the ship the night before welled up within her mind. "How strange!" Eisha exclaimed to herself. "Do dreams come true this way in this land?" Then she remembered Euphra's farewell words of advice to her when she left the Misty Isles. "All memorable dreams have messages of great wisdom. Listen to them, and they will guide you."

"In my dream, I did stop trying to escape from the alligator," mused Eisha. She looked down at the flesh and blood alligator waiting below the tree. "No! I am absolutely not ready to get near it!" she thought. "I need more time to think things over and ponder the dream before I decide what to do." Then she spoke out loud to her new friends. "I had a dream last night. Can I tell it to you? Perhaps you can help me understand its meaning. I think it has something to do with my predicament."

"Of course," replied Elim. "We always remember our dreams and tell them to each other every morning. We find them very helpful when we have important decisions to make."

"Oh good," answered Eisha. "I'm sure your experience will be help me understand my dream." Then she told them about her alligator dream of the night before. They listened very carefully, and asked her probing questions. By the time their conversation was over, Eisha did understand the meaning of her dream much better, though parts of it were still a puzzle, and she said so.

"Never mind," said Elan. "Someday you'll understand, if you keep going back to it and pondering it. Sometimes your life has to catch up with your dreams before you really know all that they mean!"

"When you do understand some of your dream's message," added Eshel, "you need to somehow act on it, or it won't do you much good."

"But how?" asked Eisha.

"You have to figure that out for yourself," replied Eshel. There was a long pause as Eisha pondered what she understood of her dream.

"I have a sense," she said slowly, "that I am supposed to go down and face the alligator, and somehow make peace with it. But when I think about doing it—" she stopped and shuddered.

"Bashda and the Swampeys hate and fear alligators," said Elim. "So they either try to kill them or run from them. Naturally, the alligators chase them! In this land, Eisha, both human and animal creatures respond to others in the same way they are regarded."

"You mean—if I treat the alligator with respect, and accept it instead of hating and fearing it, it won't hurt me?"

"That's right," assured Elim. "In fact, you will find yourself much stronger after you have made peace with it. And it might help you in some important way."

Eisha swallowed hard. She had one more question. "Have any of you ever actually done what I am thinking of doing?" she asked.

"Oh yes," chorused the three Forest Folk. "Every one of us Forest Folk have been chased into the woods by an alligator at one time or another. Every one of us had to face it and make our peace with it in the end. When we did, we were no longer afraid of it, and could even welcome alligators into our forest preserve.

If the Swampeys were to make their peace with the alligators, they would have nothing to fear, and they would be much more pleasant people to have around!"

There was a long silence as Eisha considered what she should do. Finally, she spoke. "I have decided to trust you, and trust my dream, and trust my sense of what I'm meant to do," said Eisha. "It seems the right thing to do. So—here goes!" And with these words she clambered bravely down the tree toward the alligator.

"Their bodies were lithe and limber, and they had smiles on their faces as they looked at Eisha in a friendly but curious way."

CHAPTER THIRTY-SEVEN:

SAFE PASSAGE

When Eisha was on a branch just above the alligator's head, she suddenly stopped. Was she really willing to risk her life to do the right thing? She looked dubiously at the alligator, and the alligator looked menacingly at her. Eisha knew she was not ready. Although she had courage, she had not yet taken time to consider what was acceptable and respectable about the alligator. When she looked at it, especially from such a short distance, it aroused the same old fear and rejection in her. "It's so ugly!" she exclaimed as she surveyed its long, toothsome snout and its big, dull brown, scaly body. "How can I accept and respect this creature? It would be foolish to get any closer to it. It would sense how I feel, and I'd be done for!"

Eisha sat very still on the branch and tried to relax a little. Below her, the alligator was apparently taking a short nap, for its eyes were closed, and it lay there motionless. Eisha closed her eyes too, and the memory of her time in the branches of the Sacred Tree came flooding back. She began to chant, as she had done before when she was in a fix. "Ruach, Shaddai, Eemah, Ruach, Shaddai, Eemah, Ruach, Shaddai, Eemah."

After awhile, she began to feel the familiar peace and quiet inside that the chant always created. "That's better," she said to herself. "At least I'm not full of fear and rejection anymore. But I still don't like that alligator, and I still do *not* want to get close to it. What shall I do?" The only thing she could think of was to call "Help! Help! Help!" There was a brief stirring in the branches above, as if the Forest Folk had heard, but could do nothing more for her. Beneath her, the alligator opened its eyes and looked curiously at her. Eisha shut hers again, and returned to the memory of the Sacred Tree for help. That memory reminded her of her adventure on Island of the Horses. Particularly, she remembered how she got to know the Sacred Horse—running with it, following its lead, exchanging breath with it, and riding it...

"Aha!" Eisha exclaimed, as an insight flashed into her mind. "This could be a Sacred Alligator. It doesn't look like one, but then, I don't know what one would look like, and you never can tell!" This put the alligator in a different light. Eisha opened her eyes and began to see it in a whole new way. She saw how remarkable the position of its eyes was on the top of its head, allowing it to see all around while the rest of it was underwater. She marveled at the intricate design of its scales, and the beautiful pattern of olive green, gray, and yellow on its body. When its mouth was closed and its teeth weren't showing, it looked like a huge lizard, and not all that frightening.

Then she considered how she would feel if she was feared and rejected. "No wonder it's angry," reflected Eisha. "I would be too!" She looked at the alligator with a more sympathetic eye, and the alligator opened its eyes and looked at her in a curious manner. "If only I had the Stone!" she thought to herself. But she did not. She was going to have to rely on her own inner sense. "This is much harder!" she said as she sat very still, listening to how she felt inside. After awhile, she realized that something had shifted. The loathing was gone, and the fear was manageable.

Taking a deep breath, and gathering up all her courage, Eisha inched ever so cautiously down the tree and approached the alligator. It watched her carefully, but it did not move. She fixed her mind on the sinuous curve of its body and tail, its power and agility, its ability to live in water and on land. She began to feel genuine respect and admiration for what it could do. Finally, she took the step that brought her within reach of its powerful jaws.

"Please, please," she pleaded, looking it in the eye, "don't open your jaws. I won't be able to make peace with you if you do. I'll be way too afraid to face your fearsome teeth."

The alligator looked at her—and smiled! Eisha could actually see the corners of its mouth turning up, and the smile mirrored in its eyes. Then it rolled over on its side and exposed its underbelly, as if it were asking for a scratch! Eisha was astounded. She reached hesitatingly towards its body and gently scratched it between its front legs. The alligator smiled some more. Then Eisha got a little closer, and scratched its belly. This obviously pleased the alligator. As Eisha sat there next to the alligator, scratching it in all the right places, thoughts and memories of her anger with the Lion, her irritation with the Swampeys, and her resentment at being where she was arose in her mind. "I guess a part of me sometimes feels like an angry alligator," she said, "and I might as well accept it!"

"And respect it!" said a voice from on high, and Eshel's merry face appeared among the branches above them.

"Ah—I see," responded Eisha, and she was thoughtful and quiet for quite a while, until her three Forest Folk friends came scampering down the tree, clapped her on the back, and said, "Well done, Eisha!"

"Thank-you," answered Eisha, "but what am I supposed to do? Sit here for the rest of the day with the alligator?"

"If you want to," laughed Elim. "But you said you were on a search. Do you want to get on with it?"

"Well, yes, I do," admitted Eisha. But I really don't know where to go from here."

"We know someone who can help you," said Elan. "She lives north and east from here, along the coast, past the flat swamp and forest lands. Her land is hilly, and is also cooler and drier."

"How can I get to her?" asked Eisha eagerly.

"The alligator will carry you safely and swiftly through the swamplands along the coast until the shore turns rocky and the water too cold for its comfort. That way, the Swampeys will not bother you, and by tomorrow morning, you should be safe in her territory."

"Who is she, and how will I know when I'm getting close to where she lives?" asked Eisha.

"You will have to find out for yourself who she is," replied Elim. "But if you walk along the rocky shore northward, you will come to a place where the rocks have been worn into fine, multi-colored sand. A great fallen tree serves as an entrance to this sandy stretch of beach. About a mile beyond the tree, a big pair of rocks, one on the sand, and the other in the water, marks the end of the beach. Between the fallen tree and the rocks there is fine swimming. If you swim in the afternoon with the sun behind you in the eastern sky, and face west toward the shore, you will see her sign—the sign of the full moon rising."

"Wait a minute! Doesn't the sun set in the west and the moon rise in the east?" asked Eisha in surprise.

"Not here in the land east of the sun and west of the moon," returned Elim.

"Oh!" exclaimed Eisha, "I hadn't thought of that! This is a strange land! But I'm glad I'm finally here."

"I hope you feel even more glad pretty soon," answered Elim. "Now—are you ready to go?"

Eisha nodded. Elim bent over and whispered something to the alligator. It rolled onto its belly and pulled itself up onto its short legs.

"Get on, Eisha," said Eshel. "It is ready to help you on your way with all its energy and power at your service!"

Eisha climbed onto the alligator's back, and flashed back to her ride on the Island Snake when she had left Snake Island. She gratefully gripped the alligator's body with her legs and hands, smiled and thanked the Forest Folk, and felt the alligator beneath her moving rapidly back toward the swamp at the edge of the forest.

Soon, the alligator was back in its element. It swam moving its powerful tail back and forth, and they fairly flew through the water along the coast. All around them, huge white and blue herons flapped gracefully out of their way, and fish leaped up out of the water as if to get a better look at the amazing spectacle of Eisha riding the alligator.

Once, towards evening, Eisha spied a band of Swampeys near the edge of the swamp. They spied her too, and were near enough that Eisha could see their eyes bulging with surprise. Then they disappeared, and on went the alligator through the dark night hours. A mist rose from the marsh, and hid all but the highest stars. Eisha's legs were wet and cool as they dangled in the water, and the night wind fanned her face and body. "This is a much better way to travel through the swamp than tramping along its edge in the hot sun, trying to avoid Swampeys," thought Eisha, and she laughed aloud. The hours passed swiftly, and when the sun rose in the west from behind the trees to her left, the alligator had reached the end of the swampland. It stopped to let her off, and Eisha gave it a farewell pat. "Thank you for your help in getting here, and all you taught me," she said as it slipped under the water and was gone.

"She looked dubiously at the alligator, and the alligator looked menacingly at her."

CHAPTER THIRTY-EIGHT:

THE QUEEN MOTHER

Eisha walked along on foot in the morning sun, which was warm enough to dry out her soaked clothes, but still cool enough for comfort. She could tell she was much further north, and for some reason, as she looked about at the lovely wooded hills and meadows that meandered down toward the rocky shore, she felt as if this was familiar territory.

"But of course, it can't be!" she said to herself. "It just reminds me of someplace I've been before. I wish I could remember..."

After several more hours, when Eisha was getting very tired of walking over the rocks along the shore, and very hungry and thirsty besides, she saw, in the distance, the silhouette of a huge fallen tree against the sky. Its leafless branches arched downwards toward the rocks and water, creating beautiful blue sky-spaces between them. In less than an hour, she had reached it. She paused and looked. Beyond the fallen tree lay a wide, sandy beach, with two large rocks at the far end, one jutting out of the water, and the other out of the sand—just as Elim had said. Eisha noticed one space made by the tree branches that looked just like an archway. "This makes a perfect entrance," she thought, and stepped through it onto the sand. Next, she took off her soggy shoes and walked barefoot, feeling the sand's soft warmth between her toes.

Suddenly she gasped with delight. Hundreds of orange monarch butterflies came fluttering over the golden and purple flowers that bordered the beach! "They must be migrating," she thought, "sort of like me." One of the butterflies flitted right by her face, and its wings touched her cheek as if in welcome.

Eisha looked down and gasped again. On the edge of the sand and in the calm water at its edge lay scores of spiraled coral and pink conch shells! "How beautiful!" exclaimed Eisha softly. "This feels like such a magical place!" Turning her back to the water, she looked into the woods beyond the beach and saw trees of many familiar kinds, some of them wearing bright red, yellow, and orange leaves. "It must be early autumn here," she said to herself. "I hope the water isn't too cold for my swim."

But when she stripped off her clothes and waded into the water, it was comfortably cool, and felt delightfully refreshing in the warm rays of the late afternoon sun. Eisha floated and kicked and laid on her back in the water, letting its calm, cool surface hold up her body as she gently breathed in and out. Then she swam a bit further out to get a wider view of the shore, and the forested hills and meadows beyond it. Her back was to the sun as she faced west towards the beach.

Then Eisha saw it—a round, shining, moon-like light, but brighter silver than any full moon she had ever seen. It was directly ahead of her, beyond the beach among the trees. Marveling, she swam toward shore. Still it shone. She put on her green tunic and pants, and walked across the beach and into the woods towards the shining circle of light.

As she drew closer to it, Eisha saw that it was framed by a big square window in the front wall of a pinewood cottage. "How can there be a moon in there?" she thought as she walked up to the door. Immediately it opened, and there stood a tall, plump woman with thick, wavy gray hair piled high like a beehive on top of her head. She wore a gown of yellow, with a long necklace of black pearls, and earrings to match. Her eyes glowed with the same welcome smile that lit her face.

"At last!" she said as she took Eisha into her arms. Eisha returned her warm embrace a little tentatively.

"I'm sorry I overwhelmed you a bit," said the woman, taking her hand. "It's just that I've been waiting for you for so long!" She led Eisha into the cottage, and seated her in a soft cushioned window seat under the big, square window.

Eisha looked around, speechless with surprise. On the wall opposite the square window hung a round mirror that reflected the light of the sun, just as the moon in the sky did. Between the window seat and mirror was a square pinewood table set with dishes and food and drink.

"Were you expecting me?" Eisha blurted out.

"Oh yes, my love, for many a moon," answered the woman as she bustled about putting more food out, and pouring creamy milk into two blue glasses on the table.

"Are you the one the Forest Folk said could help me in my search?" asked Eisha.

"I'm sure I am," she replied. "Come, sit and eat with me, and we will tell each other who we are, and you can tell me about your search."

Once again, Eisha told her story, and once again, discovered a great deal about herself and her search in the telling. Her hostess listened eagerly, with an occasional question. Then it was Eisha's turn to question.

"Who are you, and why have you been waiting for me, and how did you know I was coming—or even who I am?" The questions spilled out of Eisha's mouth one on top of the other.

"Let's see if I can answer all your questions before I forget them," laughed her companion. "My name is Beatrice—Bea for short. It means Blessing. I am the Queen Mother of the Bee people who live in this land."

"Bee people?" exclaimed Eisha.

"Yes, Bee People. They are called that because their main occupation is caring for bees. And they have a lot in common with them. They are busy, busy, busy all the time, and they still manage to be sweet, though they'll sting you with sharp words if you bother them when they're busy with their work. They are very hard workers. The trouble is, they take too little time to rest, or play, or think for themselves, and they hate being alone. They cluster together all the time like bees around a honeycomb. Not surprisingly, they are all very much alike. And that's where you come in, Eisha. You are very different than they are, and they have seldom met anyone different. They never want to leave work to take a vacation and travel or meet other people and see other places. They are really very conservative. Change is difficult for them. Unfortunately, few people come here from other places. It is rather out of the mainstream."

"So, somehow, you think meeting and spending time with me will loosen them up a bit and expand their minds?" asked Eisha.

"Oh, yes! I'm sure of it! That's why I've been so eager for your arrival."

Eisha's raised eyebrows expressed her surprise. "But—you don't even know me, Bea."

"Oh yes, Eisha, I know you alright. I've known you for a long time. But this is not the time to explain, nor is it my place to tell you how this is so. You must simply trust that I tell the truth and accept it, or at least let it be for the time being. Someday soon, you will know. But I can tell you how I knew you were coming." And she gave a low whistle. Two huge sea eagles flew in the open door and perched on each of her shoulders! Eisha's mouth dropped open in amazement.

"Are those Euphra's birds?" she asked incredulously.

"They are the same ones who sit on her shoulders, and serve the Lion, and winged you on your way from the Misty Isles to this land," replied Beatrice. "They often fly between the Misty Isles and this place with messages which Euphra and Lupa send me, or I send them. You see, I am their sister, and another granddaughter of the Lady you seek. Both birds, and all three of us sisters, are friends of the Lion and the Island Snake."

"What an incredible connection!" cried Eisha. "Did the birds tell you I was coming?"

"Yes indeed," smiled the Queen Mother of the Bee People. Then she whispered something to the sea eagles, who flew back out the open door and away towards the sea. When they had disappeared into the distance, Beatrice held out her hand to Eisha. "If you are not too tired, Eisha, would you go out to the meadows where my people live, and meet them, and tell them something about yourself and your journey?"

Eisha nodded, took her hand, and walked with her through the deep purple twilight into a nearby meadow. By now, the stars had begun to glitter in the sky, and the Bee People were gathered in a grassy clearing near the cluster of their hive-like homes.

"The only time they're open to new thoughts or experience is now, when they are tired from a long, hard day's work, and are relaxing a little before going to sleep," said the Queen Mother. Then she called out—"She's here, everyone! Come and meet Eisha."

At her words, swarms of people surrounded them. They all wore yellow jackets with black and yellow striped shirts and pants under them. They all had short fuzzy yellow hair, sallow skin, and little black eyes. They all welcomed Eisha at once, buzzing around her, and speaking at the same time so that she could hardly understand a word they said. Finally, at a signal from the Queen Mother, they settled down on the grass, crossed their legs and arms, and looked at her, waiting to hear what she had to say.

Eisha told them a few of the stories of her journey she guessed would most interest them, and then paused. "Any questions?" she asked. There was a buzz of voices, and one of them stood up and said, "Can you help me learn to be more like you? I think I'm way too much like everyone else here. I'd like to be a little more different—like you are."

The Queen Mother smiled to herself with satisfaction.

"I'm not sure how I can help," answered Eisha.

"Perhaps," suggested the Queen Mother, "Eisha could spend a while with us, and tell us more each evening about what she learned on her journey. Maybe she would even be willing to meet one with those of you who want to talk to her by yourself."

A buzz of approval arose from the crowd. Eisha hesitated, not knowing whether she should agree to stay, or press onward with her search.

"Eisha," said the Queen Mother, "Maybe it would be good for you to take a little time in my home to relax and reflect on your journey. As you share your story with us, not only will we benefit, you will too. You can learn a lot by putting your experience into words for us. Don't worry—you'll know when you need to go on with your search."

Eisha paused and listened and considered. Though she did not have the Stone to guide her, it didn't take her long to discern that in her heart, she wanted to accept the Queen Mother's invitation, and knew she was right about being able to tell when it was time to go. "I'll stay for awhile," she said simply. The Bee People cheered and applauded. The Queen Mother smiled and held out her hand. "My people need to go to their rest," she said, "and you do too." Once again, Eisha took her hand, and the two of them returned over the dewy meadow to the cottage of the Shining Moon. There, Eisha spent the first of many comfortable nights in a soft pink featherbed in a loft overlooking the sea and the woods.

During the days that followed, many of the Bee People came to see her one by one, asking for advice. They were curious about the things she told the gathered crowd every evening. And they wanted her to tell them again and again about how the Heart Stone had guided her.

"It worked well for me," she told them. "But now I don't have it any more. So, I have to take more time and effort to listen to my heart. I think that's what you need to do too. You've always listened to each other and wanted to be like the others around you. You've been afraid to try out new ideas of your own. And now that I'm here, I notice you're trying to be like me in some ways. But you need to just BE your own unique, special kind of being. Not just like each other. And not like me either. You must learn to listen for yourselves to the wisdom within you."

"You sound just like the Queen Mother!" they replied. "But neither of you gives us a practical way to do what you say! You had your Heart Stone to guide you until you could get along without it—and you admit it isn't easy. We don't have anything like your Heart Stone to guide us until we learn to listen to our hearts."

Eisha took their words to heart. She discussed them with Beatrice. But they were at a loss for the right solution for the Bee People. Then one evening at suppertime, as Eisha glanced at the moon-mirror on the wall of the cottage, she saw her own face reflected in it, and noticed the conch-shell earrings dangling from her ears. Immediately, Euphra's words came back to her. "Let these always remind you of the joy that listening brings."

"Conch shells!" cried Eisha. "That's it! That's our solution!" And she jumped up and down with excitement.

"Explain yourself," invited Beatrice with a smile.

"There are all kinds of beautiful conch shells on the beach near here," said Eisha. "When you put one of them to your ear, and listen carefully and quietly, you can hear the sound of the sea. Then, if you keep listening, you can hear its meaning and message."

"That's just the thing Eisha!" cried Beatrice with delight. "They will love it. It's a way that each of them can listen which is practical. Each one can have their own shell."

"Each one will hear the unique message meant for their own ears. They can listen whenever they want, and they will become much more the being each one was meant to be," added Eisha.

"I knew your coming here would be important!" exclaimed the Queen Mother. And with these words she enfolded Eisha in a warm embrace.

"Immediately it opened, and there stood a tall, plump woman with thick, wavy gray hair piled high like a bee hive on top of her head."

CHAPTER THIRTY-NINE:

AT LAST

The very next morning, Eisha gathered a large quantity of conch shells from the special beach. That evening, she showed them to the Bee People, and demonstrated how to use them. They loved them! Every one took a shell from Eisha. Some even wandered off right away to places in the meadow where they could be alone to listen to the secret guidance of their shells.

Eisha and the Queen Mother smiled at each other as they watched the Bee people sitting in the grass, holding conch shells to their ears, and listening intently. Then Eisha said, "I feel that it is time to go, Queen Mother."

"Yes," Beatrice said. "You have done what you came to do, and fulfilled all my hopes. Now you are ready to start the last part of your search. If you walk straight through the meadows and pine forests towards the full moon as it rises in the west, you will come to a huge archway of stone that marks the entrance into the desert. Go through the archway and wait until you see the Morning Star rise in the western sky. Walk towards it until sunrise, and you will come to a garden in the desert. There, you will know what to do next."

Eisha thanked the Queen Mother for her hospitality and clear directions. Then they warmly embraced. "I have a farewell gift for you," said Beatrice. She took a silver chain with a small round mirror hanging from it that looked just like a miniature version of the moon-mirror that hung on her cottage wall. "This will reveal your true self to you, Eisha," she said. "Open your eyes to your own reflection." As she hung it around Eisha's neck, she tenderly kissed her goodbye.

With high hopes, Eisha set out on the last part of her journey. As she walked towards the rising moon, she felt sad at the parting, yet excited about what lay ahead. The walk over the meadows and through the forest in the silvery moonlight was a pure delight. The fragrant smell of pine needles scenting the fresh, cool air was all she needed to refresh her and keep her going until she reached the stone archway.

It towered into the night sky at the border of the pine forest. Through it, she could see shrubs, cactus, rocks, and reddish sand stretching out to the west all the way to the horizon. She stepped out from the shadows of the pine trees into the full light of the moon, which by now was almost above her head. Then she walked toward the huge stone arch. "I wonder who built this here?" she said to herself. "It couldn't have been the Bee People or the Forest Folk or the Swampeys. Are there desert people who did this, or people who lived here ages ago?" Eisha felt a sense of awe as she stood in the shadow of the huge stone monolith. Somehow, it made her feel connected with ages past and ancient people. Taking a deep breath, she walked solemnly through the arch and into the desert to await the rising of the Morning Star. She was so tired by now that she lay down on the desert ground, put her head on a rock for a pillow, and fell asleep.

When Eisha awoke several hours later, the Morning Star was shining high in the western sky. She rose quickly and walked toward it. As she walked on and on in the silence of the desert night, following the Star, she remembered her trip on the camel with Lila under the jewel-like stars of Snake Island. The memory of Lila awakened a longing to hold the little girl in her arms again—a longing very much like the one she felt after leaving the Child in the Cave. Her thoughts flew back to her time there. She remembered the Lady's beauty, the Lion's song, the rainbow ladder, the glowing light, and the sleeping face of her beloved Child. The hours of walking through the night flew by as Eisha savored her memories.

When the sun rose in the west, turning the desert all pink and rose and orange, she saw, directly ahead, a circular hedge of shiny, deep green leaves, starred with tiny white flowers that perfumed the air even from a distance. They looked just like the white flower-crystal that sometimes shone in the heart of her Stone. "It must be the desert garden!" cried Eisha, and she began running towards it. Soon, she could see tall plumes of water cascading into the air high above the hedge. "A fountain!" she exclaimed, and kept running.

Now an archway appeared in the hedge, and Eisha ran straight towards it. When she reached it, she stopped and stood under the archway for a long moment. Then she burst into a cry of utter joy. There, in a shallow pool of water into which the fountain plumes splashed, sat the Child of her longing! It was no longer a baby, but a little girl. She had curly brown hair, and her bare skin glowed as if with light from within. She was playing with a silver ball just as she had in Eisha's dream. Next to the fountain and its pool stood the Lady, her long white hair flowing over her sky-blue robe, and her face lit with love. Eisha flew into her wide-open arms, weeping for joy. The Lady held her for a long time. And during that time, Eisha became aware that in the Lady's arms she felt again all the love and compassion she had felt from the women who had become her friends during her search. She looked into the Lady's face, and said, "I didn't know it at the time, but I was meeting and finding you all along. I have seen your face and felt your embrace in other women's faces and arms." The Lady smiled and nodded. Then she took the silver chain around Eisha's neck and held the mirror up before her face.

"What do you see?" she asked.

Eisha gazed into it, and saw in her face, for the first time, the likeness of the Lady. "I reflect you too!" she said with awe and wonder as she let the mirror drop back on her breast. They looked long and deep into each other's eyes, and smiled.

Then Eisha turned toward the fountain and knelt, opening her arms wide. "Come!" she cried. The Child looked up, and holding the silver ball in one hand, flew into Eisha's arms. Eisha held her tight, and wept again for sheer joy. She realized that when she had held the lost children, and Lila, and the children of the Misty Isles in her arms and heart, she had been holding this precious Child too. She took her little face tenderly between her hands, and saw, for the first time, that the Child's tousled brown hair and dark green eyes were her own! Once again, awe and wonder filled Eisha's soul. She stood up with the Child in her arms, and the little girl tossed the shining ball high into the air with a silvery laugh.

Suddenly, the figure of a huge Lion hurtled into the air, caught the ball, and landed softly on its great cat's feet between Eisha and the Lady. Eisha could hardly contain her happiness! She flung her arms around the Lion, and it began its purring song. Eisha felt a joy so intense she thought she could not bear it...but she did, until finally, spent with the intensity of her feelings and experience, she let go, and stood up. Her search had at last come to an end.

"Eisha," said the Lady, "now that you really know that the Child and I are part of you, and that you can find us in others, your search is over. From now on, we will always be with you and in you, and you can go back home."

"Home?" said Eisha with surprise. "The only home I ever had was my father's castle, and it fell down in an earthquake. The ship I sailed in felt like home, but I can't use the ship anymore—can I?" she asked, turning to the Lion.

"You don't need the ship anymore," replied the Lion. "Remember that I said you didn't need two homes? That is because this land is your land—the land of your birth and childhood. This is your mother-country."

"You are home already!" added the Lady with a radiant smile.

"Home?" exclaimed Eisha. "But—I've never seen the places I've been since landing here."

"Outside of the castle and its grounds, you didn't see much of your own home territory when you were a child, Eisha—only the place where Beatrice dwells," explained the Lady. "That is why it seemed strangely familiar to you—remember? Your grandmother took you there too as a little child. After the earthquake, all you saw was a piece of the desert you fled through, and a little stretch of the western forests and mountains and seacoast. You are really seeing your own land for the first time. You are finally meeting your own people. But now you need to go back to your mother's house, where you were born. When you are once again rooted there, you can continue to explore your territory and get to really know the people who live in it."

"You call this my territory, and say 'my people'," observed Eisha. "What do you mean?"

"You are of royal birth, and the Queen of this whole land," said the Lady. "And now, you are finally able to be the Queen you were born to become. Come, we will escort you to the place of your birth." Then she motioned for Eisha to take the Child and climb with her upon the Lion's huge back. When the three of them were comfortably seated, the Lion loped off into the desert, and headed north.

It was the happiest ride of Eisha's life as she sat there between the Lady and the Child on the Lion's back. "And to think the last time I was here, I was running in fear from the Lion!" she exclaimed to herself. As they rode across the desert together, the hours flew as swiftly as the Lion. By sunset, they had crossed the desert and entered the northern woods and hills where Eisha was born.

When they reached the top of a high hill from which the sea was clearly visible, the Lion stopped. The Lady pointed to a pile of old, hand-hewn, weather-beaten stones lying about, overgrown with vines and other vegetation. "The castle used to be right there," she said. "You are the only one of your immediate family who survived the earthquake. Your grandmother, who told you to escape into the desert, lives now on a beautiful island in another sea which is beyond the farthest star, and as near as your own heart. Someday you will meet her there. But you have met her three sisters here on the islands of the Inland Sea—Euphra, Lupa, and Beatrice."

"Oh my goodness!" exclaimed Eisha. "That means that my grandmother is also your grand-daughter!"

"Yes. And that makes you my great great grand-daughter," replied the Lady with a laugh of delight.

Eisha was speechless. But only for a few moments. As usual, she had more questions. "What about my mother?" she said. "I remember she left us when I was very little. What happened to her?" Eisha's eyes filled with tears.

"My dear one," replied the Lady tenderly. "I promise you that you will someday see her again, and when you do, what happened to her is her story to tell. Rest assured that she is well."

Eisha was a little disappointed, for she really wanted to know more about her mother right then and there. But since that was not possible, she asked about her grandmother. "What was my grandmother's name?" she said, for names seemed very important to her now. "And may I ask your name, my Lady?"

"Your grandmother's name is Ahava, which means Love," replied the Lady. "As for me, I have many Names, but the one I am called in this land is Shekinah, which means Glory. But enough of names and relations and family trees. The Lion and I must leave now. Not far from here you will find the house of your mother and grandmother and their grandmothers. It still stands, awaiting your coming. When you have set things right in your ancestral home, and made it truly your own, you will see your mother again." With these words, the Lady took Eisha in her arms, gave her a long and loving embrace and said, "Remember—we are always with you, even when we are out of sight." Then Shekinah mounted the Lion, and they sped out of sight.

Eisha lifted her beloved Child into her arms and walked down the hill towards the sea.

"Mother," she called, "I'm coming home!"

TO BE CONTINUED

"The very next morning, Eisha gathered a large quantity of conch shells from the special beach."

CHAPTER FORTY:

YOUR IDEAS, QUESTIONS, DRAWINGS ETC.